Ghost Ride

Fred Hurley

Fredrick Hudgin

Novels
The End of Children Series:
 The Beginning of the End
 The Three-Hour War
 The Emissary
Ghost Ride
School of the Gods
Green Grass
Sulfur Springs
A Rainy Night and other Short Stories
 (My Short Story Collection)

Short stories
A Rainy Night
Ashes on the Ocean
Being Dad
Get Them OFF!
Gina
Green Grass
Nice Day for a Ride
Sowing the Seeds
The Chair
The Last Salute
The Longest Ride
The Mission
The Second Chance
The Wiz
They Don't Have Christmas in Vietnam
When Is a Kiss Not a Kiss

Poetry Collection
Four Winds

Fredrick Hudgin

Ghost Ride

This is a work of fiction. Names, characters, places, and incidents either are the product of the author's imagination or are used fictitiously, and any resemblance to actual persons, living or dead, business establishments, events, or locales are entirely coincidental.

All names, measures of distance, time, temperatures, and math have been converted into their common English equivalents for ease of understanding. There are not English words for many of them and in their native languages, pronunciation would be impossible for human vocal cords.

No ghosts were hurt in the production of this book.

Ghost Ride

To Steve Fortson, ex-Green Beret (if there is such a thing).
He corrected my mistakes as he read it the first time,
then read it again,
because he didn't want the story to end.
From one Army guy to another,
thanks for your service to our country, Steve!

"Monsters are real, and ghosts are real too.
They live inside us, and sometimes, they win."

Stephen King

Chapter 1 – Gina

I tried to command myself to remember the war wasn't here, that these fir-covered mountains weren't hiding hard people with brown skin who wanted to kill me. Closing my eyes and inhaling the smells of the forest helped a little. It filled me with memories of pretty girls at the swimming hole, of my first .22 rifle lying on my bed for my twelfth birthday, of picking out my very own puppy from the squealing pile between the hay bales.

Afghanistan still filled my consciousness. Every puff of wind and rustle of a leaf pulled me away from the peace I longed for—peace I had felt when I sat here so many years ago. You didn't stay alive in a combat zone by relaxing. Let your guard down for one second, and that second could be your last. The little sounds are so much more important than the big ones.

The temperature had dropped with the sun, chilling the still air among the ghosts and memories. Fragrances of damp earth, ferns, and cedar filled my campsite, so close to where I grew up. The fingers of ice crystals began their nightly metamorphosis, slowly growing across the puddle outside of my tent as if some invisible night creature were doodling on a canvas of water. The pale gray of dusk had almost finished changing into the night.

This valley in central Washington was heaven on earth to a twelve-year-old boy with one pair of shoes that only got put on for Sundays and school.

"I'll name you Socks," I told the golden wiggling fur-ball with four white feet as she tried to climb up the front of my shirt and lick my face.

She was a boxer mix and the best present a twelve-year-old could ever have. Socks became my constant companion. She slept next to me in my bed, walked with me to the school bus stop each morning, and was waiting for me when I returned in the afternoon. I saved her the choicest scraps from breakfast and dinner and sneaked her some of my meals when I didn't have anything else to feed her.

I've never seen a more natural hunter. Together explored this valley from the foggy river at the bottom to the snowcapped hills at the top. We'd hunt from the moment I got my shoes off after school until the sun crawled behind those cold rock walls. If we were lucky, I would bring home rabbits, a pheasant, or whatever critter was unfortunate enough to cross paths with us.

On those days when I returned with a full game bag, Socks and I would look forward with gleeful anticipation to the ceremony of entering the house my grandfather built. I would swing open the front door and put the bag on the table, proud to contribute some tiny bit to my family's well-being, feeling every bit a man in a boy's skin.

Mom would come out of the kitchen, pushing back a lock of her graying, brown hair and wiping her hands on her apron before she hugged me. Her dresses always smelled of lemon and flour. Dad would shake his head and lament how poor the hunting would be next year since I cleaned out the hillsides of all the game. His wrinkled, leathery hands, now dark with age spots and swollen with arthritis, would lift out what critter I brought home and ask me where I found it and what it did. His eyes squeezed into sparkling slits with laugh lines that went all the way to his ears as he listened to the adventures Socks and I had that day, his ample belly wiggling with laughter that made his suspenders stretch even more.

Socks got all the parts we didn't want and sometimes some of my meal too when I figured she deserved more, crunching up the bones gleefully like rock candy.

We were a deadly pair. She would run through the woods roughly paralleling me, up and down the hills, through open forest, and down into stream beds, thick with ferns and fallen branches. Every time I heard a growl, I knew she had found something. I would creep down through the blackberries and brambles until I saw where she was. She would never move. Once I moved into position, she would pounce on whatever she had found, and I would have one shot from that bolt-action, single-shot rifle. That was usually enough.

When you work for fifty cents an hour, a box of .22 shells gets mighty expensive. The summer I got that rifle, I worked and practiced and practiced and worked, spending every penny I made on shells. By the time fall came, I could shoot the walnuts off the tree in our back yard from a hundred and fifty feet. From then on, every critter had to be on the lookout, whether it walked, flew, or swam.

One day Socks discovered a porcupine. She had never seen a porcupine before. It waddled down a dry creek bed, as unafraid of Socks as a Sherman tank driver would be of a rifleman. Nothing had ever ignored Socks before. I think it hurt her feelings. She growled and waited for me to come. I heard her, but I was stuck in a blackberry thicket. When I didn't show up for a while, she growled again, louder this time—damned blackberries! I didn't know what had happened when I heard her yelp, so I tore loose from those thorns and left some skin behind.

By the time I found her, the porcupine had fled into its den under a log, leaving Socks bristling with quills from one side of her face to the other. After that first attack, she must have hurt, and she hadn't expected to hurt. So she did what all hunters do—she attacked again and again. She had quills in her mouth, in her paws, up her nose—one even went through her left eye. She was almost blind, in pain, and running in circles, pawing at her face with her mouth wide open trying to dislodge the quills.

I rolled her up in my jacket to quiet her down and keep her from doing any more damage while considering my options. She couldn't walk, and we were a good ten miles from anything.

"Socks, what were ya thinking?"

She watched me with her good eye, trusting me to find a way of fixing what was wrong.

Nothing else to do but carry her. She weighed every bit of forty-five pounds, and I weighed maybe a hundred, soaking wet. I slung my rifle across my back with the barrel pointing down, then leaned over and gently pulled her over my head onto my shoulders.

With her paws in both hands, somehow I got to my feet and began the long walk down to Doc Johnson, Chambersville's vet.

It took me five hours to reach town, walking up and down those hills with Socks on my back. I tried to walk as smoothly as I could so I wouldn't bounce her. But, all that time, she didn't move or wiggle around. Sometimes she would whimper softly, but nothing else, even when I would stumble on a rock or have to jump across a stream.

By the time we reached his office, Doc Johnson was closing up for the day. He was a large man, tall and wide. I guess that explained why he always wore suspenders and a belt. His long hair and bushy eyebrows were snow white. Add a cherry nose and red cheeks, and you'd be close. But his eyes I remember most of all. He had hazel eyes that were always smiling—eyes so big and friendly that you could get lost in them and forget what he just said.

"So Socks discovered porcupines, did she?" he asked, looking her over. "Come on in. Let's get 'er cleaned up."

He unlocked the door he had just locked, and I followed his huge, lumbering body, carrying Socks into the back. We worked on her for almost two hours before the last quill hit the pan. He put those bloody quills in a pill bottle for me to have as a souvenir, then gave me a second bottle full of antibiotics for the infection that was sure to come.

"I don't think 'er eye's gonna make it, David. That quill went through both sides an' tore the eyeball. I've fixed it as best I can, but I don't wanna get yer hopes up. She may have ta learn to hunt with only one eye."

I counted those damned quills when I got home. That porcupine had planted over five hundred into Socks.

I worked for the doc all summer, cleaning cages and walking dogs to pay for Socks's treatment. We got to be pretty good friends. He would let me help him as he fixed people's dogs, cats, and farm animals—said I had a natural talent for it.

Socks's eye never did work again, but that didn't stop her—I don't think it even slowed her down much. However, one thing did change that summer. Socks never got over her hatred for those slow-moving, quill-covered children of Satan. I could tell every time she found one. She had a "porcupine" bark, separate and unique from all her other barks. She never got stuck with another quill, but she never tired of terrorizing those poor animals.

A couple of years later, she figured out how to kill them without getting stuck. She would wait until they would begin to climb over a log or a rock. A gap would appear between the porcupine and the ground. She would reach underneath using her paw like a hand and flip them over, exposing their unprotected belly. Never saw another porcupine in our valley after that.

She also loved to chase things that would run from her. Deer were her absolute favorite. We were walking across an old cornfield, long gone fallow, when a young doe jumped up from where she had been sleeping and took off toward the tree line. Socks went after her just as quickly. They ran across the field, the doe weaving and cutting as Socks got from one side of her to the other. They almost made it to the tree line when the doe made one more cut and ran dead into a fence post, paying too much attention to Socks instead of where she was going. By the time I got to them, the doe had died of a broken neck.

Socks pushed the doe hopefully with her nose. Finally, she looked up at me as if asking, "Why doesn't she get up? I wanna play some more."

I thought about what to do. We were nowhere near deer hunting season. Still, the doe was dead, and no one living in the country ever lets food go to waste. So I gutted her and gave the heart and kidneys to Socks as the hunter's prize. I put the liver in my game bag, wrapped in my T-shirt, cut off her head and feet to lower the weight, then slung the carcass over my shoulders.

"It's a good thing she's a yearling, Socks," I said as she ate the parts I had given her. "We wouldda had ta make two or three trips if she'd been full-growed."

Even dressed out, that deer weighed eighty pounds or more. We began the long walk back to Grandpa's house.

I don't know how game wardens know to drive down a certain road at a certain time. The state must test for it when people apply for that job. I've walked down that same logging road a hundred times and have never seen another living soul. But today, of all days, there he came.

He pulled up to me with that doe across my shoulders, took out his handkerchief, and wiped the sweat off his flushed forehead. The small amount of hair he had left made a white horseshoe around the top. His red flannel shirt had dark sweat stains under both arms and down his chest. Why a fat old man would wear a flannel shirt, long johns, long pants, and suspenders on a hot day like this was beyond me.

"Little early for deer, David," he said, pocketing his handkerchief.

"Yeah, I know. Socks ran 'er into a fence post—broke 'er neck. I couldn't leave 'er to waste."

"Well, put her in the back and get in. You too, Socks."

I climbed into the passenger seat, Socks jumped up on my lap, and the two of us sat there with our heads down, feeling like criminals.

He picked up my rifle and smelled the chamber. It hadn't been fired since I cleaned it the night before. He handed me back my rifle and turned his old truck around.

As he pulled into the dirt driveway that led up to Grandpa's house, all Dad's hounds began sounding off like they had treed the biggest coon of all time. The chickens ran every which way when he stopped, clucking their displeasure. Mom came through the doorway with her apron on and some flour on her forehead.

"Afternoon, Annalee," the warden said to her, touching the brim of his dirty old game warden hat. The Department of Natural Resources seal on the front had become so faded and grimy you could barely make it out. He'd been the game warden around here since before I was born.

"Hi, Chester," she said, smiling. "What's he done now?" She gave me the lifted eyebrow look only mothers ever master.

"Found 'im up on the 35 with that doe across his shoulders." He pointed into the back of his truck. "Said Socks ran her into a fence post, and she broke her neck. Thought he could use a lift home. That doe weighs almost as much as he does."

She laughed at that. "Well, thanks for helping, Chester. I think David would love ta give ya a hind quarter for yer trouble." She raised that eyebrow at me again.

"You bet, Mr. Quintard," I swallowed, jumping up and pulling out my knife.

He motioned for me to stop, then mopped his forehead again and looked out across the valley for a minute before he answered Mom.

"I'd love ta have some venison for dinner, Annalee, no doubt, but I can't accept it. The law is pretty clear about that."

It took a while for him to say all those words. He puffed a lot between words like he was having trouble catching his breath. I stood by the tailgate of his truck with my knife in my hand, kind of mesmerized by the wiggling of his triple chin when he talked. He got out of the truck and stared at the doe for a couple of minutes while he decided what to do.

"I'm sure the women's shelter would sure be happy for some venison. I'll be goin' right past there on my way home. Whenever I find clean 'roadkill,' they jus' turn inside out when I drop it off for 'em."

I cut him out a full hind quarter and threw in the back strap and liver along with it. Those poor kids who lived with their mothers in that shelter were skin and bones when they came to school. Mom gave him some onions, carrots, and potatoes from her garden to go along with it. We may have been poor, but we were never hungry and didn't mind sharing with people in need.

When I turned fourteen, a couple of buddies and I decided to spend the weekend camping next to the river. We brought our rifles, dogs, and coolers full of pop and food. We had just settled in for an evening of hot dogs and ghost stories when a guy we'd never seen before came running into our campsite. He didn't have a jacket or hat on and was breathing hard. He looked around with crazy eyes and fought for breath as he leaned over and put his hands on his knees.

"Have you guys seen a woman?" he managed to ask.

"A woman?" I looked at my friends. "Ain't no one up here but us. An' we been here all afternoon."

"What'd she look like, mister?" Larry asked.

"I don't know, kinda tall, dark hair, pretty in a strange kind of way. She had a red-and-blue-flowered dress on. She wasn't young, but then she wasn't old either. I've been talking to 'er for a couple a hours down by the shore." He looked around again, sighed, then started walking back the way he'd come.

"Do ya know which way she headed, mister?" Jack, my other friend, called out to him.

"If I knew that, why would I be talking to you guys?" he snapped.

He turned on his heel angrily, took a few steps back toward the river, then stopped and turned around.

"I'm sorry, kids," he apologized. "I went inta the woods to take a leak n' when I came back she was gone. I been searching for 'er for the last hour. Haven't found hide nor hair of 'er. It's like she vanished inta the river. Even with that big moon up there, I couldn't see her or even footprints showing which direction she'd gone."

He sat down next to our fire as he caught his breath, staring into the flames. I examined him more closely. He looked to be in his mid-twenties, clean-shaven, with red hair in a flat-top haircut. His short-sleeved shirt and slacks were pressed and probably expensive. His arms bulged with muscles that matched his broad chest and slim waist.

"Where ya from, mister?" I asked. "We don't get many strangers up here."

"Owens Ford, about forty miles south a here. I wanted to get away from my folks and think about things for a while. Havin' a little trouble at home. So I decided to come up here and try to figure out what to do. I had just set up camp when she came walking in."

"Did she say where she was from?" Larry asked. "We might know 'er."

"No, she didn't say much about herself. I think that's what I liked most about her. She listened and listened. Sometimes she would ask a question. But mostly, she let me talk."

I didn't know any females like *that*. All the girls I knew were all about them.

"You want some help searching for 'er, mister? Did she tell you 'er name?" We started to get up.

"No. Never mind," he said, getting up also. "I think I'll go home. She'll be all right. The funny thing is, I believe I've figured out what to do. About the time I had ta go pee, the answer came as clearly as if someone spoke it. When I come back, she was gone."

He walked away into the night, and none of us ever saw him again. However, Larry, Jack, and I never forgot the muscled man who came out of the night trying to find the mysterious woman who showed him the way. Each time we camped on that same spot, we made up stories about him suddenly appearing and bringing that woman with him. She would have wet stringy hair and be covered with weeds from the river and blood on her hands. Pop changed into beers. Girls started to accompany us on the campouts. Our bicycles became dirt motorcycles, then four-wheel-drive trucks. The woman became a ghost from a ghastly murder, searching for her murderer among the visitors to the river. Our stories of her would terrify the girls and make them snuggle closer while they looked out fearfully into the dark forest.

I grew up, and Socks grew old. By the time I graduated from high school, she was slowing down. Her puppies had come and gone. Doc Johnson spayed her after the last litter, and I helped him do it. We'd done so many operations together on people's pets we didn't even have to talk while we were working.

That fall, I joined the Army. Mount St Helens, southwest of us, had erupted, and I couldn't wait to escape the dust and tourists who had descended on us. The Army accepted me into Medic training, then Airborne training, Ranger training, and finally Green Beret training. Somewhere along the way, Socks died. Maybe she gave up on me ever coming back home. Perhaps she had gotten as old as I felt now, after thirty years of black ops that never seemed to change anything, no matter whom or how many people we killed.

Chambersville had become very different from my childhood memories. I rode my new Harley, my retirement present to myself, down that twisting excuse for a road that led to town. The logging dried up when they made these hills a national monument. When the logging ended, the lumber mill closed, and so did most of Chambersville. Almost all the people moved away to somewhere they could earn a living, leaving their houses vacant and slowly decaying into dust. The people who remained were either waiting to die next to their memories or making a living off the tourists who descended on Chambersville every weekend and all summer.

I had stopped by Grandpa's house when I first arrived. Mom and Dad were both gone now, buried behind the house in the family cemetery. No one had lived in that house for years. I walked around inside, letting the memories of my childhood fill me for a while. I was born late in their lives, an unexpected gift after thinking children wouldn't be part of their time here on earth. I hadn't returned since they died.

Dad went first, laying his lungs on the altar of tobacco addiction like so many of his generation. Mom followed him three years later. She had been so sad for those three years. She never smoked, but I think she didn't want to live without him by her side. He was her childhood sweetheart. They grew up together, then old together. I believe he was waiting for her on the other side when she passed through.

The old cabinets in the kitchen, with their scuffed finish, had worn spots next to the handles from a lifetime of Mom's hands opening and closing them. I pulled open the drawer where she kept her aprons. She always wore one of these worn-out scraps of cloth wrapped around her waist while she cooked.

I picked one up and held it to my nose—nothing left of her but a faint mildew odor.

Ghost Ride

In my bedroom, up the stairs on the second floor, my old high school stuff was still hanging on the walls. The .22 rifle from my childhood stood in the corner. I picked it up, chuckling at how light and small it was. The rifles I used in the Army were much larger and heavier.

I pulled it up to my shoulder and sighted through the window at a squirrel sitting on a branch of the ancient walnut tree beside the house. The squirrel stared back at me without moving, then turned and scampered down the limb with a walnut in its mouth—a soft brown sheen of rust covered the barrel. I pulled out the cleaning kit, still under my bed, and went through the motions of putting a new coat of oil on my old friend.

I had continued paying the taxes on this property after Mom passed but had turned the electric service off long ago. After Mom's funeral, I drained all the pipes, then let the house sit here empty, not willing to release it to another family, not ready to let some strangers begin to replace my dusty old memories with their shiny new ones.

I put some more wood on the campfire. As near as I can figure, this is where Larry, Jack, and I had camped on those summer nights so long ago. The Harley made it down the old trail as if she'd done it a hundred times. Lots easier riding on it now that the rocks and roots were gone. I had busted my ass more than once on them on my bicycle.

When President Regan declared this area a national monument, a bunch of kids with shovels, chain saws, and pry bars made this trail by the river smooth and wide. Now it has become just another trail through the woods that only tourists use, going from one place where no one lives to another place where it's much the same.

I got camp set up as night fell—a little lean-to with a poncho on top in case it rained with my tent protected by the lean-to. I had made shelters like this all over the world. When something works, you stick with it. Some people seem to love to get out in the woods so they can get cold and wet—like it is a necessary part of the "outdoor" experience. Warm and dry is fine for me. I've been wet and cold enough to last me for the rest of my life.

I remembered the guy we'd met on that night so long ago. I wonder if he'd ever found his answers. Then I thought about saying goodbye to my best friend in the world, Marley Butterhorn, six weeks ago. His friends knew him as "Doc."

I laughed as I realized I had also called Doc Johnson "Doc" when I helped him with his practice. No two people could be more different. Doc Johnson was a huge man with a heart of gold. My friend Doc in the Army was much smaller, maybe 5'8", 160 pounds, sandy hair. If you passed him on the street, you wouldn't have given him a second glance—unless you'd seen his eyes. He had gray eyes. Some people think gray eyes are really light blue. Nope, not Doc's. His eyes were gray. Those eyes could be gentle and warm or cold as ice. While he kept you alive and laughing at your injuries, you'd never know he was one of the deadliest men in the Army. He had been my teammate in the Green Berets, my companion, my savior, and my best friend through the hell and high water of thirty years of war. My mind drifted back to six weeks ago when I said goodbye to him.

After Doc and I hugged for the last time, I threw my leg over that shiny new Harley. One touch of a button, and she began her comforting purr. As I pulled away, Doc snapped to attention and gave me a crisp salute. "Bittersweet" is not a strong enough word to describe the feelings I had at that moment: the end and the beginning—the end of my career as a Green Beret and the beginning of my life as a civilian. Doc disappeared behind a building along with thirty years of brotherhood, shared dangers, and lost friends.

I cruised up to the last stop sign before exiting the base. It was time to think about the future instead of the past. As I approached the guard shack, a full-face grin blossomed from ear to ear. There *are* worse ways to begin a new life. I had a beautiful new motorcycle between my legs. The temperature hovered around 80 degrees. The sky had that unique shade of blue it gets next to the ocean with some puffy white clouds drifting around up there. Three thousand miles away, my home in Washington State beckoned me. Between here and there, a fantastic country that I hadn't seen enough of in the past thirty years was waiting to be explored. What to do next could go on hold until tomorrow, next week, or even next month.

"I think I'll name you Socks," I said to the bike as we were waved past the guard shack and into my new life. Then we were away into the wind. Names don't have to make sense to anyone else.

The ride home took six weeks. I hadn't taken a single interstate or freeway if I could avoid it. Instead, I stopped at every little Podunk crossroads I passed and talked to the people I had been defending for thirty years. Along the way, I visited every VFW, American Legion, Vietnam Veteran's club, and National Cemetery I could find. What a great trip!

And now I'm sitting next to a campfire, still undecided about what to do next. The flames had burned down until they appeared to be individual spirits dancing on the logs as they consumed the wood. I stared into the fire for a few minutes, then decided I was ready. I reached into a hidden inner pocket in my leather jacket and took out a hand-rolled cigarette.

Doc had rolled this joint for me. He tucked it into the breast pocket of my motorcycle jacket as I got ready to leave. As he pulled up the zipper on the pocket, he said, "Sometime, somewhere, you will find the place to smoke this. When you do, ask a question, and you will find the answer."

I crawled into my tent, stretched out on my sleeping bag, and pondered Doc's statement. Only one question was important to me at this moment in my life: "What the hell am I supposed to do now?" So I asked it to the air inside the tent, then lit the end of the joint. The glowing tip had the appearance of an eye in the darkness.

The jumping images of the campfire on the walls provided a kind of psychedelic illumination.

An owl hooted above my tent, so loud that the owl must have been on a branch only a foot away. I tensed, waiting for the shit storm. Whenever a big change was about to bring my life as I knew it down around my shoulders, an owl announced its arrival moments before the shit hit the fan. You laugh, but it has happened so often to me, I can't even hear an owl hoot in a movie without putting my head down, bracing for the blast. Hootie and the Blowhard—best friends forever.

"Hello, the camp," a voice said from down the hill.

Crap! Has to be a ranger, and me with this bomber just lit.

"Thanks for the warning, owl!" I grumbled. Pot might be legal in Washington State, but I was camped in a federal goddamned monument area.

I stubbed the joint out and crawled through the door, having tucked my .45 into the small of my back.

What I found wasn't what I expected. Instead of a ranger with an attitude, a middle-aged woman waited patiently while she clutched a thin gray jacket around herself like she was freezing to death. She had shoulder-length, auburn hair and a dark skirt that stopped at her knees.

"Can I warm up next to your campfire, please? I took a walk on this trail and lost track of time. Now the sun's gone down, and I'm miles from my car."

"Of course. Have a seat."

I dragged a log over to the fire for her and another one for me. I put a few more pieces of wood on the fire from what I had collected before dark.

She seemed a little ill at ease. I guess I didn't blame her. Here we are out in the middle of nowhere, and she's sitting next to a biker-lookin' guy who'd been God knows where, doing God knows what.

"So, where do you live?" I asked, making conversation.

"I live here," she said, smiling for the first time. "I've lived here all my life. My name's Gina."

This time *I* studied *her*. She didn't remind me of anyone I knew. But time has a way of changing people. She still had the beauty that must have driven the young men crazy when she was young. She had to be forty-five or fifty now.

She pulled her thick hair back into a soft ponytail and tied it with a yellow ribbon at the back of her neck.

I guess I've changed too. Every time I stare at the person in the mirror, I have to study my face longer than the last time. Then slowly I can see the young man that left home so many years ago. He's still there for now, but I wonder how much longer he will stay around and what I will do when he leaves for good.

"I used to live here, too," I said. "I guess there's a lot of people who can say that now."

She looked at *me* then and shrugged. "I don't remember you, but I don't remember a lot of things—been a few changes around here. Sometimes I feel like my world is dust. No matter how hard I try to pick some up and hold it in my hand, it slips through my fingers and drifts away."

She held her feet up to the fire. Her beat-up loafers had no socks and wouldn't have kept a mouse warm on a summer day.

I started talking. I don't know why. I told her about my childhood and growing up in Chambersville. I talked to her about my time in the Army. I told her about the good men who had died in my arms as I tried to fix them up, about the children with blown-off arms and legs who believed the big American soldier could save their lives while they looked at me with those huge dark eyes and died, about the babies women would throw into our trucks so we would take them back to the States and give them a chance they would never have at home. I talked about things I had promised myself I would never talk about. I even talked about Socks and how I was away fighting a war when she died.

I went back into the tent and retrieved the joint Doc gave me. I sat down by the fire and lit the end. The two of us passed it back and forth until I tossed the roach into the fire.

She leaned across my chest and kissed me.

"Thanks for going," she said. "There're a lot of men who are alive because you were there to plug the holes in them. You may remember the ones you lost, but you need to remember the ones you didn't. Now those men have wives and children who think the world of them, and you're the reason why. Those children you watched die were a small fraction of the ones you saved. They will never forget the tough American soldier who saved them when no one else would."

Then she took my hand and led me into the tent. The rest is kind of a blur, but I smile every time I think about it, my first and last night with the woman who healed my soul.

You might think it was weird having sex with a woman who had shown up on the side of a trail on a chilly night in October. Well, it wasn't like that. We didn't have sex. I don't know what we had. I can't remember what happened, and I've tried to remember it a thousand times. All I remember is how great I felt when we were done. Call it an out-of-body experience. Call it a healing. Call it great pot. Call it whatever you want, but I have no idea what she did.

She was gone when I awoke. I looked around the campsite, but there weren't even footprints in the dust from where I knew she'd walked. She might as well have been a ghost. What I do remember is never having felt so healthy, so alive, so in tune with everything around me as I did when I crawled out of that tent. I had been reborn and couldn't wait to start finding out what my new life was all about.

I packed the camp onto Socks, and we rode back to Grandpa's house. I got a pad of paper from the desk in my room and started inventorying what I would need to buy to begin fixing up the house. I walked outside, studying the sagging porch, faded paint, and gutterless eaves.

"Better see what tools are left in Dad's workshop," I muttered, walking around the house, then into the old barn.

I heard a noise from the back. I pulled my .45 out as I crept around some old bales of hay. There, between two bales, a litter of puppies and a mother who looked about half-starved to death stared back at me.

"Well, hello there, Mom. Who do you have here?"

Ghost Ride

A golden puppy crawled over to my boot and started to climb up, lost her balance, and splayed all four white feet up in the air. Then, she wiggled around and started up again. I reached down and picked her up. "I will call you Gina."

Chapter 2 – Rhiannon

"When can a crew get out here to turn the power back on?"

The line went quiet while the service agent at the power company checked a list on the other end of the phone connection. Who would have believed I would get four bars of service on my cell phone while I sat in my mother's kitchen? Cell phones didn't even exist up here when they died.

"Thursday morning's the best I can give ya," she replied. Today was Tuesday.

"That'll be fine." Like I had a choice! "See you then."

"Wait a minute!" she called out.

"What?"

"Be sure to turn off the main breaker. They can't hot you up unless the main breaker is off."

"Good to know. Thanks!"

I walked into the pantry and pulled open the antique blade switch in the fuse box. This disconnected the house from where the power company would install the meter. No power until Thursday. No power means no water, heat, refrigeration, or cooking. So I will have to eat downtown until Thursday.

I walked out to the barn and checked on the puppies. Mom had eaten so much dog food she could barely stand. I filled her food bowl again, emptied the last of the gallon of water into her water dish, then walked out to the stream next to the property line to refill the jug from the crystal clear water.

When I went back into the barn, the puppies were running around the barn, exploring and pouncing on each other. Gina ran up to me and attacked my boots, giving them a ferocious growl and a bark. I picked her up, chuckling, and scratched behind her ears. She tried to lick my face, licked my hand, then struggled to get down. Her brothers and sisters were having too much fun to be left out.

When I pushed the start button, Socks started instantly. The puppies dove for cover at the sound. I rode down to Chambersville.

There had been some changes in thirty years. Most of the farms I passed were overgrown and abandoned. Two deer raised their heads as I drove by, a buck and a doe, their mouths full of the hay no one harvested anymore. The antlers on the buck were fully gown out, the velvet long gone—a handsome three-pointer.

As I drove by, the light in the window of Mountaintop Diner said "OPEN". I used to drink sodas and eat burgers there after football games—maybe I would recognize someone.

I turned Socks around and swung into the parking area, paved now. Inside two farmers sat in one booth, and a guy with greasy cover-alls sat at the counter. The waitress, a cute middle-aged woman, smiled as I entered.

I sat at the counter, feeling a massive déjà vu. I could still remember sitting in this exact seat in a blue tuxedo while my prom date and I ate burgers and fries before heading over to the dance.

The waitress walked over. "What you havin', honey?"

I snapped out of my daydream and got to study her up close—full lips, hair the color of spun gold, and eyes so blue I had to force myself not to stare at them. Instead, I studied the menu to keep from making a fool of myself. She smiled, making the laugh lines next to her eyes crinkle up. I suspected she was used to being stared at.

"Three eggs, over medium, hash browns with gravy on top, sourdough toast, and coffee, black."

"You're out of luck with the gravy, honey. The tourists clean us out by now every morning."

"You don't still have some a that homemade apple butter, do you?"

My mouth watered at the memory of apples, sugar, and cinnamon. I hadn't found any since I came home to bury Mom.

She studied me a little harder then, as if trying to see inside my shell to the guy inside.

"Not that we sell, but I have some in the fridge in the back I use on my toast. I'll get you some."

"Do I know you?" she asked when she returned and put a small dish of apple butter on the counter. "No one's asked for my apple butter in ten years."

"Doubtful. I'm David Peterson. I'm moving back into my folks' house up on Davis Ridge."

She had a puzzled expression on her face, one eyebrow higher than the other. "David?"

Suddenly I remembered her. Rhiannon. Rhiannon McNeil. We dated once in high school. She had been the captain of the cheerleaders. She married the quarterback and started popping out babies, or maybe the other way around—it had been a long time ago.

"Rhiannon," I said, more of a statement than a question. "It's been a long time."

She checked around the diner—the farmers talking quietly, greasy cover-all guy sipping his coffee. No one needed anything. She got a cup for herself and sat down next to me. That got me a dark look from the guy in the greasy cover-alls.

"Where have you been? When did you get back? The last I heard, you were in Iraq or Afghanistan or somewhere. What *happened* to your beautiful hair?"

My hair had just begun getting long enough to be wavy again like it had been for most of my childhood. Oh, how Mother had cried on my first trip home after basic training, mourning my hair lying on the floor of the PX barbershop. She kept running her hands across my head, as though my hair would reappear if she wished for it hard enough. It had been "high and tight," a classic military haircut for the last thirty years. My "suntan" and vaguely African/Indian features were a genetic gift from my great-grandparents and grandparents. My mother's father and mother were also Cowlitz Indians. Those features had helped me fit into places where lily-white Americans would have had a lot of trouble.

Rhiannon smiled at me with those wide-open blue eyes. Freckles ran across her perfect nose from one cheek to the other. And I had forgotten how full her lips were. I stared into my cup of coffee again. Thirty years had gone by since I last saw her, and I felt like a high schooler again.

"I got back yesterday—retired from the Army six weeks ago and bought a motorcycle. How have you been?"

I was staring at her again and couldn't seem to stop. She smiled like it was a private joke. The sun came out from behind the clouds when she smiled, or it must have. I swear the room filled with light.

"Oh, I'm OK. My kids are all grown, still got two in college. The rest are gone to the four winds. Joe left me for a cute young thing he met on a business trip about twenty years ago. Then he got AIDS and died. So now I'm pushing fifty and swimming around on my own."

The cook, a black man with almost white hair, rang a bell and slid my food onto the warming shelf for Rhiannon to pick up. She put it in front of me, then walked around the diner filling the coffee cups of anyone who needed it. She leaned over the back counter and whispered something to the cook. I enjoyed watching her trim figure stretch to the window. I hoped I looked as good when I pushed fifty.

"Uh, David," that little voice inside my head chimed in. "Don't know how to tell you this, but you *are* 'pushing fifty.'"

I told the voice to shut up, but it didn't listen.

"And why would you like to look like a cheerleader anyway?" the voice continued, laughing. "Is there something you haven't told me?"

I ignored her.

"So, what are you going to do now?" Rhiannon asked, sitting back down with another cup of coffee. "Relax and hang out, or do you have some other plans?"

She crossed her legs and put both elbows on the counter, looking at me. Her waitress uniform clung to her body in a most sensual way; the swell of her breasts peeked out where her top buttons were undone.

"I've been thinking about opening a first aid station," I said, forcing my eyes up to her face instead of her cleavage. "I've had a little experience fixing up hurt people."

"Well, there's nothing like that around here anymore. Nearest medical care is on the other side of the mountain, at least two hours away."

"Do you know anyone who works on cars? I'd like to see if Dad's old pickup is worth fixing."

She leaned around behind me, pressing her breast into my back.

"Tommy, can you slide over here a minute?"

The young man in greasy cover-alls walked over with his coffee cup and sat on the stool next to her. His eyes were a little too bright. Acne sores covered his face and neck. His four-day growth of beard didn't fit his hollow cheeks. I tried to ignore how much he irritated me.

"Whaddaya need, gorgeous?"

His discolored, rotten teeth showed when he grinned. She blushed a little, then smiled at me self-consciously and introduced us.

"Tommy, this is David Peterson. He's just out of the Army. He wants to know if his dad's old pickup is worth fixin'. Do you think you could help him out?"

"Sure thing." He leaned over so he could see me. "Does it run?"

"Not in fifteen years. Two tires are flat."

"Well, I should tow it to my garage, so's I can check it out. Where is it now?"

I gave him my address.

"Be up there early this afternoon. See you then."

He got up and threw some money on the counter.

"Bye, gorgeous. Gotta get back to work."

Somehow I didn't think he was talking to me.

"So are you and Tommy a thing?" I asked after he left.

She looked down, then away for a minute before answering.

"Well, he thinks so. Me? I like to go out on Friday nights as much as the next girl. Not a lot of options around here. Tommy and I have been casually dating for a year, on and off. He wants to get a lot more personal. I'm not ready—not with him. He's only twenty-nine, for God's sake."

She gave a little shiver and looked away. I got up and put fifteen bucks on the counter for a ten-dollar breakfast.

"See ya, later, Rhiannon."

"I hope so," she called as I walked through the door toward Socks.

I looked up before I rolled Socks out of her parking spot. She was still smiling at me. I waved. She waved back. I headed out to see what else had changed while I fought in the wars around the world.

Tommy called in the middle of the afternoon. Dad's pickup truck needed a new battery, a tune-up, a brake job, an oil change, and four new tires.

"Go ahead with that stuff—some good mud and snow tires and ceramic brake pads. Change the gear oil in the transmission while you have it, Tommy, and the differential oil in both axles and the transfer case, the antifreeze, and purge the old brake fluid. How are the hoses and belts?"

"They're cracked. I'd replace 'em."

"Then do that, too. Can you replace the vacuum hoses as well?"

"Sure. Should be done tomorrow."

While he worked on that, I went to the local DMV office to change the title over to my name and register it. The office manager, Shawn Kozup, had my application in his hand. He had also been on my football team during high school.

"I should have a copy of your dad's death certificate to do this."

"Shawn, you knew my dad. You were at his funeral."

"Yeah, I know," he sighed and glanced around to see who would notice. No one paid any attention to us at all. "OK. Here are your tags and title."

"Thanks, buddy."

"You doin' anything after work?"

"I don't know. Whaddaya have in mind?"

"I thought we might get together tonight ... maybe lift a couple. Whaddaya think?"

"An offer I can't refuse," I replied solemnly, then broke out into a grin. "Wagon Wheel? About 6?"

"I'll be there."

A call to my insurance company got the truck insured. I called Tommy to find out what progress he had made. He said the truck would be ready around noonish tomorrow.

The Wagon Wheel was about half full when I got there. Shawn already had a table at the back with a couple more old friends from our football team. They bought me beers and shots until either I stopped or I replayed some other less pleasant parts of my high school memories. I slept on Shawn's sofa until dawn broke through the window. The cold ride back to Grandpa's cleared out most of the cobwebs from my poor, hung-over brain. A cold bath using a bucket at the creek took care of the rest.

As I poured the last bucket over my head to rinse off the shampoo and soap, I looked up at the snow on the hills over Grandpa's property. The water I used to bathe was maybe a couple of degrees above freezing. It had to have been snow two or three hours ago. *At least the water is clean,* I thought to myself. *Better than that time in Congo. You could jump from clump to clump in that water. And some of those clumps were corpses!*

At lunchtime, I rode Socks to town to check on Tommy's progress with Dad's pickup.

"The suspension and steering are worn but still serviceable. The shocks should be replaced. I put new wiper blades on. One headlight was out, and both taillights were bad. You should be good to go."

I gulped at the bill. Almost $2,000, about half of it was labor. A thousand bucks for eight hours' work. Not bad wages.

Tommy smiled at me, wiping his greasy hands on a dirty rag. "Yeah, it do add up."

Four parallel scratches were deep in his left cheek. They looked new.

"How'd you scratch yourself, Tommy?" I asked, trying to make conversation while the total on the bill sank in.

"Oh, cleaning some blackberries out from around my house last night. Pretty normal for up here."

I handed him my credit card.

"We don't take credit cards or checks, David." He smiled that empty smile again. "Been stiffed too many times by the tourists. But, the bank's still open. You can get cash there."

I looked at the credit card dongle hanging off the side of his computer. His face smiled, but his eyes were as cold as a winter storm. Without saying another word, I turned on my heel and walked across the street to the bank, my lips pursed into a hard straight line.

The branch manager greeted me. He was bald without even a whisper of hair on his head. Odd for a man around forty-five or fifty, I thought. His suit of fine quality wool seemed a couple of sizes too large for him. I introduced myself and inquired if I could cash a check.

"Well, what I'd like you to do is open an account and deposit some money," he said, a little breathlessly. "You can withdraw the money when it clears in seven days."

"I need the cash today to pay for some repairs on my truck. Tommy won't take my credit card."

He stared across the street at Tommy's service station for a moment, then shook his head and sighed.

"Sure, David. I'll cash your check. You don't remember me, do you?"

I looked at him more closely and drew a blank.

"Nope. I sure don't."

"I'm Frank. Frank Everest. I was two years behind you in high school. I was the only guy on the football team who never got invited to the campouts by the river."

The image of a fat boy with pimples who followed us around like an abandoned puppy came to the surface.

"You've lost a lot of weight, Frank."

"Yep." He looked even sadder. "I guess life doesn't give everyone a happy ending."

I didn't know what to say. He handed me an envelope full of cash.

"Watch out for Tommy. Rumor has it he isn't the most honest or reliable mechanic in town."

I walked back to Tommy's office and handed him the envelope. He counted it, handed me back seventeen dollars and some change, marked the bill paid in full, and walked into the back of his shop without saying a word.

The key to Dad's truck was on Tommy's desk. I walked out with it to where the truck was parked and sat behind the wheel. Everything looked normal, but I felt it—hell, I could almost hear it screaming—something was wrong. After thirty years of people trying to kill me and somehow staying alive, I paid attention to my "feelings." Always.

I walked around the truck. Everything looked as it should. The new tires were properly inflated with new balancing weights on the rims. I popped the hood and started checking Tommy's work: engine oil—clean and filled to the dipstick's full mark; oil filter—new and tight; hoses and belts—new, connected to the right places, and clamped securely; brake fluid reservoir—on the full line; antifreeze reservoir—on the Cold mark where it should be; radiator—full without a trace of the rusty water that had been there; spark plug wires—new and plugged into the new distributor cap, all routed to the correct new spark plugs.

I slid under the truck, grateful it had enough clearance to move around under it—nothing loose in the suspension. The oil drain plugs on the engine, transmission, and differentials were tight. The brake rotors were shiny and newly cut. I could see the new brake pads inside the calipers. Then I noticed a drop of brake fluid fall to the ground next to the right front tire. Reaching up to the brake caliper, I found I could turn the nut on the brake line by hand. I checked the brake lines of the calipers on the other wheels. They were loose also.

The brakes would have worked fine until the brake fluid reservoir emptied, then ... nothing. Then I noticed the emergency brake cable hanging loosely when it should have been tight and out of sight. So not only would the brakes have failed, but I would also have had no emergency brake. In the mountains around this town, that would have been a death sentence.

I walked back into Tommy's work bay to his toolbox, and got a 3/8-inch line wrench, a pair of ½-inch open-end wrenches, and an adjustable wrench. I walked back out to the truck, tightened the brake lines, then adjusted the emergency brake cable back to where it should have been. It had been deliberately loosened, based on the clean threads on the adjustment screw. When I finished, I checked the pedal pressure on the brakes and the emergency brake—worked fine. I crawled back under the truck and removed the filler plug from the transmission. I couldn't feel any oil as far down as I could reach with my finger. It should have been overflowing. I returned Tommy's wrenches and got the gear oil pump. I filled the transmission, both differentials, and the transfer case. Based on how much oil they took, I figured they had been dry, probably drained, then not refilled. Tommy didn't come out of his office or even acknowledge I had entered his garage.

From the hardware store across the street, I bought ten gallons of light brown paint, a couple of gallons of gray trim paint, and a gallon of mauve accent paint, pausing to think about what else I was going to need.

"Add rolls of 14-, 12-, and 10-gauge copper wire," I told the kid helping me. I figured him to still be in high school. "I know I'm going to need them. Do you have 250-foot rolls?"

"Sure do."

"Give me two of each."

He went to retrieve them. When he returned with the rolls of wire, he asked, "Do you need brushes, tape, window paper, scrapers, painter's rags, drop cloths, a wire stripper, wire nuts?"

I hadn't seen a paintbrush anywhere in the barn. Almost all Dad's tools had "disappeared" while the house stood empty and unoccupied.

I laughed at myself. "Of course I do. Thanks for reminding me."

"How about a paint sprayer?" the kid asked. "Make the job go a lot faster. We rent them by the hour, day, or week."

"Show me what you've got."

This kid had really impressed me. His hair was short, and no tattoos or piercings were visible. I liked him more with each word that passed between us. He rented me the sprayer for a week, showed me how to use it, and sold me a gallon of cleanup solvent to go with it.

"That paint is supposed to be self-priming." He pointed to the brown paint. "You'll need to do two coats on that dried-out wood. Or you can prime it first. I'd go with the priming. It's a lot cheaper than two coats of paint and will make the paint stick better."

"Then add five gallons of white primer. Is there a discount tool store anywhere near here? I need a bunch of tools for fixing up my place."

He looked around to make sure the owner wasn't in the store.

"Well, Harbor Freight is over the mountain. So is Sears, Home Depot, and Lowes, but you didn't hear it from me. It's a hike, but you'll get a lot more for your money there than you do here. Pull your car around back to the loading dock, and I'll put all this stuff in."

I backed up the truck to the loading dock and realized the edge lined up with the bed. And at the side of the loading dock had a gentle ramp that went down to the driveway.

"Would you mind if I used your loading ramp to put my bike in the back? Tommy had my truck, so I rode my bike down to Chambersville."

"Bicycle or motorcycle?"

"Harley."

He got a big grin on his face, then he looked around for his boss again and said softly, "Old man Beckitt don't want nothin' to do with motorcycles. Thinks only hoodlums ride 'em. He don't know I got my first dirt bike when I turned six. But he's over at the café having some coffee. Go get it quick. I'll load your paint."

When I pulled the shiny new Harley up the ramp, his eyes got wide. I thought he was going to wet his pants.

"How cool is *that*!" he exclaimed. "It must be brand new. Can I sit on it?"

"Of course."

"Oh, man. If the kids could see me now!"

He postured like the Fonz, in *Happy Days*, leaning one way then the other, making motorcycle engine noises. He sold me a couple of tie-down straps then helped me secure the bike.

"What's your name?" I asked the boy.

"John Nelson."

"I knew a Jack Nelson when I went to high school here."

"That's my dad!" he said proudly.

"Well, tell him David Peterson said 'hi.'"

"I sure will, Mr. Peterson."

He watched the Harley longingly until I disappeared around the corner of the building. I had to smile, remembering those same feelings when I was his age, and I saw *my* first Harley.

As I passed the diner on my way out of town, something said as clearly as a passenger next to me, "How about some food before you go up?"

I shook my head and laughed. *I must be losing it. Hey, everyone, the old soldier in the pickup truck has gone around the frigging bend.* I shook my head again, then started back up the road, then slowed down and pulled over again. Anyone watching me would have laughed as well. On the other hand, I didn't have any food in the house. Or any way to cook it, if I did have any food. Why not stop? The power won't be on until tomorrow. The chance of seeing the golden-haired woman from my past had nothing to do with it. Really!

Rhiannon wasn't working.

"She called in sick this morning," the cook said when I asked. "Not like her. She ain't been sick a day since she started fifteen year ago."

I ordered a cheeseburger, fries, and a vanilla shake. From the moment he'd said Rhiannon had called in sick, a cold lump had started growing in my gut. Call it dread, prescience, premonition, whatever. I didn't like it. The other times in my life when that lump appeared had not ended well.

"Where does she live?" I asked the cook when he brought me the food. "I think I'll check on her—make sure she's all right."

"You that Green Beret guy everyone's talking about, ain't cha?"

I didn't know *anyone* was talking about me. I'd only been home for two days. "Yeah, I guess so. So who's talking about me?"

"Well, Rhiannon was. Her boyfriend didn't like it and told her so. She told him to ... well it weren't exacly polite English, if ya know what I mean."

He cackled a little, remembering the scene.

Well, that explains Tommy and my truck—explains it, but doesn't forgive it.

"She lives about a block away. Sixty-five Elm Street. But you didn hear it from me."

"What's your name, old-timer?"

Even with his white hair, he still looked to be in pretty good shape.

"Gus. Gustophe Schwartz, but everyone calls me Gus."

I blinked, not expecting such a German name for a black man.

He cackled some more. "My daddy's German. I get that a lot."

"Well, I'm David Peterson." I extended my hand. "Thanks for the info."

He shook my hand firmly. "Sure thing, young man. I served too. Twenty-Fifth Infantry Division, Mekong Delta, '65-'67. Glad I could help. Tell Rhiannon I'm worried about her."

As I finished the burger, I saw a picture hanging on the wall behind the cash register. It showed a much younger Gus. He rippled with muscles as he posed beside a 4.2-inch mortar. The base plate on those mortars weighed a hundred and fifty pounds—a tough job in a tough war. I paid the tab with an extra five bucks for a tip and walked over to 65 Elm Street—a small yellow house with a fenced yard, neatly trimmed shrubs, and hanging flower baskets around the full-width porch. A two-person swing rocked slightly in the breeze near the front door. I walked up to the door and knocked.

"Whoos der?" came a muffled voice.

"It's David Peterson."

"Dvid, dis idn't a gud tim." I could hardly understand her. "I'll thee ya tomorra'."

"I came to see you because Gus said you weren't feeling well. What's going on?"

"Pleez, Dvid ..." I heard a small sob.

I grabbed the doorknob and turned it—locked, but the door pushed open. Someone had smashed the door frame. From the footprint next to the handle, I'd say it had been kicked in. Rhiannon was standing behind the door in her bathrobe. She turned away when I entered and tried to cover her face with her left hand. I stepped up to her and pulled her hand away.

She had a blackened left eye, almost swollen shut and turning colors. The left side of her jaw was severely bruised. The right side had a split lip with bruises to match. She held her right forearm gently across her chest. Another bruise was visible on her wrist.

"My God, Rhiannon ..."

She stepped into my arms and started to cry. I held her gently until her tears slowed, then stopped, then lifted her face so I could wipe her nose on my shirt sleeve. All those years of carrying a handkerchief and the one time I really needed it, I'd left it on my dresser at home. I examined her face carefully—no apparent broken bones. Her shoulder was clearly dislocated.

"I need to get you to a hospital. Where else do you hurt?"

"I hur evywhere," she moaned, closing her good eye.

"Can I do a quick exam?" I didn't want any surprises when I was transporting her.

She looked into my eyes, then shrugged as if nothing could hurt her more than she already hurt. "Sure."

I opened her robe. She was naked underneath. No surprise there. How would you put on underwear with a dislocated shoulder? There were bruises on her breasts, abdomen, and thighs, but no lacerations or obvious broken bones. I checked for broken teeth or dentures, but everything in her mouth was intact. Her abdomen, while bruised, was not swollen. "Lie down on the couch," I told her.

I palpated the four quadrants of her abdomen. Nothing was screaming out as an injured organ would other than general soreness. Both her irises were reactive, coordinated, and equal. Her heart rate was a little high, as were her respirations—completely normal, given her injuries. I helped her rollover. There were some more bruises on her back and possibly a broken rib over her lung on the right side, but the site was not depressed—no danger to the lung. I ran my hands down the length of her spine from her neck to her pelvis, then down both legs, checking for deformities, pain, and bruising—nothing. I pulled her robe back over her.

"You can get up. Are you taking any medications? Insulin? Antibiotics? Illegal drugs?"

"No." She hesitated a second, then continued. "I smok sum pot fer da pain. Tuk sum Advil an hor ago."

"Your shoulder is dislocated. I need to reset it. You OK with that?"

"Sur."

"I know you hurt bad, but I need you to relax everything, or I'll just be fighting you. The pain from your shoulder will pretty much go away when the joint is back together."

"OK. Jus do it."

She closed her eyes and visibly relaxed her muscles.

Tough girl, I thought to myself. I had seen soldiers cry like a baby for a lot less.

I lifted her arm, and the ball snapped back into the socket with a loud pop. She gasped at the red hot moment of pain, then let the air back out as the pain went away.

"OK. Thas bettr." She lifted her arm a little and winced. "It's ba, but nt as ba as havin' a baby."

I laughed. "I know that's right!"

She smiled back in a distorted, bent kind of way.

I put her arm in a sling I made from a bath towel, then retrieved my truck from in front of the diner. We drove over the mountain to the hospital.

I filled in the ER doc, a Dr. Chung, about my examination, what I found, and how I had reset her dislocated shoulder. Then, they wheeled her into the examination room.

An hour later, the doc returned with a heavyset Hispanic-looking cop beside him. The cop wore a protective vest that made him appear even bigger. Neither of them was smiling.

"You were right about the broken rib. It should heal fine. We need a DNA sample from you so we can eliminate you from the samples we got from under her fingernails and the semen. We also need a copy of your driver's license. Nice job on shoulder reset."

"I've done that a few times before." I left out the part about the bullets and explosions going on while I did it.

He swabbed the inside of my mouth. I handed the cop my license and retired military ID.

Twenty minutes later, the cop brought them back. "Sergeant Major Peterson, I'd like to shake your hand. I've never met a for-real hero before."

"You saw all that, huh," I said nervously. I never wore all the medals I had been awarded. They seemed like bragging to me. "Don't be too impressed. The difference between a hero and a corpse is usually about half an inch. I was at the right place at the right time and didn't get killed. You'd have done the same thing."

"I'd like to think so—hope I never have to find out. What were all the classified awards? They wouldn't even tell me what the medals were, let alone why you got them."

"Nothing important. Spooks give out medals to impress themselves."

"I don't know about that. But my name is Xavier Sanchez. Let me know if you find any leads on this case. Rhiannon won't tell me anything about who did it or why. That's why we swabbed you. Here's my card. My phone number is on it. It rings right here."

He patted his cell phone on his belt, right next to his pistol, a Glock 17.

An hour later, Rhiannon and I were going back over the mountain. Rhiannon spent the whole two-hour trip looking out the window without saying a word while I quietly pondered the events of the day. Semen. The doc said he had found semen. Somehow I didn't think it was from consensual sex, not with the bruises I'd seen on her thighs.

Dusk set behind us as we crested the pass. By the time we pulled up in front of her house, stars had filled the night sky.

She looked into my eyes, touched my cheek with her hand, and tried to smile. "Thnk you, Dvid." Then she got out and walked through her ruined front door.

I drove back to the hardware store. John had just locked the door but opened it again when he saw me. I bought the stuff I needed to replace Rhiannon's door jam and make her front door secure. All of those new tools were things I would need to fix up Grandpa's house, so I didn't worry too much about how much they cost. I slid a twenty-dollar bill across the counter to John as he ran my credit card for the total.

"What's that for?" he asked, handing me the credit slip to sign.

"That's for staying open. I appreciate it. And I'll bet you aren't getting paid for working late."

"Old man Beckitt barely pays me for the scheduled hours I work."

"'Nuff said. Buy your girlfriend a burger. Thanks again."

About halfway through fixing her front door, Rhiannon walked out of the bedroom—showered and dressed.

"Wha're you doin, Dvid?" she asked.

"Fixin' your door." I would have thought it was pretty obvious what I was doing.

"Why're you doin' tht?"

"It's broken. I figured you would want to lock it."

"Yeah, lokin wud be gud."

She crossed her arms in front of her chest protectively and looked down, trying hard not to cry.

"You want to talk about it?"

She hung her head again and shook her head. "No. I wanna forgt abou it. I wan it t' disapper. I wan it t' nevr'v happnd."

She started to cry again. I held her until she stopped. She didn't move away from me. Instead, she laid her head on my chest, her arms around my waist. Her hair smelled clean and floral. I liked holding her a lot.

"Did you tell them about Tommy?" I whispered in her ear.

"Tommy? Who sed anythin abou Tommy?"

She pulled away from me.

"Didn't Tommy do this to you?"

"It wad't Tommy!" she screamed, her eyes wild. "I nevr seen 'im before. He was ... black and ... had a scar on his cheek."

She pulled away from me. "You havta lev!"

"I'll leave when I finish your door." I turned back to the job, deliberately ignoring her. She watched me for a minute in silence, then walked back into her bedroom, closing the door. I could hear her crying.

When I finished, I studied the job with satisfaction. I had replaced all the screws holding the door and door frame with four-inch grade eight steel screws and added twenty more screws around the door jamb for extra insurance, each one shimmed and tight. I added a steel door jamb reinforcing plate around the deadbolt then used some foam from a rattle can to seal the gap around the door frame. No one was going to kick their way through *that* door with *that* deadbolt!

I left the keys to the deadbolt on her kitchen counter with a note that told her to lock the deadbolt, and that I would come back in the morning to attach the trim.

Chapter 3 – I've Been Called Worse

The next day, I started the morning with a five-mile run to clear my head. The rolling hills and country roads around Chambersville were perfect for getting my blood pumping. Autumn colors were in full bloom everywhere. The hills were a riot of deep green from the fir and cedar trees interspersed with yellows, reds, and golds from the alders, maples, and oaks. The clouds that usually fill the sky in October were gone for a day, replaced by a freshly scrubbed blue.

On a beautiful day like this, I get a momentum when I run. So when I got back to the house, I didn't want to stop. But duty called.

As I cooled off, I walked out to the barn and checked on the puppies. Mom even wagged her tail a little when she saw me. I filled her food and water dishes again, played with the puppies, then walked back to the truck. Socks was easy to unload with the help of the ditch beside my driveway. With the truck's back tires in the ditch, the tailgate was at ground level, and the bed sloped gently toward the rear. Socks rolled out the back with hardly a bump. The paint, the tools, and the supplies went into the barn where the puppies couldn't reach them. Then the house scraping began in earnest. Somehow the tool thieves had missed the extension ladder in the barn's loft.

Beyond having to go up and down the ladder a lot as I moved around the house, the scraping effort wasn't nearly as much work as I'd feared. The old, flaking paint came off easily. With the temperature in the sixties and a light breeze out of the west, I couldn't imagine a more perfect day for mindless physical labor— exactly what I needed after the drama of yesterday. It felt wonderful to use my muscles again.

Lunch time, I headed down to Chambersville to eat and get some hornet spray for the nests under the eaves. Rhiannon hadn't come into work again. I filled Gus in on what had happened yesterday. From the look on his face, I suspected Tommy wouldn't be eating at the diner anymore. People who've served in the combat arms of the military tend to be pretty protective of people in their unit.

I picked up some trim wood and a chop saw at the hardware store, then dove around the block to Rhiannon's house. A custom-painted pickup with a twelve-inch lift kit and huge off-road tires sat in front of her house. It had more lights on the front grill and light bar over the cab than a sideshow at a carnival. I remembered it being parked next to Tommy's service station.

I heard shouting from inside the house as I walked up.

Tommy opened the door and bellowed back into the house. "You even see him again, you whore, and yesterday will be like child's play."

He slammed the door and came up short when he saw me in front of him.

"I might have something to say about that, Tommy," I said quietly.

He went white, then red, then white again. I laughed. He looked like a blinking traffic light. He tried to push past me. I put my hand in the middle of his chest and glared into his eyes, his being about six inches from mine.

"You touch her again, I'll tear off your head and shit down your throat."

He did the blinking traffic light thing again. I tried not to laugh.

"Fuck you."

Before the "you" had left his mouth, he was lying on the ground with my left hand cutting off the air in his windpipe. The fingers on my right hand had stopped about a quarter of an inch from gouging out both of his eyeballs. My knee was in his solar plexus.

"Did you know a finger can penetrate the brain when you enter through the eye socket?" I paused for effect. "It's usually fatal. Do we understand each other?"

I hadn't raised my voice above deadpan. If you want to be heard, speak quietly.

He nodded.

"Good. If I were you, I'd leave town. Find some shithole to slither into far, far away and never, *ever* come back. I'd really *hate* to have to hurt you."

He was turning purple, and his mouth opened and closed like a fish out of water. When his eyes started to roll back into his sockets, I released his throat and pulled out my handkerchief.

"Spit," I commanded.

"Wha wha what?" he stammered.

"Spit into my handkerchief. Are you deaf as well as stupid?"

His mouth had gone dry. It took him a couple of tries before he hocked up some adequate spit. I released him.

He scrambled upright then ran to his truck, the front of his pants dark with a spreading water stain. He fell once climbing in, then tore a six-inch-deep trough in the dirt with both wheels. When he went around the corner at the end of the block, the truck went up on two wheels and almost tipped over. I watched it wobble, miss a parked car, come down heavily on all four wheels, and disappear past the house on the corner.

I knew it wasn't over yet, between Tommy and me. But you have to try to make idiots understand. It just never works. They *are* idiots, after all.

I realized Rhiannon had watched the whole thing from her front door.

"Hi. Ready for me to fix the trim? And I need a clean Ziploc baggy."

She ran to me and threw her arms around my neck. And I let her. OK, so I'm easy. I've been called worse.

Chapter 4 – Good Times Autopilot

By the time Tommy got back to his service station, he was shaking with fury. The kid he'd hired from the high school a couple of weeks ago on a work-study program looked up as he came in. *Jimmy. Yeah, Jimmy was his name.*

The kid walked over to him as Tommy unlocked the door to his office. Jimmy had an athlete's physique with a dark brown crew cut and a soul patch under his lower lip. A small diamond earring glittered in his left ear lobe.

"Spilled some coffee," Tommy spat as he changed clothes, trying to get his anger under control. "That Taurus done yet?"

"Nah, needs a new timing belt. Got to take apart the whole front of the motor. You OK?"

"Stupid tourist cut me off. Spilled my coffee all over my lap."

Jimmy pursed his lips and shook his head. Everyone in Chambersville had a stupid-tourist story.

"You clear the repairs with the Taurus's owner?"

"Yep. He stopped in. I showed him. He said go ahead. They're camped out at the Oak Tree Motel," the kid snickered. "I think his wife and him are like having a second honeymoon."

"Cool! That'll be a fat bill. And you'll get a fat commission," Tommy added, grinning his rotten-tooth grin. "Make a list of the parts you need. I'll pick 'em up tomorrow morning. I have to make a run over the mountain anyway."

"Will do." Jimmy returned to the Taurus.

Tommy closed the door to his office, then got out his mirror and stash. He laid out a fat line of meth and snorted it. The familiar bite brought tears to his eyes. *Fuckin' Green Beret, son of a bitch.* The humiliation of what David had done to him began to sink in. *And in front of Rhiannon! Dammit! And he'd just got her straightened out. Fuckin' whore!*

She was the whole reason he lived in this shithole. He met her where she worked on the other side of the mountain, then followed her over here after work one night. Chambersville looked like a great place to live for a while. They had even dated a few times, but she never took him home. A kiss on the cheek and off she would go into her house. He'd even made an appointment with the local dentist to fix his teeth. *Well, guess what wouldn't happen now.*

The more he thought about it, the angrier he got. The meth he'd put into his body fanned the flames. *We'll see about this, Davie Boy!*

The phone rang.

"Yeah?" Tommy was in no mood for customers.

"Mr. Santanini?"

Only one person called him by *that* last name. He rubbed his face and took a deep breath, trying to clear the meth buzz out of his brain. "What's going on with Mom?"

"Hi, Mr. Santanini. This is Joan in the billing department. Your mother is healthy and happy."

"She just can't remember her name," Tommy mouthed so quietly the woman wouldn't hear him. Then he spoke at regular volume. "That's good news. So what's up? Why did you call?"

"The money you put into her bill pay account is almost gone. We're assuming you want to keep her here. You'll need to add some more money before it runs out."

Christ, did I forget to do that again? he thought to himself. To the woman, he said, "Thanks, I'll take care of it immediately. Thanks for calling."

He used his cell phone to connect to his private account on the other side of the mountain and set the transfer up in under a minute.

Tommy's mom was the only person in his family he still talked to. Well, OK, he spoke to her when she had a good day—when she could still remember that she had a son. He tried to recall when she'd had her last "good day". He couldn't. It had been years ago. His asshole older brother had split when he turned fourteen. His little sister left when she got tired of their dad climbing into bed with her—maybe twelve when she walked. He thought again, maybe not quite twelve. Turning tricks in Vegas, last he heard—crawled into a crack pipe and never looked back. Only Tommy stuck around to care for his mom after his dad went belly up in the county morgue.

Pissed off the wrong dude in a fight outside a bar, didn't ya, Dad?

Tommy laughed out loud at that. *He'd* been that "wrong dude" and lost count of how many times he'd wished he could've pulled that trigger more times than he did. His father's death had been way too fast. Tommy had been fifteen but could still remember the feeling as he squeezed that trigger—pure ecstasy. That son of a bitch would never beat up him or his mom again. While blood poured out the holes in the back of his father's chest, Tommy pulled up his father's head by the hair and put the pistol barrel into his mouth. He studied his father's face for a moment, trying to remember every detail. His father's eyes had opened wide.

"Fuck you!" were the last garbled words his father said.

Tommy pulled the trigger three times. He would have pulled it more, but the gun went empty. Not a lot left of his dad's head when he finished—a little smoke coming out of his nose. His dad's eyeballs had popped out of his head while the bullets turned his brain into mush on the alley floor.

Tommy started living on the street after that. Whenever he made some money from whatever he could steal and sell, he'd give it to his mother. Then, when his mother got diagnosed with Alzheimer's, he found a place that would take care of her and paid for her treatment with his auto repair scams as he hopped from one backwater shithole to another.

Then he met the folks out on Black Mountain Road. They needed a local business to wash some money clean. He got all the speed he could do, making money to boot. He'd never done drugs before that—no money for it. So now he had lots of money, lots of drugs, and the world had settled into a "good times" autopilot. At least it had been until David Peterson showed up.

"Gonna have to do something about you, Mr. Sergeant Fucking Major Peterson," Tommy whispered hatefully. "Yup, gonna have to do something about you."

He got out his shotgun, cleaned and loaded it. Then he cleaned and loaded his pistol. He laid out another line and snorted it, then pulled the slide on the gun back and let it chamber a round, the sound of the slide going home hanging in the air of the office. Finally, Tommy aimed the pistol at where David's chest would be if he walked through the door, said "Bang," then smiled coldly.

Chapter 5 – A Successful Friday Night

I had missed the electric company visit, but the note they left said they had put in the meter and hotted-up the line. At the bottom of the note, the technician added that the transformer on the property would only supply100-amp service. So if I wanted to install anything like a heat pump or modern appliances, I would have to request an upgrade.

I unscrewed all six of the glass fuses in the fuse panel. Underneath the sixth fuse, I found a penny. The fuse had blown at some time in the past, and someone, probably Dad, had bypassed the fuse with the penny, leaving that circuit unprotected and a fire hazard. Holding my breath, I pushed the blade switch home. This turned on the power to just the fuse box. And ... nothing happened. So far, so good. None of the circuits were labeled. Grandpa had been a wonderful man and a loving husband, but he was no electrician.

I screwed in the first fuse. The circuit it protected had a dead short—blew that fuse faster than you could say "pop." The second fuse didn't blow—either the circuit was good, or the wires were completely broken. The third delayed for about thirty seconds, then popped. The fourth and fifth stayed on. I screwed in the sixth fuse, expecting it to blow. It didn't. Six fuses protected the whole house. That it had never caught fire still amazes me.

The job of figuring out how Grandpa had wired the house began in earnest. I pulled the blade switch again to turn off the power, then removed the cover from the fuse panel. Inside I found a rat's nest. Literally. Well, OK—a mouse nest, but mice are just small rats. I cleaned out the chewed-up paper, bits of wire insulation, and mouse turds, then studied the remains of the wires with less and less hope of being able to save them.

After spending a large part of the day under the house with the mud, spiders, and mouse droppings, I finally realized how big a mess the house wiring had become. Using the new wire from the hardware store, I created safe circuits to the water pump in the well, the water heater, and the stove. The furnace would have to wait. The outlets in the kitchen were on the same circuit as the stove and had survived. They would have to last until I could rewire the house. Unfortunately, most of the wall outlets in the rest of the house were dead, casualties of the field mice who had reigned unchecked for fifteen years.

Amazingly, the pump in the well still worked, but I could have cast an engine block from all the rust that came out with the water. I let the water run until it became clear and tasted clean. The stove clicked and stunk, but the elements got hot.

I turned on the refrigerator. The light inside went on, and it hummed softly at first, then louder and louder. Finally, it gave a loud click, a pop, and went silent. Even the light inside turned off. I checked the fuse for the kitchen circuits—blown. I put in a new fuse. It popped before I could finish screwing it in. I felt like playing taps over the fridge. I grew up with that fridge. A yellowed photograph of Socks and me posing with our first deer was still taped to the front.

I got into Dad's truck and drove down to the hardware store in Chambersville. John told me that no one in town sold appliances, but his dad had an old refrigerator he used for beer in his garage. I could probably buy it from him. So he made a phone call.

John gave me his address. I drove over to his dad's—a charming ranch house set on about ten acres. Jack was waiting for me.

"It's been a long time, David," Jack said, walking up to the truck.

I got out and hugged him. "Yes, it has. Too long."

He'd put on a little weight since I saw him at Mom's funeral but still looked very distinguished with gray hair at his temples, an expensive haircut, and a chiseled face. Somehow, even his T-shirt and blue jeans looked expensive.

"How's Ethyl?" Ethyl was Jack's wife. I had known the two of them since high school.

"Ask her yourself. She's right behind you."

I turned around, and she hugged me also. "Welcome, David."

I kissed her on the cheek and hugged her back. "Thanks, Ethyl," I whispered. "You're a sight for sore eyes."

She'd put on a little weight, too, probably a left-over from having their three kids. Nevertheless, her hair was still light brown and beautiful without a trace of gray.

"I hear you need a fridge." She glanced at Jack while she said it.

"I guess John told you about Mom and Dad's fridge dying when I turned it on today."

"Yep, he did. Well, I would love to get rid of the one in the garage."

She turned to Jack and gave him the same raised eyebrow my mother had used on me. The ability to do that must be genetic—somehow tied to the X chromosome. I laughed at the memory. Ethyl turned back to me quizzically.

Jack sighed. He knew he'd been beaten—no man can win against The Eyebrow. "Sure. If anyone gets my beer fridge, I'd like it to be David. How about fifty bucks?"

"Sold!"

I handed him the cash.

We muscled the fridge up into the truck, leaving it standing, then strapped it in with the tie-downs that John had sold me for securing Socks. You should never put an old fridge on its back. Not if you want it to work when you plug it in again.

"Do you need some help unloading it?" Jack asked hopefully.

I knew where this was going. "Oh, I don't know, only all I can get."

"Give me a minute."

He came out of the house a few moments later with a bag under his arm that looked suspiciously like a six-pack. "Ready?"

"Bye, Ethyl," I called as I got into the truck.

She waved and walked back into the house.

We started up the road to Grandpa's house. Jack reached into the bag and pulled out a beer, handed it to me, and got one for himself.

"Now this brings back some memories," I sighed, popping the top. "Speaking of beer, where's Larry? I haven't seen him since we left high school."

Larry, Jack, and I had been the gruesome threesome until we'd each gone our separate ways after graduation.

Jack looked at me sadly. "Larry's still around. He went from one job to another but never found anything he could get his teeth into. He even enlisted in the Army, but he got kicked out for drug use, then spent some time in jail for getting mixed up in a real estate scam where he sold houses that didn't belong to him. I guess he thought since the owners had left, no one would notice."

"Wow. That sucks."

"Yep. Last I heard, Larry worked at the Kubota dealer on the other side of the mountain washing tractors or some such."

We arrived at Grandpa's house fifteen minutes later.

Jack and I got the old fridge out of the house and the "new" one in. It fit the spot where the old one had been. I plugged it in, and it hummed away happily.

"I've got a bunch of trash and things I need to get rid of. Where do people throw away stuff around here now? I saw the closed sign on the old dump."

"There's a new landfill on the other side of town. They have a recycling center there also. They'll take your old fridge off your hands. They got tired of people heaving them into the gullies and streams around the county."

"Excellent! I'll take it down there tomorrow." The.house scraping called to me.

"Or this afternoon. You have to take me back home, remember? It's not that far out of our way. I'll show you where it is."

We got the old fridge into the back of the truck. In retrospect, loading the old fridge today had been a good idea, even if that meant not finishing the scraping. It would have been impossible to get that heavy beast into the truck by myself.

Jack handed me a beer, and off we went to the recycling point. Maybe someone had a boat that needed an anchor.

After dropping Jack back at his house, I visited our local grocery store. I may have set a record at the store as I paid the bill. The other two checkers cheered when the kid checking my groceries announced the total—a personal best for me. Then, for the first time in my life, I accepted the kid's offer to help me out with my three carts of groceries.

The shelves in Mom's pantry had been a disaster. First, I washed them with warm soapy water (the water heater worked!), using Mom's old Dutch oven as a washbasin and one of her worn-out aprons as a washrag. When I finished washing the shelves, the water resembled that river in Congo. I poured it down the drain, filled the pan again with clean water, and went over the shelves again. Field mice were fast becoming my least favorite critter. After I dried the shelves off with another apron, I loaded the groceries onto the shelves and took a step back. My heart filled with pride. A full pantry! Cans, jars, boxes, and bags lined the shelves from floor to ceiling. A missing piece of my childhood had been restored! I could almost feel Mom's approval. It's the little things that make the best memories.

I opened the fridge and looked with satisfaction at the milk, eggs, cheese, and butter that filled the top shelf. The fresh vegetables and fruit were tucked into the bottom drawers. The second shelf held my favorite three kinds of beer. Frozen vegetables, steaks, TV dinners, and a gallon of ice cream filled the freezer. Life was good!

I walked upstairs, used the toilet, then took my first hot shower in the house in fifteen years. About halfway through, I remembered it was Friday night, my first Friday night since I had returned home. Time to see if Friday night in Chambersville had survived the downsizing. I changed clothes and headed down to the Wagon Wheel Tavern. It wasn't the only place in town, but I had very warm memories of Friday nights past. Or at least I think I did.

A really successful Friday night is kind of hard to remember the next day. If you can remember it, you probably didn't have a great time.

Before I went to the bar, I stopped at Rhiannon's. I saw her through the front window, sitting on the sofa wearing a comfortable-looking robe with her golden hair pulled back into a ponytail, watching TV.

"Come on in, soldier boy," she called out when she saw me walking up the sidewalk.

I stopped at the screen door. "I was wondering if you'd like to go out tonight."

Her bruises were in full flower, but the swelling had mostly gone down.

"I think I'll stay home until these go away." She hesitated, then smiled at me. "You could always watch a movie with me." She patted the couch beside her. "I think we could both fit here. Gino's makes a pretty good pizza."

"Wait a minute, let me think." I scrunched up my face in mock concentration. "Oh, OK. But pizza needs something to wash it down. Would you like beer or wine?"

"Tough choice." She considered the two, trying hard not to laugh. "Beer, I think, something lite—go better with the pizza."

By the time I got back with the beer, Rhiannon had picked up the house. An interesting-sounding movie about a guy advertising for a time travel companion waited for her to press the play button on NetFlix.

A knock sounded on the door. In a flash, I had my .45 out and stood beside the door jam. I motioned for Rhiannon to answer it.

"Gino's Pizza," the delivery kid called out through the door.

I shook my head, feeling a little foolish as I returned the .45 to the small of my back. Maybe I expected too much from Tommy.

Rhiannon opened the door and took the pizza. I paid the kid. He kept adjusting where he stood so he could maintain his view of Rhiannon as she put a couple of slices of pizza on plates for us. She *was* looking pretty yummy. Her robe kept falling open, giving an almost complete view of her right breast. Finally, she caught him looking and gave him a big smile as she tightened up her robe.

The kid left, and Rhiannon turned off her porch light.

The movie turned out to be excellent in a non-Hollywood, Indie kind of way. The actors were young and excited about being actors. The script had lots of imagination. We laughed all the way through it.

I missed the actual ending. I'm sure the leading guy got the leading lady, but I became a little distracted. It turned out Rhiannon was as glad as me that I was beside her. It had been a long time since I kissed a woman who could speak English. I had forgotten how well she could kiss, but I was sure grateful for the opportunity to refresh that memory. It could take years of practice to figure out how to kiss her back just right. The Special Forces taught me that you couldn't practice anything too much. Guess they were right about that, too.

Maybe I'm getting old, but that particular Friday night turned out to be one of my most successful ever, and I remember every single thing.

Chapter 6 – Leaving Town

In the morning, Rhiannon fixed me a big breakfast while I slept. Not only was she great-looking and a fantastic lover, she was also a terrific cook. I usually cooked trail meals in a can or had diner meals at whatever greasy spoon crossed my path when hunger started gnawing at my gut. Only rarely did either one leave me wanting more of the same. Rhiannon had cooked ham, hash browns, sausage gravy, pancakes, fresh-squeezed orange juice, and good black coffee. The smells from her kitchen that greeted me as I woke would have raised the dead.

My fork hovered over the stack of pancakes dripping with maple syrup and melted butter, when I realized she had drawn a set of paratrooper wings in the top pancake. I looked up at her in surprise.

She stood in the doorway to the kitchen, waiting for me to notice. "Did I get them right?"

I studied her culinary artwork. She even had the correct number of risers. "You did! How did you know what to draw?"

"I've had a lot of practice with six kids. I can draw almost anything in pancake batter with my baster. You draw the picture on the griddle first, then pour the background of the pancake over it after the picture is cooked for a minute. My kids grew up with Bert and Ernie and Big Bird pancakes. Now they're doing it with their kids. I thought you might like it since you have those wings tattooed on your chest."

I have a warm memory of going to that tattoo parlor in Columbus, Georgia, when I graduated from jump school at Fort Benning. Every one of the men in my class got a tattoo. My tattoo had been touched-up half a dozen times since then, keeping the detail of the wings and chute perfect. Every Green Beret has one thing in common: pride in those wings.

But I never realized those wings could taste this good. I could have eaten three plates of Rhiannon's breakfast and still wanted more. It was past ten by the time I pried myself out of her kitchen chair. Then she wanted to kiss me goodbye and then ... well, I got out the front door about eleven.

All four tires on Dad's truck were flat, the knife blade slits visible in the tires' sidewalls.

"I seen who done it," an old black woman across the street called out to me from her front porch swing.

I walked over to talk to her. She had her white hair tied up in a bun behind her head and was sipping a cup of coffee while she rocked back and forth on her swing.

"You that Peterson kid, David, right?"

"Yes, ma'am. I sure am. What did you see?"

"I knew yer ma," she continued. "Sold me them blackberry preserves every fall at the farmer's market. Never figured out how she made 'em so good."

I smiled at that. Every August and September, Mom made me fill her big plastic buckets with those fat, ripe blackberries. I would crawl through the forests of thorny vines in the meadows down by the river for hours, dragging one of those white buckets behind me. By the time her buckets were full, I looked like me and a wildcat had gone round and round. Later that day, she always fixed me fresh, hot biscuits with a big scoop of the season's new blackberry jam spooned over the top as a reward, the jam still hot from the cookpot.

"Mom didn't use pectin from the store to thicken her jam," I whispered, looking around for the Jam Police to bust me for divulging state secrets. "We have a quince tree out back. She'd use the quince fruit instead of pectin."

She cocked her head when I said that, considering the flavor combination of the quince and blackberries. "If Annalee were still here, she'd skin you alive for givin' away her secret."

"I'm sure Mom would want you to know, now she's gone. So Tommy from the service station did it, right?"

"No surprise there, young man," she snickered a little. "After you showed him the door yestaday, I was laughin' so hard I thought I was gonna wet my pants." She chuckled some more, coughed, then spit.

"When did he do it?"

"A little before dawn. Maybe five o'clock. Gus lef fer the diner a couple a minutes earlier. He always put a cup o' hot coffee on the table for me before he leave. I drink it out hyer when it ain't too cold."

"Are you Gus's wife?"

"Yep. Been that way fer almost fifty years. Name's Desireé."

I turned around and stared at Dad's truck, sitting on those four flat tires. Both of us were quiet for a moment.

"That boy never did have no sense." She spat again. "Chasin' after Rhiannon and her bein' twice his age. What you gonna do? Call the cops?"

"Nah. I think I'll talk to Tommy myself."

That made her laugh. "I wish I could be there to see that, David. You take care, ya hear. Tommy carries a pistol. Got a shotgun behind the counter."

The front door of Tommy's service station was open when I got there. I didn't see Tommy or his stupid truck anywhere. Instead, a muscular kid working on an old Taurus looked up as I walked through the door. The name patch on his shirt said "Jimmy."

"What you need, Mr. Peterson?" he asked, walking up to me, smiling while he wiped his hands. "How's your truck runnin'?"

"Tommy around?"

"Nah. He went over the mountain for some parts for this Taurus. He ought to be back after lunch sometime."

"Someone slashed my tires. I need my truck towed over here and new tires put on."

"Those were brand-new tires!" The kid was incredulous. "Who the hell wouldda done that to new tires? When did it happen?"

"Got me last night."

"They didn't hurt your Harley, did they?"

I looked at him carefully. "How do you know about my Harley?"

"I saw it when you picked up your truck. John Nelson at the hardware store is a friend of mine. We're both on the football team. He told me about you loading it into your truck with his loading dock."

"Bike's fine, as far as I know, Jimmy. Up in my barn where I left it, I hope. It's my truck that got hurt."

"Fuckin' tweakers!" Jimmy said spitefully. "They got nothin' better to do than tearing up other people's stuff. See somethin' new, and they got to tear it up."

"I don't think that was the problem this time. Can you tow it over here? You got any tires left that'll fit it?"

"Sure. I can tow it. Where is it?"

"Two blocks away on Elm Street."

"I'll lock up the place and go get it."

I gave him the truck keys and walked across the street to a café for a cup of coffee. Half an hour later, I watched the tow truck come back with Dad's pickup on dollies behind it. Jimmy put the truck up on jack stands and had the wheels off before I had finished my coffee and walked back over.

"Damned shame!" Jimmy fumed as he took the ruined tires off the rims and mounted new ones back on. "Brand-new tires! What a waste! Good thing we got our winter tire order in."

Tommy pulled in as Jimmy took Dad's truck off the jack stands.

"Hi, David," Tommy said, walking around Dad's truck, trying hard to hide the smirk on his face. "What happened to your tires?"

"You slashed them this morning, Tommy."

"The hell you say!" Tommy yelled at me, flecks of spit flying out of his mouth. "You got no proof a that! I was nowhere near your fuckin' truck last night."

"I got an eyewitness saw you do it."

Tommy's face got even redder. "The hell you do! You owe me for a new set a tires!"

"I don't owe you shit."

Tommy reached under the counter and pulled out a sawed-off, double-barreled shotgun. "That truck don't leave this property until you pay me for them tires!" he spat, his voice as cold as ice.

"Tommy, you just made the second biggest mistake of your life," I told him calmly. "I'm gonna tell you one more time: Get the fuck out of town. This is your last warning."

"Why? What you gonna do now, tough guy? You gonna Kung-Fu some double-ought?"

"Nope. No need."

I walked toward him with a faint smile on my face. This would be fun. After so many years of kicking the asses of people I didn't even know, I was finally going to do it to someone who desperately needed and deserved it.

The shotgun hammers clicked on the empty chambers as I walked around the counter. A moment of panic crossed Tommy's face. I had found the shotgun and unloaded it while I waited for Jimmy to finish with the tires. I put the two shotgun shells next to the cash register. He tried to hit me with the shotgun barrel, but I blocked him and took the gun away. Thirty seconds later, Tommy was on the floor, out cold. I kicked him again, good and solid, right where it would hurt most. I figured he should have a little souvenir from raping Rhiannon. Jimmy still stood in the doorway with his mouth open. I smiled at him.

"Thanks for the tires, Jimmy, and good job on the tune-up." Then I walked out of the shop.

Tommy did leave town. Three big U-Haul trucks appeared bright and early in front of his garage the following day. A bunch of skinny kids with tattoos in saggy pants, rude T-shirts, and hats on sideways spent all day loading the stuff from the garage into them.

Tommy didn't help much. He spent most of the day sitting on a thickly padded office chair, telling everyone else what to do. The only times he did get up were to pee, waddling like a duck to the restroom with a pained look on his face.

About dark, they headed out of town toward the road over the mountain, a four-truck caravan with Tommy in the lead.

Chapter 7 – The Special File

Grandpa's farmhouse had turned into a forty-foot-tall white dollhouse with a black roof in the middle of the yard. The windows and doors were gift-wrapped with paper and tape. All of them had needed to be re-caulked where the trim met the siding—many of the window panes needed to be reglazed also. I had made significant progress with the painting. The pile of empty caulk tubes looked like used artillery shells in the trash pile I had accumulated. John had been right about the sprayer. I can't even imagine how much work it would have been to paint the house with brushes. In a few days, my "dollhouse" would morph back into the house of my childhood.

As I painted the top parts of the house, I saw the state of disrepair of the roof—amazing it wasn't already leaking. After I finished painting, the roof would be next. I didn't look forward to putting on a roofer's harness and tying myself to the chimney. One slip on that 45-degree slope, and that would be all she wrote. I sighed, wondering again why Grandpa made the roof so steep.

An old red Corolla pulled up the driveway. Rhiannon got out carrying a box wrapped in a towel. "Hi, David," she called, waving. "I brought lunch. The house looks great!"

I pulled down the tailgate on Dad's truck and ate some fantastic roast chicken, potato salad, and fresh bread while we sat there. I had learned the hard way to ignore hunger when I was elbows-deep in something else. But when food presents itself, you eat all you can.

"You don't have an ounce of fat on your entire body!" Rhiannon said in amazement as I finished the last of the chicken and helped myself to yet another heaping spoon of potato salad. "How do you do it?"

"Clean living!" I lied.

In a combat zone, there was always something more important to do than eat. And Rhiannon had made *good* food, not a gut-bomb from a greasy spoon. So I ate until my stomach cried out in surrender. "No more! Or you won't like what happens next."

I burped happily and took her hand. "Thanks, Rhiannon. I didn't know I was that hungry."

Hand-in-hand, we walked around the house. The few shrubs that had survived their fifteen years of abandonment, I had pruned away from the house and covered them with drop cloths. I liked the natural look of the fieldstone foundation, so I had taped and papered it off also.

"What are you going to do about the yard?" she asked.

In the fifteen years without people around to cut them down, volunteer trees had sprouted and grown. Twelve-inch diameter alders and firs, now forty feet tall, filled the yard. They were almost as high as the top of the house.

"Clean 'em out!" I said, looking around. "A house should have a yard that kids can play in. And I thought I'd leave a horseshoe of poplars around the barn to shade it in the summer. Maybe do the same thing with a fir next by each house corner. I like the sound of the wind as it blows through them."

"You sound like you have kids, too."

"One daughter—she's twenty-one and lives with her boyfriend in Los Angeles while she's getting her law degree at UCLA."

"Where's your ex?"

"Don't have any idea. She wanted US citizenship, and marrying me was how she got it. Of course, I didn't know any of that when we were married. She left me a week after we flew back from Thailand."

"Are you close to your daughter?"

I hung my head. My daughter was a tender subject. "I've never met Amy. Her mother wasn't interested in me being Dad—she just wanted the child support money the divorce court assigned to me. And the Army kept me pretty busy running around the world. I once tried to get the court's permission to see her, but her mother fought me until I finally gave up."

I decided to change the subject. "What do you know about Frank Everest? He looks like he's dying."

"He *is* dying. Of cancer. He found out about six months ago."

"Has he ..." Her eyes made me stop.

"Has he done chemo?" she finished. "Has he gotten a second opinion? Is there any hope?"

I nodded.

"Yes, yes, and no."

A police cruiser pulled up the driveway and parked behind Rhiannon's Corolla. A slightly overweight cop got out and walked up to us. A drooping, mostly gray mustache filled the front of his face, which was framed by longish, mostly gray hair. The baseball cap on his head said Chambersville PD. He had to be seventy.

He smiled and nodded at Rhiannon, then did a double-take on her fading black eye.

"Hi, Rhiannon." He looked at me cautiously. "Are you David Peterson?"

"Yep, I am. What can I do for you?"

"Hi, David. I'm Josh Parker. I'm chief of police here. That sounds a lot more impressive than it is." He smiled, but only with his mouth. His eyes never left mine, and there wasn't a hint of a smile in them. "I'm the only cop on the force." He paused. "Well, here it is. Tommy Sandouval left town in a hurry a couple of days ago. Before he left, he swore out a complaint against you. He said you stole a couple of gallons of gear oil, some wrenches, a set of tires from him, and assaulted him as well."

Rhiannon looked back and forth between us, not believing what she heard. I coughed a little. "That's not exactly what happened," I said. "Here's the real story."

After I finished my side, I showed him the receipt for Tommy's repairs that I pulled from the glove box of the pickup and told him what Desireé had passed on to me. Next, I described the confrontation in Tommy's shop. Then I told him about Rhiannon's assault and rape.

The further into the story I got, the harder his eyes got. When I got to the part about making Tommy spit into my handkerchief, he interrupted me.

"Do you still have that baggy? The one with the handkerchief?"

"No, I overnighted it to Officer Sanchez on the other side of the mountain." I showed him Sanchez's business card.

"I know Xavier. I'll give him a call." He looked at Rhiannon. "Rhiannon, is there anything else you'd like to add to David's story?"

I saw his hand drop to rest on the butt of his pistol. It could have been a casual gesture, but I remembered making that same move when questioning some farmers in Zimbabwe. There's careful, and there's stupid. Chief Parker was being careful.

She pursed her lips and looked at him, then at me. "Tommy said if I told anyone what happened, what he'd done, he would kill David *and* me. He held a gun to my head and made me promise to keep quiet. He scared me so bad I wouldn't even leave my house until David showed up and took me to the hospital. It wasn't until David 'explained' things to Tommy that I decided to ignore his threats and let myself begin to get pissed off."

"Would you testify against Tommy, assuming the DNA in his spit matches the DNA the hospital collected?"

"Oh, yes," she said, smiling coldly. "I would *really* like to do that."

He moved his hand off his pistol butt and smiled, with his eyes this time.

"I wish you two had come to me sooner. Pictures of the bruises on the day of the injuries are such great evidence at a trial."

"The hospital took some," she said. "I'm sure they would give you copies."

"Well, this trip didn't turn out like I expected," he said, relaxing a little. "All I knew about you when I started up here was you were an ex-Green Beret with a bunch of medals. Didn't know quite what to expect."

His description amused me. "If I can help out with the investigation, let me know." Most of my medals were classified, including the big one.

"Actually, you *can* help me out." He peered around the property for a moment, thinking about how to choose the right words. "Are you looking for a job?"

I blinked ... twice. "Excuse me?"

"The city council authorized me to hire a deputy about a year ago. Unfortunately, I haven't found anyone who is even remotely qualified. No one has replied to my advertisements in any of the metropolitan newspapers across the state. I guess being a cop in a backwater town like this isn't romantic enough for most people."

"I'm a soldier. I don't know the first thing about being a cop."

As I thought about many of the things I had been told to do in the Special Forces, I figured most of them wouldn't stand up to a courtroom critique.

"Well, we don't get much high crime around here. Mostly it's explainin' to people about the difference between right and wrong and tryin' to cool off hostilities between neighbors before they start shootin' at each other. It sounds like you have a pretty good understandin' about that. For the rest of it, well, there's a one-semester course at the local community college on the other side of the mountain for beginnin' cops. It starts in January."

"Let me think about it for a couple of days. Then, I'll let you know."

"Until you finish the course, I could hire you into the Police Auxiliary. It's minimum wage and doesn't have any benefits, but you carry a badge so people wouldn't object to that .45 you've got tucked in behind you. I'll give you all the hours you want."

I liked Chief Parker more and more. I could do a lot worse than work for this man.

"Chief, I wanna open an emergency care clinic here in Chambersville. That's my goal. I don't know how long that's gonna take to set up. I could be your deputy until that happens."

He studied me for a minute. "Chambersville needs a clinic, no doubt." He hesitated again, then shook his head. "Who knows what the future will bring. I need a deputy now. Let tomorrow take care of tomorrow."

He held out his hand. I shook it warmly and smiled. He smiled back.

"I knew this was going to be a good day! I love it when Indian Summer gets here. So come down to the station tomorrow and fill out an application. I'll swear you in."

"What happens with the complaint Tommy swore out against me?" I asked, changing the subject.

"I'll talk to Desireé and Jimmy to get their stories, and then I have to give it to the city prosecutor."

"And then?"

"Then he'll thank me, read it, and put it into a special file. It's kind of round and sits on the floor next to his desk." Chief Parker shook my hand again. "See you tomorrow, David."

He gave Rhiannon an awkward hug like she would break, then got back into his patrol car.

Chapter 8 – The Foot

I moved in with Rhiannon the next day. It made sense to me to live somewhere else while I worked on getting Grandpa's house livable again. She suggested it. I think the idea that Tommy might pay her another visit still spooked her. I didn't exactly resist. I didn't resist much of anything with Rhiannon.

Our life together had its ups and downs like any couple. She squeezed the toothpaste from the middle. I squeezed it from the bottom. I picked up all my dirty clothes and put them in the laundry hamper as soon as I undressed. She left them lying where they fell until the morning. It was a learning process. Neither of us had been a live-in companion for a long time.

Rhiannon worked a second job over the mountain three nights a week. I hated that she did and worried about Tommy lying in wait for her every time she left. But she told me I would have to accept that she wouldn't stop—something about paying for her kids' way through college.

My drinking was the hardest part for *her* to accept— sometimes, at night, the monsters from the id would reawaken in my subconscious and slither out to wreck any hope of a good night's sleep.

What is "monsters from the id," you might ask. That's a line from an old science fiction movie called *Forbidden Planet.* The lead scientist had discovered the lost civilization of the Krell. The Krell had perished in one night after a long and brilliant climb up the ladder of technologically assisted living. They had invented a way for people to create anything they could think of. Anything you want! Picture it in your mind and Shazam; there it was, right in front of you. They expected it to usher in a new era of happiness and social growth.

The first night after they activated it, everyone died. The monsters from the id got them. Everyone has something of which they are terrified. Something so frightening, they are helpless to prevent it from overwhelming them when it appears. The "id" is your subconscious. That night, everyone's subconscious took over in their sleep. Every one of the Krell awoke to their personal worst nightmare, alive, in the flesh, right beside them. When morning came, there wasn't a single Krell left alive.

After thirty years of black ops, I had acquired my personal set of "monsters from the id:" ghosts of friends who died in my arms, images of children blown beyond recognition by "friendly fire," politicians who ordered us to go on suicide missions, booby traps that killed the rest of the team, rifles aimed at the back of my head, civilians who were collateral damage.

When one of them arrived in my sleep, I had trained myself to wake up automatically—the only way I could escape from the monster. Unfortunately, the only way to get back to sleep after a visit was to drink myself into oblivion.

Tonight, the worst monster of the bunch had arrived, the one that still haunts me when all the rest of my nightmares have given up and slithered back to where they hid inside my brain, the one so frightening that I had never even tried to talk about it with another human being.

I fell back on my only remaining line of defense: Johnnie Walker.

Rhiannon woke up with a start. She reached out to where I was supposed to be, next to her in bed—nothing there but cold covers. She got up, pulled her robe around her, and walked into the living room.

I had heard her wake then enter the room. No lights were on. The streetlight outside her house provided a pale illumination.

"What're you doin' up?" she asked, sitting down at the table and yawning. The almost empty bottle of Scotch stood on the table next to me.

"Couldn't sleep," I slurred back at her.

"You wanna talk about it?"

"Can't."

"Can't or won't?" she asked.

"Can't. Too bad."

She picked up my hand and looked into my bloodshot eyes. "There's nothing you can say that will make me think any less of you. You are my hero and my savior. I haven't yet seen a monster from the id that doesn't turn into nothing when it's exposed to the light of day."

I jumped at her use of "monster from the id." I think that was what made me turn the corner and start to talk to her about it. I stared through the window into the dark street and collected my thoughts through the Johnny Walker haze. "I'm not th' nice guy ya think I am."

"Who said I think you're a nice guy?"

"I'm a murderer."

She reached out to my hand and took it gently into hers. "Killing in war isn't murder."

"This wasn't war. Or at least declared war."

"Tell me about it."

"I can't. If I tell ya, you'll leave me." It wasn't a threat, just a statement.

"Let me decide that." She squeezed my hand again and smiled in encouragement. "What happened?"

I looked out the window again. Fifteen years ago I had been in Colombia.

"You c'n never tell anyone wha' I'm about t' tell ya or I'll go t' jail, proba'ly for the res' of m' life."

"I promise. I'll never tell a soul."

I closed my eyes, took a deep breath, then let it out unsteadily. Fifteen years ago—fifteen years and I could still remember the smell of the temporary hangar we used as an HQ as clearly as if I were still standing in it—jet fuel, tent canvas, dust, sweat, and jungle. In a monotone, I began to tell Rhiannon the story of Colombia, the story I had tried and tried to drink into dust. As I started recounting the story, the effects of the Scotch evaporated. Some things are too painful to hide inside a bottle of booze.

"We've found another factory," Captain Matthews handed me the intel.

The packet contained color pictures of four-wheel-drive jeeps and SUVs backed up to a cinderblock building with people loading small bundles wrapped in plastic and tape into the vehicles. They appeared to be kilogram bricks of cocaine. I checked the coordinates in the packet on my map—a small village named Poco Pito, way up in the hills south of Medellin.

"How good is the intel?" I asked.

"Won't know 'til we get there. The team departs in one hour. A Blackhawk gunship will insert us ten klicks away ... right here." He indicated a hilltop on my map. "The gunship will rendezvous with us at the village at dawn in case we need firepower support."

An hour from now would be 3 A.M. There would be no moon tonight. Ten klicks (kilometers) is seven miles, seven miles of walking along the hilltops of Colombia in total darkness. I left to alert the team. I became the senior enlisted member after Jamie had returned to the US on emergency leave. It seemed odd to have a medic as second-in-command, but rules were rules.

We inserted uneventfully then made our way along the ridges to an overlook above the village, arriving at 6 A.M. Not a soul was moving. The village should have been crawling with people starting their day.

"Something's wrong," I told Captain Matthews. "I don't see any movement."

The gunship arrived and circled overhead.

"Yeah. It smells like a trap," he agreed.

I checked the coordinates again on my GPS. Yep. This was the village. Captain Matthews motioned us to move down into the jungle beside the outlying houses. One of the embedded Colombian Security Police triggered a trip flare—probably accidental, but you never knew with those guys. Many of them are on both Medellin's payroll and the government's. We never included them on the intel until we were in the air and on our way. This whole operation began to stink to me. It didn't feel right. Where *was* everybody?

Fredrick Hudgin

An automatic rifle opened up from a house. We returned fire. The rifle went silent. The cinderblock building from the pictures was on the uphill side of town.

We began a house-to-house search, moving up the hill. We found some terrified women who were in the process of fixing breakfast—but no weapons, weapon fire, children, or men. One pregnant woman tried to attack me with a butcher knife. Based on the size of her belly, she was almost full term. I disarmed her without doing any harm to either her or the baby, then cuffed her to a roof support pole in her house. I left her sobbing quietly as I slipped out the back and rejoined the team going up the hill.

The last house had a clear view of the factory. There were no cars or trucks or SUVs in front of it. The village was spooky silent.

Four automatic weapons opened upon us from four different windows in the building.

"Withdraw!" Captain Matthews ordered.

We went back up the hill a little way, to where we had an unobstructed view of the whole village. We received intermittent fire as we withdrew.

"Paint them!" Captain Matthews told me. He got on the radio and told the Blackhawk to expend all ordinance on the paint.

I painted the building with my laser while he called the gunship. This whole operation was weird. Why hadn't we seen any children or men? Typically, these villages had kids everywhere, running and playing. I looked up at the Blackhawk. It circled around to get the shot. As its tail went up to fire, I finally figured out what was wrong. There were no supplies outside the building. Around every coke factory I had ever seen, there were lots of 55-gallon drums. They contained the chemicals that were used in cocaine manufacture. And there were no jeeps or Suburbans the security people were fond of. And on the outside of the building were paintings of kids playing.

"This is wrong!" I shouted. "It's not a factory!"

I sent the laser off the building into the jungle, but the rockets were too far down their trajectory. So instead of landing on only the factory, they slammed all over the village and exploded

Page 64

with tremendous flame balls and concussions. Burning fragments were sent high into the air, blasting bits of that village over the surrounding countryside.

"Why?" Captain Matthews demanded.

I told him what I saw. He looked back at the village and blinked at the destruction.

"I hope you're wrong," he said, already knowing I wasn't. "Alpha Squad—approach the village. Bravo Squad—cover."

With me in command, Alpha Squad began the walk down the hillside to approach the burning village cautiously, moving from one place of cover to the next. Bravo Squad took cover and watched for snipers.

About halfway to the remains of the village, I got hit in the head by a foot—a child's foot, still in a sandal, still warm. It had been blown straight up when the rockets hit the building and finally fallen back to the earth. I recognized it immediately for what it was.

The building was not a cocaine factory. It was a school. The carnage we found inside will haunt me until I die. I lost everything inside my stomach as the reality of what I had done sunk in. I puked until I couldn't puke anymore.

Captain Matthews reported all this to HQ over our encrypted radio.

"Shit," was all the response we got from Major Daniels. Then he said, "Wait in place. I gotta tell upstairs."

I told the squads to search the village, checking for survivors. They found several, but those people soon died of their injuries. I went from one injury to the next, trying to save someone, to no avail. I had killed the whole village. Finally, I came to the house farthest away from the factory. I found the pregnant woman who had attacked me with the knife. She had a piece of shrapnel in her chest, unconscious and bleeding out. From her agonal breathing, I knew she would die within minutes. But her baby was still alive! I cut off the plastic cuffs and did a meatball C-section. A girl! She cried as I pulled her from her mother's womb, covered in blood. I clamped off and cut her umbilical cord, then slipped her inside my tunic, secure and warm. Her mother had died while I did the section.

As I finished, I heard Captain Matthews's radio crackle to life. "X-ray niner five seven, do you copy?"

"This is X-ray niner five seven. Over."

"X-ray niner five seven. This is Kilo Foxtrot. Are there any survivors?"

Kilo Foxtrot was General Hoskins.

"One infant," Captain Matthews told him, looking at the bulge in my tunic making baby sounds.

"But no one who can say what happened?"

"Roger that. Everyone else is dead."

"A chopper will arrive shortly with weapons and chemicals—plant weapons on all corpses. Make sure the magazines are partially used. Then, add the chemicals to the remains of the building. Do you understand?"

"Copy. X-ray niner five seven out."

General Hoskins was telling us to put weapons on the dead villagers, make it appear that a firefight had taken place, and plant cocaine and production chemicals in the "factory."

The next day all the news wires ran a story about a massive drug bust in Colombia with a blown-up coke factory and many dead workers. Pictures of people killed, the factory remains, and the bags of coke on display were prominently featured.

We found out later from a CIA spook that Pablo Escobar, the head of the Medellin drug cartel, had personally chosen Poco Pito and given the tip to the intel officer along with all the pictures. He'd also provided all the weapons to the villagers and said the Americans and the Colombian Security Police were coming to kill everyone. He'd told the villagers the safest place to be was in the school building. The people shooting at us were parents trying to protect their children. There had to have been forty children and most of their parents in that school when we called in the strike that blew it up and killed them. I had painted a school full of kids instead of a cocaine factory. Escobar did this to embarrass the United States and the Colombian government. And we played right into his hands.

\-

Rhiannon remained silent for a while after I finished. Then, finally, she asked, "Could you have done anything to prevent that from happening?"

"I've gone over it a thousand times. I've never found a way I could've stopped it after it started. Once we received fire, our training took over. Once we blew up the school, the situation became a recovery from a terrorist attack—Pablo Escobar's—not ours. The children and their parents became collateral damage in the war between Pablo Escobar's drug empire and the CIA. I understand all that. But *I* moved the laser and caused the rockets to hit the village as well as the school, not Pablo. It's me who'll meet the pregnant woman again when I die."

"If you hadn't moved the laser, what would've happened?"

"No way of telling. The school would've been blown up. Most of the village, too. It might've ended the same way. The pregnant woman would probably have lived. Her house was farthest from the school. But that would've created its own set of problems. I think, in their warped way, the two governments were grateful that I moved the laser. It made covering up the whole mess that much easier." I stopped my narrative for a moment, then gave Rhiannon a cold, bitter smile. "I settled the score a little, about two years later."

"What did you do?"

"I was in Medellin when Pablo died. I had been implanted there as an observer for the CIA while the Colombian Security Police tried to capture him. I saw Pablo escaping from the building the police had entered. They went in through the ground floor doors and windows. Pablo and his bodyguard exited an upper-floor window and ran across the rooftop. The police were still inside the building and hadn't seen them escape. Someone had wounded Pablo, but not mortally. He was preparing to jump into an alleyway where a car waited when I shot him through the head. The bullet went in one ear and out the other. Pablo had always bragged he would never surrender to the police. He'd said over and over that instead of surrendering, he would shoot himself between the ears. I just helped him out a little. The only thing I regret about *that* kill was that I couldn't do *it* over and over again, once for each of the people who died in Poco Pito."

I looked out the window onto the dark street outside her house. Nothing could hide the bitterness in my voice. "But the cartels that run the cocaine business now import ten times more cocaine than Pablo ever did. All we really did change was who was in charge and made them smarter. The war on drugs has failed to accomplish anything except getting a lot of people killed, making more of the world hate the United States, and putting our country even further in debt. Those people in Poco Pito could have stayed alive, and it wouldn't have changed a thing."

Rhiannon held me, not knowing what to say. "What happened to the child?"

"I gave her to the MASH unit that supported our anti-drug efforts there. The nurses took over immediately. It was like I had given them a Christmas present. After that, I never saw her again."

That wasn't entirely true. I had kept track of the girl. Her name is Pájara Benito, named after a beautiful bird that visited the MASH compound every morning, hunting for scraps. One of the nurses created a birth certificate, listing herself as the child's mother to bring her back to the US when the MASH unit returned from Colombia. Pájara lives in Topeka, Kansas, and is a sophomore in high school. Her mother has risen to the rank of Colonel in the Kansas National Guard. I stop by at least once a year to ensure she's all right. That had been one of the stops I made when I rode Socks across the country from MacDill. Neither she nor her mother ever knew I was there or if I even existed anymore.

"Why did you save the child? Why not let her die with her mother?"

"I don't know. I've asked myself that a hundred times. It was a snap decision or maybe even a non-decision. That child had nothing to do with our war on Pablo Escobar. I had seen and done so much killing and death; I think a part of me finally rebelled. I remember hearing a voice inside my head say, 'Enough!' In the blink of an eye, I switched from being a killer to a medic. Two minutes later, I pulled a living, breathing baby girl into my hands."

Ghost Ride

Something inside of me finally let go, and I began to cry. I cried the tears I had held in for fifteen years, afraid that, when they started, they might never stop.

Chapter 9 – Stay Safe

The painting was done. I felt great pride in the result. I had added the shutters that Mom always wanted, and Rhiannon showed up with window boxes that she and John Nelson made without me having the slightest clue they were doing it. The roof was another matter entirely.

Instead of replacing the roof next, I decided to rebuild my poor, sagging front porch. As I ripped it out, I discovered a carpenter ant infestation that went into the main support beams of the house—time to call a professional. Rhiannon knew a contractor she trusted named Herman Goldstein. He listened quietly while I told him what I'd found. I didn't know what to expect from the deep voice over the phone. He turned out to be short, wiry, with a thin mustache and dark wavy hair. He walked like a runner with a spring in his step. I liked him immediately. After introducing ourselves and showing him what I had found, he poked and prodded around and under my house for a couple of hours.

"I can fix it, but I'll have to jack up the house from inside the crawl space using I-beams and timbers. I'll cut out the infested wood, put in new wood, then lower the whole house back down onto the foundation. I would recommend removing all that pretty fieldstone and putting in a cast foundation while we do it. The mortar has disintegrated, and the foundation walls are ready to collapse, which would total the house."

"A cast foundation will be much stronger and will true the frame. The downside is all the plaster in the house will crack and break because the existing foundation isn't true. When I finish the foundation and framing repair, you should pull all the remaining plaster down and replace it with plasterboard. While you're at it, you can rewire, re-plumb, and insulate everything. I would put in a modern heat pump at the same time. Your old furnace is a fire waiting to happen. The upside of replacing the foundation is I can give you a full basement as part of the job."

He looked at the house for a moment in silence. "Here's the thing: carpenter ants only eat wet wood. They got into your main house beams, which means the beams were damp. That dampness came from water in the crawl space, which came from improper drainage uphill of the house. I recommend putting a French drain system around the new foundation to divert the water flow coming down the hill and put plastic sheeting under the slab we'll pour on the basement floor. You need to put gutters on the roof and have the downspouts drain away from the house and downhill from it. That should solve your problem for good."

The tab for the new foundation and replacing the ant damage came to a little less than $50,000, payable in $10,000 increments as the job progressed.

I had been able to save a little over $200,000 while in the Army. Most guys blew their reenlistment bonuses on cars, motorcycles, and women. I socked mine away. One of my company commanders showed me how to choose stocks and balance my investments between stocks and bonds. His advice lived longer than he did. He bought it in Iraq, compliments of an IED.

I tried to ignore the cold fingers around my heart as I committed to spending a quarter of my life savings. I wrote him a check for $10,000 and told him to begin as soon as possible.

Six weeks later, a pile of mortar-encrusted fieldstone lay next to the barn. I watched as a tractor covered the French drain around the foundation. I hadn't been able to save the few surviving shrubs that were still alive after all those years the house had stood empty. Rhiannon said she wanted to try her hand at the landscaping—an offer I gladly accepted. I had other things to deal with.

Not only had the plaster cracked and fallen like twenty-pound snowflakes, the roof now leaked like the proverbial sieve, and the fall rains had begun with a vengeance. I needed the house reroofed, and I needed it done yesterday. The tarps I had nailed over the existing shingles were holding for the time being. To put them on, I had crawled around the roof in the rain like a drowning spider attached to a rope around the chimney. I didn't want to do that again.

I called the roofer Herman recommended—a guy named Abe Rabinowitz.

Abe was large, in an NFL linebacker way. If I got into a fight, I wanted him on my side. His arms were bigger than my legs. He came out and looked at the roof, then examined the attic.

"The roof's in pretty good shape considering it's been up there for over forty years. I didn't find any dry rot. Apparently, it didn't leak before Herman repaired your foundation. There are three ways to go. You can get a traditional asphalt shingle roof installed over your old one for about $10,000. A fancy textured shingle roof will cost you about $18,000, mostly because we have to remove the old shingles first and put down plywood. This option also takes the longest and can only be done after the rain stops. Or I can put a metal roof over your existing shingles for about $12,000. All the options include new felt and flashing around your chimney. If it were me, I'd go with the metal roof. I can get it done in half the time, and you get a fifty-year warranty with it, which means it will outlive both of us. Finally, I can add gutters and downspouts for another thousand bucks."

I signed up for a metal roof with gutters.

"What color metal do you want?"

Roof colors? I hadn't thought about it.

"There must be forty different colors you can choose from. Don't matter to me. I just need to know what to order."

I flipped through his book of colors, holding them up to the house and trying to imagine what each would look like with my light brown paint and gray trim. Most were pretty easy to eliminate. White, blue, red, bright green. I mean, really, a white roof on a house? Then I thought about living in Phoenix. White might make a lot of sense down there.

"Could you leave me with the color book and let me think about it overnight?"

"Sure, no problem."

After he left, I perused some old *Architectural Digest* magazines that Mom kept around to dream and drool over. I paged through them for hours until I got tired of searching for inspiration. Lots of pretty houses I couldn't afford. I mean, who cleans those monsters? Not the people who own them, I would bet. I got a beer and watched the sun going down over the mountain through the kitchen window. The clouds in the sky were turning into a pallet of reds, golds, and purples. When I came back to the magazines, one lay open. I remembered closing them in disgust when I got up to get the beer. I picked up the magazine. The picture of a brick house with a copper roof filled two pages. It was magnificent.

The next day Abe came back out. "Decided?"

"Can you make me one in this color?" I showed him the copper roof picture.

He laughed. "Sure, but it won't be real copper like that one. You don't want to know what *that* roof cost. But they do have a metal roof with copper paint that looks almost as good and won't turn green in a year like that one did."

A week later, my grandfather's house began to get a copper-colored metal roof. I liked it very much.

Rhiannon drove up to watch as one of the roofing workers finished the final touches on the gutters. I could see a big package in the back of her car. She whispered into Abe's ear, and they both walked to her car. She opened the back door and pulled out the package.

"Stop work!" Abe called out in a loud voice. "Everyone come down here but Ted. Ted, keep your harness on and get up on the roof peak. We forgot the most important piece."

I looked from Rhiannon to Abe to Ted. "What's going on? What did you forget?"

Abe ignored me. "Ted, throw down that line. I'll tie the missing piece on, and you can haul it up. You understand 'careful,' don't you?"

"Yes, darling, I understand 'careful,'" he called back down.

The rope hit the ground. Rhiannon carried the mysterious package up to the rope. Abe removed the paper from around the object as gently as he would have a diaper from a newborn's bottom. He slowly uncovered the most magnificent copper weather vane I had ever seen. Abe secured it with the rope until he felt it would be safe during the pull up the side of the house. The weather vane was an eagle with a green-tinted beret on its head, its wings spread out wide behind it, talons grasping in front, red eyes staring straight ahead at some invisible foe. Its mouth was open and screaming, the tips of its beak and talons dripping blood. An enameled Special Forces patch had been attached to each side of the eagle's body.

"Go ahead, Ted. Haul it up."

I didn't know what to say, so I turned to Rhiannon. She smiled at me with a tear sliding down her cheek.

"I wanted to tell you so bad!" She gave me a big hug and a kiss.

"*Where* did you *get* it?"

"From them." She pointed at the ten men in DCUs (Desert Camouflage Uniforms) and green berets who stepped out of the woods surrounding my house. My old A-team had come to visit.

Doc walked up and hugged me. "We miss you, brother."

The rest of the team gathered around for hugs and handshakes.

"What are you guys doing here? Doc, you were in Kandahar. Smitty, you were ..."

"Never mind where I was," Smitty said smiling. Some things are better left unsaid.

"How did she find you guys?"

"I asked Officer Sanchez if he knew how to contact them," Rhiannon said, smiling at me with a look that made my insides melt. "The next day, I got a phone call from Doc. Some weird set of numbers I'd never seen before made up the caller-id."

Doc jumped in. "When Rhiannon contacted us with the idea, everyone liked it: an eagle turning into the winds of war without a thought for himself. We found a fabricator who could do it. He is the same fabricator who made all those cool weather vanes in the movie *Twister*. Two of these weather vanes were made. The one up on your roof is the first. The second one sits on the roof of our team HQ at MacDill. All of us flew back from around the world so we could be here when she gave it to you."

Ted finished attaching the weather vane to the peak of the roof. A wind sprang up from the east. The eagle swung around into it, its talons clawing at the wind.

We went down to the diner for a meal with the team. Gus made us all steaks and wouldn't let anyone pay.

"Thanks, you guys," he said as he served the plates. "The SF saved my patrol's ass one day in the Mekong delta—never got a chance to say thanks. Now I can."

"None of us were there," Smitty said. "It wasn't us who bailed you out."

"Don't matter. This is a 'paying forward.' I'm sure some soldiers are alive somewhere because of you guys. Thanks again."

After dinner, we posed for group pictures outside while Rhiannon snapped away. We almost caused two wrecks as people rubbernecked on their way through town. It's not every day you see ten Green Berets in one little backwater village—unless you are an enemy—then count on it being your worst nightmare.

Gus headed back inside the diner to print the pictures in his office. When he came back out, he asked those warriors to sign the one he selected. It would be displayed behind the cash register, next to him and that mortar. Finally, the pictures, handshakes, and hugs were done. My friends got into their cars and headed back to where they came from. As I watched them leave, a not small part of me wanted to be right beside them.

"Good luck, my brothers," I whispered. "Stay safe."

Chapter 10 – They Must Have Known Each Other

I had almost filled the rented trash trailer with the stuff I had pulled out of the house—plaster, lath, boards, old pipes, mouse-eaten wires, insulation, odd shapes of plasterboard, and bits of hot air ducts. I filled the mouse access holes with foam from a rattle can as I rewired and re-plumbed the house. For some reason I didn't understand, mice won't chew through the foam. Replacing the foundation also eliminated numerous mouse holes. The tide of my war against the rodents had turned in my favor.

The windows and doors were all re-caulked and sealed. The house had become noticeably warmer, even without the heat pump that hadn't been installed yet.

I paid the electric company for a 300-amp transformer at the end of the driveway then dug a two-foot deep trench by hand from the new transformer to the meter on the side of the house. The cables in the bottom of that ditch were an inch thick. I ran another set of cables out to the barn. I took great pride in the new fuse box with thirty breaker slots to distribute power throughout the house. Each room would have two breakers assigned to it, one for lighting and one for outlets. I put another fuse box out in the barn to wire those outlets and lights later.

All but two of the pups had found new homes with the workmen as they put my new foundation and beams under the house. Only Gina, one of her sisters, and Mom remained. Gina followed me everywhere, becoming as great a companion as I had hoped. She reminded me very much of Socks from my childhood. I looked forward to teaching her to hunt. Somehow I would find a way to keep her from having to go through the porcupine ordeal that Socks endured.

I spent every other night at Rhiannon's house. We were getting very comfortable being around each other. She said she needed those other nights to work her second job on the other side of the mountain. She laughed when I asked her why she worked two jobs.

"With two kids still in college, I don't have much choice. I've had at least one and usually two in college for the past ten years. One would graduate, and the next would start. My ex left me high and dry after he died: no insurance, no estate, no money. I either had to work a second job or tell my kids to find another way. At least they went to the community college first then transferred to Washington State. And all of them worked part-time jobs all the way through. That helped a lot. Two of them got scholarships, and that helped with the tuition."

"So, where do you work over there?"

"I clean motel rooms where they rent them by the hour." She rolled her eyes.

"And that pays enough to make it worth your drive over the mountain?"

"Well, I'm also room service. I delivery beer, wine, liquor, and food from the all-night diner/liquor store that's next door. Those guys always leave big tips to impress their 'dates.'"

One night after we finished a movie rerun about a kid who could see dead people, I told her about my meeting Gina by the river right after I retired from the Army.

She pulled away from me and sat on the edge of the sofa, looking into my eyes with an expression I had never seen before—almost angry. Then she got up without saying another word and walked into her bedroom. A few minutes later, she returned with an old photograph—a woman, a man, and two young children—one child a girl and the other a boy. The children were posing on a horse. The woman held the horse's bridle. The man stood behind the horse, holding the kids.

"Is this her?"

I studied the picture. The woman in the photo appeared much younger than the one I met. But they could have been the same woman. They had the same basic body shape, height, and facial contours. I'd never seen the man or children.

"Could be. When was that picture taken?"

"1950—right before she died."

"Then it couldn't be her. She was as alive as you and me."

"Her name was Gina."

"That's not an uncommon name. So what's this all about?"

"Yours isn't the first story about people meeting a woman by the river, a woman who helped them work out their problems, then disappeared without a trace."

Suddenly I remembered the man who had stumbled into our camp when Jack, Larry, and I were fourteen. I told her about that as well.

By the time I finished, Rhiannon had crossed her arms and hugged herself, shivering.

"Who was Gina?"

"My grandmother. That little girl in the picture is my mother. Grandma died in a train wreck while going to help a woman give birth. She was a midwife and healer to this side of the mountain."

"Sounds like I would have liked her," I said aloud, then, to myself, I thought, *maybe even loved her*. I still saw her sometimes in my dreams.

"She's the reason I went to nursing school," Rhiannon continued. "I wanted to be just like her. I spent all that time commuting to the other side of the mountain while I raised babies and tried to be a housewife—eight years it took me to get my RN Then, the summer after graduation, the clinic over here closed along with the rest of the town, and here I sit, waiting on tables."

"Is your grandfather still alive?"

"No. He passed about ten years ago. When World War II started, he joined the Marines—fought in the Pacific from Guadalcanal to Okinawa. Got a Silver Star and a field commission."

"I *know* I would have liked *him*," I said with a twinkle in my eye, "even if he was an officer."

"He remarried about two years after Grandma died. His new wife was a good woman and a wonderful mother to Mom and Uncle Donald, but she could never replace Grandma to me. And while Grandpa loved her, his heart always belonged to Grandma. He became the shining star of my childhood with his stories of how he'd asked Gina to marry him, how she'd learned to barrel-race horses from her mother, and how she visited him after she'd died. I still have the plaque the vets gave Grandma for writing to them while they were fighting in World War II. I found a stack of letters in Grandpa's stuff after he died. They were tied up with a ribbon. Grandma Gina saved every letter he wrote to her while he was in the Marines. He saved every letter she wrote to him in the Pacific. I never knew he had included poems in the letters he wrote while fighting the Japanese. I read and reread those letters. He always had something good to say about people. Even when Joe left me, Grandpa said it was for the best, that someone was waiting to be my companion, that I would meet him eventually, and the wait would be worth it."

A tear rolled down her cheek as she missed her grandfather again. When she could continue, she said. "I was too overcome then to believe him. I was angry that I was alone, that I had to wait to meet my soul mate. It was the only time in my life, I shouted at him. I said, 'How do you know that? How do you know I'll meet someone else?'"

"What did he say?"

"He said Gina told him. And if she said it, then it was true."

I put my arm around her and kept quiet. Sometimes the most comforting words are the ones you don't say. She turned her head to my shoulder and cried silently.

"How about *your* grandfather?" she asked a few minutes later. "What was he like? You said he built your house."

"Grandpa was old when I was born. He died when I was two. At least that's what Mom said. I don't remember him. His name was Jacob. He was the son of an Indian and a black woman who settled near here over a hundred years ago. He was a full-fledged member of the local Indian tribe. His Indian name was Black Eagle. He married another member of the tribe, Jane Fish. "

"That must be where you get that beautiful wavy hair and perpetual suntan."

"My wavy hair is from my great-grandmother. She was the daughter of two slaves and a midwife to this whole area. Mom said she learned it from her mother."

"I wonder if my great-grandmother knew your great-grandmother? They must have known each other. There weren't that many people out here then. They were both healers and midwives."

"Must have. No way of knowing now."

Chapter 11 – You Think You've Gotten Even

Spring was beginning to show around Chambersville. The drive up to the house took a little longer than usual. I stopped to look at a field of daffodils as they swayed in the breeze and enjoyed the beauty of this spring day. But the house called to me to get to work. As I finished the drive, I went over what I had accomplished and what remained.

All the wiring and plumbing were complete, along with the insulation and plasterboard. The new heat pump was wired in and connected to the ducting I had added while the walls were down. I had finished the mudding of the plasterboard yesterday. The house was starting to look like a house again. Today, my mental task list had "sand the plasterboard mud." It should be dry by now. John had rented me an electric sander connected to a shop vac. Using it, he said I should be able to sand the whole house in only one day. I doubted it but hoped he knew better than I did. Sanding plasterboard mud is one of my least favorite things to do.

The kitchen still awaited the new appliances, holes reserved in the cabinets where the dishwasher and stove were destined. Mom had wanted a dishwasher her whole life. Now the kitchen would have one. Instead of simply replacing the old cabinets Grandpa made, I had refinished them. Putting in new cabinets would have felt like I was throwing the away memories of Mom and Grandpa with the old cabinets. I didn't want to diverge too much from the kitchen Mom used.

Stripping all those layers of paint had been a lot of work. The cabinet wood turned out to be birch. I had been amazed by the closeness of the graining in those boards as I stripped away the layers of paint. The cabinet doors were made out of *single boards*, two feet wide. You can't even buy wood like that anymore. Initially, I planned to paint them like they were when Mom commanded the kitchen but decided the wood was just too pretty. So instead, I put six coats of clear varnish on them, sanding between each coat then using steel wool before the last coat. The cabinets gleamed now.

However, I did replace the worn-out Formica counters with granite. A new stainless steel sink sparkled under the brushed nickel faucet.

The dogs didn't run out to greet me in the morning when I got up to the house. Unusual. I walked out to the barn to check on them. When I opened the door, I expected them to come bounding out. Instead, smoke poured out through the opening. Mom and the female puppy I hadn't been able to find a home for were dead, hanging from a rope over Socks, my motorcycle. Someone had disemboweled them while they hung and struggled over my bike. Their guts and blood covered the seat, gas tanks, and windshield. Across the windshield, someone wrote in their blood, "Fuck You!!!" Whoever did this had poured paint remover on the tanks and fenders and dogs' entrails. It took a long time for those poor dogs to die in horrible pain. The paint still bubbled.

I went into autopilot mode. My .45 came out, and I stepped away from the door, studying the entire inside of the barn, absorbing every detail.

A bloody handprint was on the inside of the door I had opened. I could see boot prints in the dust under where the dogs were hanging. My toolbox had been stolen along with most of my carpentry tools. Someone tried to start a fire with some hay bales, but the bales had smoldered instead of burning. They were smoldering still. Around Socks, someone had drawn a large pentagram in the dirt.

I heard a noise beside me. I dropped, rolled, and came up pointing the .45 at the source, ready to pull the trigger.

Gina came out from behind my workbench, limping. Her front leg appeared broken. She hobbled up to me without even a whine and looked up into my eyes. I examined her quickly. In addition to her broken leg, she had some broken ribs and assorted cuts and bruises. I picked her up gently and closed the door to the barn again.

After putting her into the truck, I went behind the barn to the back door and pulled the smoldering bales out so they wouldn't hurt anything while they continued to burn.

I walked to the house, braced for what I knew I would see. Most of the damage had been hidden by the trees in the yard when I drove up. I saw my furniture lying in the grass under the smashed windows; the drop cloths I taped to them were still attached. I stepped through the ruined front door, the wood and glass crunching under my feet.

The walls inside were covered with spray-painted graffiti: "Fuck You!!!" "Green Berets are pussies." "Green Berets suck my cock." Some elaborate, meaningless tags.

Most of it was pretty amateurish, almost funny in a sad way. But one caught my attention and held it—on the wall next to the fireplace, someone had spray-painted, "She was mine, asshole." Underneath that, the single letter "T" had been added.

The cabinets and countertops in the kitchen hadn't been touched. Strange. The shelves in the pantry were still intact and untouched, the food and supplies still on them in neat rows. But every other door in the house had been destroyed, every window smashed, Jack's refrigerator mutilated with a sledgehammer, and a crowbar stuck out of the heat pump's compressor. Upstairs had received the same kind of damage: windows and doors in pieces, holes in the plasterboard, graffiti, all my tools were gone.

But the beautiful wide board, fir floors Grandpa had cut by hand, and I had carefully sanded and finished were untouched. I couldn't figure out why the vandals stopped their destruction.

More graffiti filled the walls of my new basement. Three separate shit piles and urine puddles were on the floor. Now I knew how many of them were here.

I walked back outside and looked around again, then up. The eagle on the weather vane glinted in the sun. Maybe it was my imagination, but the eyes seemed to glow malevolently. I guessed the vandals had missed it in the dark. It pointed southwest. Odd, the breeze was from the east. Then I noticed the wind kept trying and failing to bump it around to the east. The weathervane seemed to be fighting the wind as it kept pointing to the southwest. I would have to climb up there and see what the problem was.

Twin, wide, six-inch-deep troughs led away from the house where a vehicle had spun its tires as it left. They appeared to be the same width and distance apart as the dirt tracks Tommy's truck had made in front of Rhiannon's house. That didn't make any sense either. Why would they leave in a hurry? They had all the time in the world. What could have spooked them like that? The nearest person was Mr. Griff, and he was over ninety.

I looked at the hills around the house, letting my anger fill me like an erupting volcano. It was time to make a statement. "Tommy, you think you've gotten even. You are playing at being a Hollywood badass. What you don't understand is I do black ops for real. And I'm really good at it."

I closed my eyes then started turning circles. I wanted to try to feel which way he had gone. When I stopped and opened my eyes, I faced southwest. Sometimes it works, and sometimes it doesn't. It's a starting point.

"Ready or not, here I come." I spit on the ground, sealing the covenant.

I got in the truck to take Gina to the vet. At the end of the driveway, I saw some big off-road tire prints turn up the mountain, then disappear about a hundred yards farther up the road as the dust slung off them. I pulled out my cell phone and took a picture.

On the way down to the town, I called Chief Parker and filled him in. He said I lived outside of the city limits. My house was in county jurisdiction. He'd contact the sheriff's office and have them do their thing. I called Rhiannon at the diner. She hadn't seen Tommy or his truck, but she would keep watch for them.

"Do you have your pistol with you?" I asked. We practiced almost every afternoon when we were up at the house.

"You damn betcha!" she said under her breath. "And I've got a welcoming committee of seventeen, waiting for that son of a bitch to show up here."

Her pistol's magazine held seventeen rounds. She wasn't ever going to be surprised again.

I could tell when she thought about Tommy during our practice sessions. She would tuck, roll, and put three rounds in the man's chest on the target, followed by three in his forehead. Then she would get up, aim, and put one in his crotch. All seven shots took maybe three seconds. Her groupings were about the size of a silver dollar and getting smaller every day.

In half an hour, an A.P.B. had been issued for Tommy and his truck. Not that it would do any good. There'd been one out for him ever since the assault and rape charges had been booked, but no one had seen him yet. In a way, I was glad. He would be all mine. For an old, retired Green Beret, this was going to be fun.

Chapter 12 – Picking Up the Pieces

My old friend, Doc Johnson, had retired twenty years earlier and sold his practice to a young man right out of vet school. Unlike many other businesses, the vet practice had survived the downsizing of Chambersville. I hadn't met the new vet veterinarian, although I drove by his office every time I went into town.

I carried Gina through the door into the reception area. A bell attached to the door rang, and a middle-aged man walked out from the back. I took him to be about forty. He had shoulder-length brown hair, tied in the back into a ponytail, a rolled-up, tie-dyed bandana around his forehead, and a gold peace sign hanging from his neck. The embroidered name on his green clinic tunic said "Dr. Nigriny."

He greeted me warily, "Hi. What's up?"

I started to introduce myself. "You're David Peterson," he interrupted. "The Green Beret. I've heard all about you. What happened to your dog?"

"Gina's leg is broken, and she has three broken ribs I can feel."

"You have a bit of a temper?"

I looked at him coolly. "Some vandals killed my other two dogs, robbed me, and trashed my parents' house. Can you fix her, or should I take her over the mountain?"

I could see he didn't like me. I didn't care. Gina needed help.

"Let me X-ray her and see if there's any other damage." He lifted Gina gently and carried her into the X-ray room. She watched me from his arms as she disappeared through the door.

Fifteen minutes later, he came back. "That was all the damage besides the bruises and a couple of minor lacerations. As far as I can see, her vital organs were not injured." He looked down for a second, then into my eyes. "I called Chief Parker, and he filled me in on the break-in and damage. I apologize for the way I sounded earlier. We get a lot of abused animals in here. I'm pretty tired of fixing them up only to find them dead on the side of the road a week later."

"I don't blame you, Doctor Nigriny. That would piss me off, too."

That got a laugh. "Leave Gina with me for a couple of days. I'll set her leg and get her started on healing. She looks pretty healthy besides her injuries. I expect she'll be fine. Puppies are pretty tough."

"Go ahead and give her the puppy vaccinations, too. And thanks."

We shook hands, and I walked back out to my truck, then headed toward the center of town. I needed the stuff to secure my house—I wasn't going to be unprepared again. I called my insurance company and started the claim for the damage. The adjuster would be out that afternoon. The service agent said to have all my receipts ready. My policy specified complete replacement after a thousand-dollar deductible.

I called Doc's cell phone number. I knew he wouldn't answer. Cell phone numbers in black ops are encrypted voice mail drop boxes. He would retrieve it when he called in to get messages. To anyone else, the message would be noise.

"Hi, Doc. I need a favor. I need a satellite scan of the seventy-five-kilometer circle centered on my house." I gave him the GPS coordinates. "Look for a white Ford F-350, regular cab, short bed, two years old. All I need is the coordinates of whatever you can find. Fifty percent partials and up are OK." I hesitated, knowing Doc would be curious about why I asked for this. "Call me for justification."

The spring foliage had begun to sprout on the hardwood trees. The firs and cedars still had their green on, of course. Tommy would have a harder time hiding his truck with the leaves off. Not that Tommy would try to hide anything. He was too stupid to plan for danger from the air or even to realize it might be there.

I knew he would come back. He figured he'd gotten away with saying "fuck you" to a Green Beret. I didn't care about that at all. I'd had that done in at least twelve different languages by guys a lot tougher than Tommy. But to people like Tommy, it called them like a drug. You had to have more. He'd be back, and I would be ready.

But until then, the preparation for Tommy's revisit would keep me pretty busy. I pulled into the parking lot of the public library. Inside the library were computers with a broadband internet connection available to the public—time to spend some money.

Next, I stopped to see John at the hardware store. I loaded the truck with fence posts, T-posts, fencing, shock wire, insulators, fencing tools, a gate, a solar-powered gate opener, and a 50,000-volt cattle fence shocker.

"Add twenty bags of ready-mix concrete and a framing hammer too, the one with the cross hatches on the face. Oh, and I need a T-post driver."

"I heard about your house. We have a police band scanner at the store. Do you know who did it?"

"I have a pretty good idea. Know of anyone with a four-wheel-drive tractor for sale?"

"No, I sure don't. And you wouldn't want one from around here. Everything's worn out."

"Guess I need to go over the mountain."

I dropped off the stuff I bought next to the barn. The sheriff and his crime scene team were there. I introduced myself. He looked like Jackie Gleason in *Smokey and the Bandit*, complete with a round belly, mirrored sunglasses, and a brown Smokey-the-Bear hat. I figured him to be fifty-five to sixty. Uniformed officers were everywhere, photographing and collecting samples. I guess this county didn't see this kind of stuff very often. I was surprised at the number of people. This was vandalism, not murder.

"We don't get much crime out here beyond someone's Jon boat getting 'borrowed' or a poacher hunting deer offseason," Sheriff Crook explained. "I thought it would be good to give everyone a refresher—makes it a lot easier when we get a serious crime if they get to practice once in a while on something not quite so serious. That, and you're a cop, at least a cop-in-training. We protect our own, David. Damn shame about your dogs."

"Yep. I took the one survivor down to the vet. He said he can fix her broken leg."

"You think Tommy was into Satanism? That drawing around the motorcycle has everyone spooked."

"Nah. I expect he put it there because he thought it looked cool. Maybe it was a misguided attempt to throw us off the track. Wiccans don't have anything to do with Satanism. That's pure Hollywood."

"Yeah. You're right."

"Are you going to be able to get any DNA from the urine in the basement?"

"Don't think so. I expect the lime in the new concrete corrupted the sample."

"How about fingerprints? That bloody handprint on the door to the barn looked pretty complete."

"We've got that already and the boot print samples from the dirt all around the motorcycle. The blood will probably be the dogs, but we can hope one of them bit him. We might get lucky and get some DNA from that."

"How much longer do you think you'll be? The insurance adjuster from over the mountain will be out here after lunch. I know he'll want to look around for himself."

"Another hour ought to do it. Then we have to wait on the lab to see if we've got anything that will stick."

"Did you get a picture of the tire prints turning up the hill at the bottom of the driveway?"

"No. Damn! And they're gone by now." He shook his head ruefully. "I guess I need some practice, too."

"I have a picture of them on my cell phone. It won't be as good as your Nikon, but I'll send it to you. What's your phone number?"

He gave me the number. I keyed it in and sent the picture.

A woman drove her car up the driveway with the logo of my insurance company on the door. She parked the car behind the police cars and got out. She had on a beige pantsuit, carried a clipboard and camera, and looked to be all business. She could be Asian Indian or maybe Pakistani, middle-aged—maybe 35 to 40.

But the thing that I found most striking about her was her hair. She had the thickest, most beautiful black hair I'd ever seen. It was braided down the middle of her back all the way to her waist, with not a single gray hair in sight. A small diamond glinted from the left side of her nose.

"Hi. I'm David Peterson. Are you the adjuster?"

"Yes, sir. My name is Geeta Palivela. I am here to begin the repair process. Do you have some time to talk?"

"Nothing but time today. Where would you like to begin?"

"Let's start with the house."

I called out to the sheriff. "Sheriff Crook, are you done with the house? The adjuster wants to look around."

"Sure. Go ahead."

We walked in, and she began taking notes and pictures. When she got to the kitchen and saw the destroyed fridge, she turned to me. "Where are the rest of the appliances? Were they stolen?"

"No. They weren't installed yet. They're still at the store waiting for me to pick them up."

"I love those cabinets and counters!" She ran her hand over the graining. "Are they original?"

I nodded. "My grandfather made them from trees that grew on this property."

"How lucky those weren't ruined as well." She took a picture of the fridge, then pursed her lips when she saw the heat pump and took some more pictures.

When we got to the cut pipes and wires pulled out of the plasterboard, she asked, "No water damage?"

"Nope. The power to the well isn't on yet. The only damage from the water lines being cut was to the pipes and the plasterboard. But I'll have to restring the wiring, which will mean I have to pull down a lot of plasterboard. Code won't let me put a splice without a box, and all boxes have to be accessible. I don't want a bunch of cover plates in the middle of my walls."

"The windows will be tough," she said, examining them. "No one makes these anymore, and the frames are ruined. So we may have to put in something a little more modern. Same with the doors. Is that OK?"

"Sure."

Forty-five minutes later, she was done. I showed her the receipts for the tools and materials I bought. She scanned them with a portable scanner in her car and handed them back.

We walked out to the barn.

"Are you sure you're ready for this?" I asked her before we went in. "They killed my dogs and left them hanging over my motorcycle."

Her eyes got hard. "Who could do such a thing?"

"When I find them, I'll let you know."

When she saw the motorcycle and the dogs, she gasped and looked at me with tears in her eyes. Then, she wiped her eyes and took more pictures.

Five minutes later, we walked outside. "Mr. Peterson, I will have to get some bids from contractors to do the repairs and some research to find out how much the replacement things will cost. When I'm done, I can either give you a check or have the contractors bill me directly. I should have a final number in about a week. Since we also have your auto insurance, the same deductible will cover your motorcycle. Let me know if you want us to get the repairs done or arrange for them yourself."

I considered what she'd said. I knew and trusted the contractors I had already used. I didn't want to go through all that again with a new set of people.

"I think I'd like a check. I'll use the same contractors I used before."

"That's fine. If you don't want to wait on the final settlement, I could give you some starting money. I have a pretty good feeling about what the final number is. So today, I could be giving you half of what I think that will be, and then, when all the numbers come in, I'll be giving you a second check minus the deductible."

"Good. Do that. Then I can start right away."

She sat in her car, wrote the check, and handed it to me— very healthy five figures. I could certainly get started with that. As she drove back down the driveway, I called Herman Goldstein, the framing contractor. He said he would come out tomorrow. Next, I called the heating and cooling company that installed the heat pump. They would be out tomorrow also.

After I washed off as much of the paint remover as I could, two deputies helped me push the motorcycle up into the bed of my truck. Most of the paint was ruined, along with the plastic and rubber. The seat had been destroyed. The bike would have to be disassembled, repainted, and re-assembled with all new plastic and rubber parts.

I named the female puppy Tabitha. Nothing should be buried without a name. Then I buried Tabitha and Mom together in my family graveyard, right next to where Dad buried Socks. After I'd filled in their grave, I got into the truck and began the ride over the mountain to deliver Socks to the Harley dealership.

Last January, I began the cop class at the community college. Two evenings a week—rain, snow, sleet, or ice—I would get into Dad's truck and drive over the mountain, grateful more times than I could count for its four-wheel drive and new tires. I had driven this winding road so often I felt like I could navigate those turns with my eyes closed. The classes were four hours long. Most of it was pretty interesting—rules of evidence, grounds for arrest, when you can use deadly force and when you were breaking the law, techniques for cuffing and taking down a suspect, techniques for approaching a vehicle, how to write a ticket, how to testify in court. A steady progression of senior working cops gave us real-life stories of mistakes and successes. Sometimes I had trouble not laughing as I remembered the things I had done in the Special Forces. We didn't have quite so many rules or lawyers to pay attention to.

Chapter 13 – A Tough Job

I headed over the mountain to the Harley shop to drop off Socks.

The service manager promised to have an estimate by the end of the day tomorrow. He only asked one question, "Do you want to keep it stock?"

I said I would have to think about that. For the insurance company, I needed the stock restoration number.

We unloaded Socks, and I drove to the Kubota dealership.

"Can you deliver it? I don't have a trailer yet."

The salesman and I at the Kubota dealership had been going back and forth for over an hour. I knew what I wanted to pay, and he tried to wring every penny he could get out of me. We finally settled on a price that I thought was fair, and he said it would cost him his commission. So now, we're talking about getting the tractor back over the mountain to my property.

"Let's see, four hours at sixty dollars an hour plus a hundred and fifty miles at fifty cents a mile. That's over three hundred dollars to deliver it. Tell you what, add another two hundred dollars to that three hundred, and I'll sell you an old trailer I have that can carry your tractor. Then you'll have one. No one living in the country should be without a trailer."

"Sold. Load it up."

The Kubota dealership also carried Stihl chainsaws. I bought one that someone had traded in on a bigger model. The guy behind the counter suggested a couple of spare chains and a chain sharpener, then threw in some two-cycle oil for the gas.

I hooked up to the trailer, then watched them load my tractor onto it. The dealer threw in the tie-downs and chains for his cost. The tractor had four-wheel drive with a hydrostatic clutch, a removable backhoe, and a bucket loader on the front. I also got a brush mower to pull behind the tractor, a posthole digger with a twelve-inch auger to dig the holes for the fence posts, and a blade to level the driveway. The salesman showed me how to hook up the posthole digger to the back of the tractor. Building the fence would be a total breeze with this. As we loaded the posthole digger into the back of Dad's truck, I got an interesting idea.

Tommy thought his trashing of Grandpa's house and Socks and killing the dogs was payback for my luring Rhiannon away from his sorry, meth-addicted ass. What would he think about me having a new tractor? What if I dragged that shiny orange beast all around town and in his face on that trailer? He would never let me have something so cool. He would have to respond. And I would be ready!

Then I noticed the guy putting my tractor onto the trailer. "Larry?"

He turned to look at me. His hair was too long and greasy, like it hadn't been washed in a while. He had on a filthy baseball cap with "Kubota" on the front. It matched his dirty, worn-out clothes. "Do I know you?"

"Larry, it's David. We went to high school together."

"David?" He blinked a couple of times, then a crooked kind of smile crept onto his face. "Hey man, how *are* you? It's been a long time."

"I'm good. I got out of the Army a few months ago. I moved back into my folks' house. Jack told me you were working here."

"How is Jack? I haven't seen him in a while either."

"He's still married to Ethyl. They have a couple of kids. I met his son, John. Where are you living now? We'll have to get together."

He looked around, coughed, and spit. "I'm living right here."

When I gave him a confused look, he laughed but without much enthusiasm. "I live in a little travel trailer on the back of the property. I double as the night watchman."

"Well, it's easy to get to work! But, man, talk about a great commute!"

"Hey, David, I'd love to talk, but I got a bunch of stuff to do."

"Well, let's get together another time then."

"Sure, man, see ya."

He walked away around the corner of the workshop, lighting up a cigarette as he went. I watched him go. His shoulders were hunched over. He shuffled his feet and stared at the ground in front of him as he walked. He looked like an old man.

Seeing Larry sure took the edge off my excitement at buying that shiny, new tractor.

I stopped at the auto parts store and picked up some gas cans, two big ones and a little one. Before I headed back over the mountain, I filled them up at a gas station, along with the truck and the tractor. The big ones were for gas and diesel, respectively. The little one had gas-oil mix for the chain saw.

On the way over the mountain, I got a text from Doc. A friend of his at the NSA had run the scan on one-week-old data. There were a hundred and seventy-seven hits. He e-mailed the coordinates along with the percentages. The higher the percentage, the more the subject truck fit the parameters.

When I got back to Chambersville, I stopped by the US Forest Service office. They operated a storefront for the tourists who wanted to explore the Mount St. Helens, Mt. Adams, and Mt. Rainier national forest areas. They had USGS (United States Geological Survey) topo (topographical) maps of the whole area. I bought 1:250,000 maps covering the entire county. These large-scale maps weren't good for much but to give the general lay of the land. But they would be great to plot the coordinates that Doc's e-mail listed and see what smaller-scale maps I would need to investigate the hits.

I dropped by the diner to show Rhiannon the tractor. I know it's hard to imagine, but she was more excited about it than me. As soon as she got off work, she wanted to get it unloaded and try it out. I told her I wanted to park it in front of her house tonight and drive around town with it a few times while still on the trailer. She thought I was bragging. Nope. I was fishing—for Tommy. Sometimes you have to troll a while before you get a bite.

"Do you know where Tommy lived?"

She put my cup of coffee on the table in front of me and looked out the window with a bemused expression on her face.

"No. I sure don't. He never talked about it. I never thought to ask. I was usually trying to get rid of him."

I sat in the corner booth of the diner. After I called my insurance company and added the tractor to my homeowner's policy, I began to plot the coordinates that Doc sent me on the topo maps. As you'd expect, most of the hits were on the flat, bottomland where the farms were. A few were in the hills—probably homesteaders or survivalists. Once I had a good feeling for where the hits clustered, I went back to the Forest Service office and bought 1:100,000 maps of the areas containing the hits. Those maps contained six times the detail the 1:250,000 maps did.

I decided to examine the hits based on percentage—the highest percentages first. Once I put eyeballs on the high percentage item, I would check out the lower percentage items in the immediate vicinity before moving on to another area. With any luck, one of the hits would be Tommy's truck.

My phone rang—some number I had never seen before. Doc's voice greeted me. "Hey, brother."

"Thanks for the scan, Doc."

"Glad to help. What's going on?"

I filled him in. After I finished, silence came through the phone, followed by a low chuckle. "So the Black Ops King can't escape by retiring? Is that it?"

"I didn't make this happen, Doc!"

"Well, be gentle with poor Tommy. He has no idea what he's signed up for."

"Scout's honor." I held up my hand in the Boy Scout salute then crossed my fingers.

"By the way, I have some other info for you. It's in an encrypted e-mail I sent to you. Do you remember the name of that bar in Tangiers where you met that beautiful woman who turned out to have 'guy' equipment?"

I shook my head at the memory. "I would rather forget it, but, yeah, I remember."

"Well, that's the decryption key."

We never give away decryption keys over unprotected phone calls.

I hung up and checked my e-mail on my cell phone. The one from Doc prompted me for a decryption password. I keyed in "Scylla" then read with more and more fascination what Doc had sent me.

The DEA had a top-secret investigation going on, searching for a methamphetamine lab they suspected was located in my county. If they were correct, this lab produced enough meth for the entire three-state region. The DEA had failed so far in narrowing down the search. The lab had succeeded in keeping the production underground and didn't allow any distribution of the meth within a hundred miles of the lab. That hundred-mile circle was centered in my county. The DEA had also not been able to infiltrate the operation, find the supply lines, find the distribution network, or even find the money trail. I remembered the sores on Tommy's face and the skinny kids who helped him move the stuff out of his shop. Maybe Tommy wasn't so stupid after all. Or maybe he wasn't in charge. Or maybe he had nothing to do with the lab. I couldn't see how a professional meth lab would allow something as flashy as Tommy's truck anywhere near it.

A lot of questions but no answers—everything revolved around finding Tommy and his stupid, very expensive truck. How could Tommy have bought such a thing? Extorting tourists on auto repairs couldn't be that lucrative.

I deleted the e-mail, emptied the "deleted" folder, then ran a special safe-delete program that wrote zeros and ones three times to every unused byte in the cell phone storage. While that was running, I looked around the map for the other towns in the county. Since I had no idea where Tommy lived or hung out, I would have to pull my shiny new tractor through them also. The names of the towns were a tour down memory lane. I had played football and wrestled in about half of them in high school. The other towns were too small to have a high school back then. The end of logging must have been even worse for them than Chambersville.

I walked over to the bank to see Frank Everest.

"Frank's not in today," the teller said. "He called in sick."

This kept happening to me. Someone, please tell me Tommy hadn't visited Frank as well.

"Could you give me his address? I want to stop by to say hi."

"No. I couldn't. We don't give out personal info on anyone."

"Frank and I went to school together. We were both on the football team together."

"The best I can do is take your name and phone number and give it to him. If he wants to, he will call you back."

"That'll be fine." I gave her my info. "Thanks. See ya."

The police station for Chambersville was next door. Calling it a "police station" was a stretch—it was a storefront. It didn't even have a jail, just a holding cell. Chief Parker came out of the door as I walked up. "Hey, David. Ready to start getting some hours?"

"I've got a pretty full plate right now."

"How's the investigation going out at your place? Sheriff Crook gave me a thumbnail yesterday. Are you sure Tommy did it?"

"That's the only thing that fits. I have to meet the contractors up there tomorrow to get the repairs going."

"Anything I can do to help?"

"Do you have a home address for Tommy?"

He gave me a blank look, then said, "Well, let's go see."

He unlocked the door to the station again and walked to his computer. He pulled up DMV's website and keyed in "Tommy Sandouval." No hit for either a driver's license or a vehicle registered in his name. He tried "Thomas Sandouval," then "Tom." No hit. He pulled up the Secretary of State's website, looking for a business license on the service station, and got no hit. He looked for an officer in an LLC named "Sandouval." A "Jasmine L. Sandouval" was CFO for a corporation in Seattle, but no Tommy. He brought up the Social Security Administration website and checked for an account for Tommy. No hit in this state. He did a Google search on Tommy Sandouval. He got a lot of hits about a professional skateboarder, but nothing about a guy running a service station in Washington. He pulled up the IRS website and searched for Tommy's past tax filings. No hit for a Tommy Sandouval in our state. He went to the county Better Business Bureau website. There were a lot of hits there, but they were all complaints about being overcharged and underserviced.

Apparently, Tommy Sandouval didn't exist, a least not the one who ran the service station in our little town. All that meant was "Tommy Sandouval" was an alias for this asshole, not his real name. And that was interesting enough, all by itself. Why would a shyster running an auto repair service need or want to have an alias? What was he hiding from? Other illegal activities in other places? Other warrants?

Rhiannon had just gotten off work when I stopped by again. "You feel like driving over to Clarksville?"

She laughed like I had said the funniest thing she'd heard all day. "Clarksville? If you think this town is dead, you can't even imagine Clarksville."

I explained my plan of trailering the tractor through all the towns in the county. She jumped into the front seat and slid over next to me, trying to keep a straight face.

"Well, let's go to Deadsville, I mean Clarksville. Then we can go over to Williams Crossing, then, hold on to your hat, Higginston. That should set your hair on fire!"

She was right, of course. Higginston didn't even have its streetlights on. We only found one business open—a combination bar/gas station/general store.

I pulled up out front and parked. "How about a beer?"

She gave me a sultry look. "Why sure, you silver-tongued devil!"

I got out and opened the passenger door for her. OK. It was kind of a corny thing to do, but I believe in opening the doors for women. And I do the dishes too. Dad would always smile when he did them. I remember one of his favorite sayings: "No man has ever been shot by a woman while he was doing the dishes."

Like he had anything to worry about from Mom. Every time he said that she would chuckle and say, "I'd wait 'til he finished." Sometimes she would get out her pistol and clean it.

The store had two sections, divided by a wall: a bar and a convenience store. Two swinging, louvered doors separated the passage between them. We walked through the swinging doors and entered the bar. A couple of kids dressed like farmhands were in the corner with half-empty mugs of beer in front of them. OK, they must be at least 21 to be drinking, but they still looked like they should be in high school. The only other customer was an old guy at the end of the bar with his head on his arms. A Seattle Mariners game played on the TV. I walked up to the guy behind the bar and ordered two mugs of beer from a local microbrewery.

"Five bucks, pardner. It's still happy hour." The glasses were frost-covered with a little beer sliding down the side. I threw seven on the bar and carried them back to our table.

"I haven't been in here in maybe sixteen, seventeen years." Rhiannon grinned at the memory. "Joe got into a fight, and we got thrown out. I was so embarrassed."

As I looked at the bartender and sipped my beer, an idea occurred to me. I got up and walked over to him. "Kind of slow in here tonight."

"Kind of slow in here almost every night," he said with a grin. "But the building is paid for, and I make enough to pay the bills. Winters and summers, we get a bunch of tourists, and that tides me over."

"Would you mind if I asked you a weird question?"

"I guess that depends on how weird." He had a twinkle in his eye.

"I'm looking for a group of kids who come in together, keep to themselves, never make trouble, then leave at the same time. They would always pay their tabs and leave a good tip."

"Don't know anyone like that," he said, shaking his head. "But I wish I did—sounds like a bartender's dream. What do you want 'em for?"

"Oh, on a whim, I asked the bartender at the Wagon Wheel in Chambersville the same question. He was bitching about how all the young kids wanted to play rap music so loud his head hurt. He made me a twenty-dollar bet I'd never find them. I keep trying. I might have to end up paying him."

"If you ever find them, send them over here. I could use a whole bar full of those guys."

"OK. I'll do that. Thanks."

"What was that all about?" Rhiannon asked when I got back.

"I have a friend who is a Navy Seal. He said that to catch a boomer, you had to listen for where the sound wasn't."

"What in the world is a 'boomer'?"

"A nuclear missile sub. They are so quiet when they are underway the only way to find them is to listen for where there is no sound at all. The ocean makes noises continuously—waves, currents going over rocks, whales calling out. The subs create a kind of noise vacuum. So I had the idea that the way to find Tommy's friends is to look for quiet people instead of noisy ones. Find Tommy's friends, and you find Tommy."

"Why do you think Tommy's friends are quiet? I don't think I've ever seen him with a friend."

"The kids that helped him move were very quiet. I watched them for an hour while they were loading the truck with his stuff from the service station. They were all business. No joking. Not even talking, other than a few words about where to pack something or what to pack next." And I thought to myself, *That's exactly what professional meth lab people would be like—low key, no waves, no attention, under the radar. Even in a noisy honkytonk, you'd never know they were there.*

I sighed. Now I would have to visit every bar in the county. I know, I know—a tough job, but someone has to do it.

Chapter 14 – Alternative Medicine

Frank Everest called me the next day. "Hi, David. Here's my number."

He gave me his phone number and address.

"How are you feeling?"

"Oh, I don't know. Like shit, I guess. I think I'm trying to fight off a cold. Hard to tell. One bad thing pretty much runs into another these days. How are you? I heard about your house. That sucks."

"Yep. I'll find Tommy. We'll even things out. Would you like to come over for dinner at Rhiannon's? Say 6 P.M? I do a pretty mean meatloaf."

"That sounds wonderful. I don't know how much I can eat. Usually, the great nausea god claims my meal."

"I've got an idea about that as well. See you at 6."

"Bye. And thanks, David." The line went dead.

I called Rhiannon at the diner. Dinner with Frank was fine. She would bring home a pie from the diner and pick up the fixings for a salad.

I got out a set of my military desert camos and pulled off all the insignia. I did this automatically. We never wore insignia when we worked, and it *was* time to go to work. The contractors weren't going to show up at the house until after lunch. So I had all morning to begin examining the coordinates Doc's scan turned up. I had sorted the list Doc gave me from highest percentage to lowest. The first one on my sorted list was a 100-percent scan about fifteen klicks northwest of my house. I picked up my binoculars, camera, compass, and map, put them in a camo backpack, then grabbed a couple of bottles of water as I went out the door. I drove to the coordinates and parked nearby in a hunter's turnout.

Half an hour later, I stood on a hillside staring down at a white F-350 Ford with a short bed and standard cab, but hay bales filled the bed, it didn't have a lift kit, and the custom paint came from mother earth. It was a muddy old farm truck. I took a picture, made a notation, and then on to the next dot on the map. Mark off one from the list. Only 176 to go.

I had three other partials nearby. The closest one was about three klicks north-northeast. So I headed off in that direction. It turned out to be a GMC pickup parked under a canopy with its bed sticking out—hence the partial. It looked like it hadn't moved in months.

I didn't find a vehicle at the next coordinates. I figured that would happen a lot—the data was nine days old. Most of these trucks would be in use every day. I examined the house next to the coordinates—just a farmhouse with a barn behind it. A plump woman with white hair came out of the house and started putting some clothes on a clothesline.

I made a notation indicating I had seen the place, but not the truck, took a picture, then on to the next partial.

A little before one o'clock, I pulled up my driveway. Herman Goldstein, the framing contractor, was there waiting. Gina sat in the passenger seat of my truck—her front leg in the walking splint Doc Nigriny had put on her. She jumped out when I opened the door and ran around on it like she'd been wearing it from birth. The doc told me to keep her quiet for another three weeks.

"Hi, Herman," I called out as I struggled to put a leash on Gina. She didn't like it at all and kept trying to wiggle out.

"Hi, David. What happened here?"

"A gift from an old friend. Let me show you around."

I put Gina back in my truck and rolled the windows partway down. I would have to build a cage for her to stay in until her leg finished healing.

He looked at the holes where the windows and doors used to be and ran his fingers around the smashed frames.

"With such friends, who needs an enemy?" he asked, shaking his head.

He agreed to begin the repairs as soon as he could get the windows and doors, probably a couple of weeks. He said he'd send his foreman up this afternoon to tarp over the holes. He measured all the openings and wrote them down. I would have to settle for double-pane, double-hung windows. They were close to how the old ones looked, except these would have a lot less heat loss and wouldn't need reglazing for a long time. The exterior doors would have to be fiberglass. But he knew where he could find interior doors that would look almost identical.

"Any damage in the barn?"

"Nothing serious. Tommy tried to set a fire with the hay bales, but it never got past a smolder." I told him about the dogs and the motorcycle.

"I hope you catch the son of a bitch," Herman said grimly and spat on the ground.

"Yep." Sometimes there's nothing else to say.

The heating and cooling contractor pulled up the drive as Herman left. They waved as they passed. I showed him the damage done to the heat pump.

"I hear about this stuff happening in the big cities, but not out here. What would make someone do this?"

"It's a story as old as humanity—ego and jealousy."

"I'll order the compressor—it should be available from our supplier's warehouse. Tomorrow soon enough?"

"Tomorrow's fine. See you then."

I got the tractor off the trailer, set up the posthole digger, then spent the rest of the afternoon drilling postholes and setting the posts with concrete. While the concrete cured, I began driving the T-posts between them. It felt good to be sweating and working again. The fence line would encircle the house. The two ends met where the driveway entered the road. That was the only opening— a gate across the driveway would seal the enclosure.

I loaded the tractor back onto the trailer and washed the dust and dirt off. I wanted it to look brand new. Then I headed down to Chambersville, stopping by the grocery store to get the fixings for my world-famous meatloaf.

I heard Doc laughing at me from the back of my mind. "World Famous? Really? The last time you made it, we needed a chain saw to slice it."

OK. "World-famous" didn't necessarily mean "Good." I would have to remember to turn the heat down to below 500 degrees.

Frank did indeed look like shit. He was pale, and his cheeks were sunken. There were dark circles around his eyes. Rhiannon fluttered around him like a hummingbird, making sure he was comfortable, that he had something to drink, that the stereo wasn't too loud.

The smells of the meatloaf cooking filled her little house. Rhiannon had immediately turned the heat down to 350 degrees when she walked through the door. While the oven cooled down, she moved the loaf from a bread pan into a meatloaf pan that allowed the grease to drain out. Then she covered the meatloaf pan with some aluminum foil. I figured there was a lot better chance of it being edible now.

I sat down next to him. "Frank, have you thought about using pot to control your nausea and get back some of your appetite?"

He looked at me like I was insane. "Pot? You're kidding, right? I haven't smoked pot since high school. And nothing happened when I did."

"Maybe you didn't inhale." I snickered, remembering Bill Clinton's famous line. "It's actually prescribed by doctors now. And Washington passed a law making it legal. It's not against the law anymore."

"I hear the Feds don't see it that way."

"They'll come around. They did the same thing during Prohibition. The states started passing laws allowing alcohol, and finally, Congress repealed Prohibition. It's all about money and power. As soon as Congress realizes how much money they can generate by taxing it and that they won't get kicked out of office for legalizing it, it'll be allowed the next day. If you'd like to try an experiment, we can see if it helps you tonight."

He still couldn't believe I was serious. Finally, he shrugged. "What the hell. Nothing else is working. Let's see."

Fredrick Hudgin

I got out Rhiannon's bong and stoked it. "Put your finger here and suck on that pipe stem. The water will cool the smoke and remove a lot of the bad stuff. When the smoke gets to the pipe stem, let your finger go and keep sucking."

Frank did as I instructed him. He blew out a thick stream of smoke.

"Nothing," he said, disappointed.

"Try again."

He finished the small bud of pot I had put in the bowl.

"Dinner's on," Rhiannon announced.

Frank sat at the table like he'd forgotten what it was for. He speared a little piece of meatloaf with zero enthusiasm and put it in his mouth. Then he blinked a couple of times, started chewing, and then reached for another bite.

Rhiannon and I watched Frank clean his plate while we ate what turned out to be a passably good meatloaf. He didn't talk while he ate. He kept piling the food into his mouth, chewing and swallowing.

"This is really good," he said as he poked the last bite into his mouth.

"Think you're up to some apple pie with ice cream, Frank?" Rhiannon was already preparing him a plate.

"That sounds good too." He tried to smile as he swallowed. "I haven't eaten like this in two years."

"How do you expect to fight this thing off if you don't eat?" she asked him as she put the pie in front of him. "Your body needs some fuel to fight the good fight."

I don't think he heard her. He was focused on the pie, and the pie was losing.

I let Frank smoke another bowl after dinner to keep his nausea down. It seemed to work.

"Frank, did Tommy have a bank account with you?"

"I can't tell you that. We pride ourselves on keeping customer privacy."

"Would it help if I gave you a county sheriff case number?"

"Yes, it would. And you'd have to have the sheriff give it to me."

"OK. It'll be on your desk tomorrow."

"Then in that case, yes, he did."

"What kind of activity did the account have?"

"Pretty normal for a successful retail business. Tommy did all of his transactions in cash. The AML guys at the bank were always questioning me about him."

"AML?"

"Anti-Money Laundering," Frank explained. "The Feds have pretty strict reporting requirements on cash deposits. I told them over and over that Tommy did his business in cash. He'd deposit fifteen, twenty thousand dollars at a time into his account. Damned red flags were always popping up with his name on them."

"Did his account have an address associated with it?"

"I'm sure it did. I don't know what it was, probably his business address."

"Was it a personal or business account?"

"I think it was personal with a DBA."

"DBA?"

"Doing Business As. A lot of small businesses do that. Less overhead for them than starting an LLC and having to register it with the state."

"Is his account still active?"

"Don't know. I could tell you tomorrow."

"Great. How about a movie?"

Together we watched a movie about a kid in India trying to run a hotel his parents left him after they died. The "great nausea god" must have been sleeping that night. Frank watched the whole movie with us without looking distressed at all. He *did* laugh a lot. It was good to hear. I had the feeling he hadn't laughed much in a while.

Rhiannon followed me while I drove Frank and his car back to his house. I didn't want him trying to drive after all the pot he'd smoked. He clutched the little bag of pot I had given him like his life depended on it. In one way of thinking, maybe it did. I had found out many times how hard it was to fight when you hadn't eaten in days.

Chapter 15 – The Homestead

Frank called me the next day. He sounded in much better spirits and filled me in on Tommy's account information.

Someone had closed Tommy's checking account the day he left Chambersville. There had been almost a quarter-million dollars in it. A wire transfer moved the balance to an account in the Cayman Islands. The statements were sent to his business address. The account had no phone number, alternate address, and no additional signers associated with it.

I continued my examination of the coordinates Doc sent me. The next group was twenty-two klicks southwest, a cluster of four, with one being 99%. The first three ended up being two more farm trucks and a Dodge. The last one, a 55% match, was located up in the hills, away from all the farms and the other hits on Doc's list. According to the map, it was also in a deep ravine.

An hour later, I stood over the ravine but still could not see the truck. "How did it get up here?" I wondered aloud. Then I noticed a narrow road winding up the hillside from the farm area as it went in and out of the tree cover. The road didn't appear to be used much. I studied the area with my binoculars but couldn't see anything through the trees—firs and cedars filled the whole ravine. I would have to go down for a closer look.

As I began the climb down the hillside, I heard the unmistakable sound of a round being chambered into a rifle. Close. Behind me. Followed by a voice. "You know any good reason why I shouldn't blow yer head off?"

"Now, why would you want to do that?" The fact he hadn't *already* blown my head off was very hopeful. "I'm a bird watcher looking for a snowy egret. I heard they were up here and wanted to see one."

"Bullshit." Not angry, just a statement.

Well, a lie didn't work. How about a half-truth? "I'm searching for a pot field I heard about. I got a friend who has cancer." It was a gamble. If he was growing pot, I might have a problem.

"Ain't no pot up here. You a Fed?"

Damn, let's see if the truth works. "Nope—used to be a Green Beret; retired a few months ago; live down below in my folks' old house."

"That house wouldn't be the Peterson's, would it?"

"Yes, it is. Do I know you?"

"I knew yer mom, yer dad, *and* yer grampa. Used to buy 'shine from me."

OK—*now* I understand. "I remember drinking it with them when I was a kid. Can I put my hands down?"

"You armed?"

"Got a .45 in my belt in the back."

He pulled it out. "Nice piece. Well taken care of."

He unloaded it and handed it back, keeping the magazine and the round from the chamber.

I put it back in my belt behind me so he could watch me do it, then turned around, my hands in clear sight. He was an older man, thin and weathered, maybe sixty or seventy—hard to tell. He had a mouth full of tobacco and a scruffy beard—looked to be tough as rawhide.

"Have you got an F-350 Ford?"

"Why do yuh want to know?" He spit on the ground next to his feet without letting his eyes leave mine. He held his rifle with the confidence of years of practice, the muzzle not pointing directly at me, but I had no doubt it would be pointing at the middle of my chest in a split second if I gave him cause to do it.

"I'm searching for a kid named Tommy Sandouval. Drives a white F-350 short-bed with a twelve-inch lift kit. Got fancy tires and wheels and a pretty paint job."

"I got a F-350. Ain't got no stupid lift kit or fancy paint on it. It's already higher than a kid on pot." He paused a minute, sizing me up. "I seen the one yer looking for, though. Let me see yer map."

I handed it to him, chuckling to myself that he knew I had one.

He studied it for a minute, looked up at the sun, changed the orientation of the map, so it fit the hills we were standing on. He put his finger on a ravine about eight klicks away. "Last I seen it, it were turning up this here road. What that kid done to you?"

I told him about the house, the barn, and the dogs.

"I sat in that kitchen for dinner with yer folks many a time. Yer ma put great store in that kitchen. I see 'im, you won't have to worry about findin' 'im. Don't have no truck with people hurtin' dogs. Here's yer magazine and bullet."

"How long ago did you see 'im?" I slipped the magazine and bullet into my pocket.

He pondered my question a moment. "Been 'bout a week. How'd you know I had a F-350 parked up here?"

"Satellite scan."

He looked up with a faint smile. "Good to know. Leave the way yuh come in."

He stepped back into the woods and ... disappeared. My concealment instructor in SF school couldn't have done it as well.

It was noon when I got back to the truck. I wanted to check out the place the old man indicated on my map. None of Doc's sightings were anywhere near there. The fencing could wait.

I found a hunter's turnout on the road as I approached the ravine and parked the truck. The "road" that the old man had described looked to be more like a driveway than an actual road, gravel but well maintained. The hills went up steeply from the driveway. A stream came splashing down the hillside into the ditch beside the road beside where I was parked, joining the stream that came out beside the driveway. I started up the hillside. Twenty-five minutes later, I came out on a ridgeline that looked like it paralleled the driveway and stream. From where I was standing, I had a partial view of them as they wound up the ravine. Nothing moved on the driveway or n the hillsides beside it. Then I had a feeling, so I sat down and waited to see what would happen.

I waited there for half an hour, no movement anywhere beyond some birds flying around. Finally, I began to walk up the ridgeline, moving from tree to tree. I stopped beside each tree, looking for movement, paralleling the way Tommy would have gone if he'd driven up that gravel road. About a mile and a half later, I looked down on an ancient homestead with a house built into the side of the mountain. Some chairs were on the porch in front. In front of the house, two people were working in a large garden. Dead plants from last year still lay in neat rows as they turned the soil, getting the garden ready to plant. I studied the people and homestead through my binoculars—a man and a woman, mid-forties, worn clothes, no sign of Tommy's truck. An old, beat-up Impala was parked in the driveway, next to a worn-out Chevy pickup with a cab-high railing around the bed built of old, weathered boards. A small shed stood open next to the house with garden tools visible through its door. I took several pictures, then moved back down the ridgeline toward my truck.

....

High above David, a camera in a tree turned as he walked, following him down the ridge. One camera after another watched him until he got into his truck. The couple in the garden heard a soft bell chime. Wordlessly they put their tools back in the shed, closed and latched the door, then walked into the house.

Chapter 16 – Tommy Floats to the Surface

I dove into the routine of checking on the coordinates in the mornings, working on the house in the afternoons, then either going to class or pulling my tractor around the county at night. I figured I would finish the coordinate list by the middle of summer, about the same time as I would finish the house. As I visited all the little towns, villages, and wide spots in the road around the county, I left pictures of Tommy and his truck in all the gas stations with the phone number of Sheriff Crook's 24-hour dispatcher and my cell phone.

So far, no one had seen Tommy or his truck. I never got any phone calls from people with information. I also drew a complete blank on the quiet kids in the bar. No one had seen anyone like them. I met a lot of good people, though. My deputy badge helped a lot. You put enough lines in the water; one of them is bound to get a bite sooner or later.

....

There were four weeks left in my cop class. We were assigned to real cops and spent a whole shift once a week, dogging them as they did their job. Once they found out I was a retired Green Beret, they relaxed and let me do the work. I really appreciated it. Only once did my partner order me to back off and let him take over. We were on a domestic disturbance call. The guy had beat the shit out of his wife for not having cold beer in the fridge when he came home from work. Apparently, I "helped" him to the floor a little too vigorously after he swung at me. His cheekbone will heal eventually. They should have had carpet, for God's sake.

On another call, I almost delivered a baby. We made it to the ER as her baby crowned with a headful of curly black hair. I showed the mother how to breathe differently to make the contractions less intense so she could have the baby inside the hospital instead of in the police car. Between contractions, she said she would name the baby after me if it were a boy, but it turned out to be a girl. She was born in the hallway of the ER on the gurney as the orderly waited for the elevator to Maternity. I stopped by to check on them at the end of my shift before I went back over the mountain. Mom and daughter were both doing well.

But I spent most of my time on the house—every afternoon and all weekend. All the electrical work was done and approved, as were the plumbing, heat pump, and ducting. The new stainless steel appliances were beautiful next to the natural birch cabinets. Mom would have loved them. *I* really loved the new windows and doors. It was hard for me to say, but in a back-handed, weird way, I kind of appreciated Tommy trashing the old ones because the new windows and doors were air-tight and insulated.

I bought another smaller "beverage fridge" and a chest freezer for the basement. Jack approved. He brought over a case of his favorite beer to keep in the downstairs fridge.

As the weather got better, I dropped most of the trees that had grown up on the lawn since Mom and Dad died. The woodpile under the barn's eaves grew larger, and my stomach grew flatter. Grandpa had always resisted getting a chain saw until we bought him one as a group Christmas present. The first time he used it, he came back in laughing. "It's no less work—yuh just get more wood."

I split all the wood by hand with wedges and a sledgehammer. Then I had fun blowing the stumps out of the ground with the dynamite John sold me when no one was looking. I had always liked demolitions. But the guy at the explosives store wouldn't sell me C-4. Now *C-4* is fun! Chief Parker came out when he'd gotten some calls about the noise.

"You're supposed ta have a demolitions license and get a permit," he told me, knowing he was wasting his time.

"I've blown things up a few times before this, Josh."

He shook his head and got back into his car.

After the stumps were out and burned, I plowed and disked the yard, then raked it smooth and put in grass seed. Gina was out of her cage now with her splint off and loved digging holes in the soft dirt. I would fill them in, smooth the dirt over, and re-seed them, again and again.

Rhiannon began putting in the new landscaping. I gave her a budget, and she stuck to it to the penny. The outside of the house looked as good as the inside. The new porch was on and painted, complete with a swing. Rhiannon put hanging baskets of flowers around the freshly painted eaves.

Abe Rabinowitz, the roofing contractor, let me be the labor when he put the roof on the porch. He bought the stuff. He told me what to do. And I did it. Not much to it once you learn how. I guess you could say that about a lot of things.

Rhiannon and I were snuggled up on her couch on a rare night off when I got a phone call from a blocked number. A man's voice said "Tommy's at ..." and he gave me some GPS coordinates. Then he hung up. His voice had been electronically distorted. I went out to Dad's truck and got my maps. The coordinates were way out of my search area, at least eighty miles from Rhiannon's house. I called Chief Parker and told him. He wanted to wait until morning. I worried about Tommy not being there by morning, so I drove over to the coordinates. I needn't have worried. When I found the coordinates, I found Tommy's truck with Tommy inside, dead. Based on the level of decomposition, he'd been there for months. He had three rounds through the head.

I called Chief Parker. He called Sheriff Crook. Sheriff Crook called the county coroner and the crime scene team. In two hours, there were cops all around Tommy's truck. I let them do their job and went back to Rhiannon's house. We had a movie to finish.

It turns out Rhiannon had other plans. She wanted to celebrate Tommy's death. I guess I can't blame her. His loss was *definitely* my gain. She can be downright celebratory when she wants to be.

The phone company unblocked the phone number the next day when the sheriff asked them to. The phone call had been made from a GoPhone. The sheriff's office traced the phone to a Quik Mart about a hundred miles away. They had sold the phone a week earlier to some guy who paid for it with cash. The closed-circuit, black and white camera in the Quik Mart showed a youngish bearded white man in an unmarked gray hoody pulled up over his head. He wore jeans and sunglasses—no visible birthmarks or tattoos. He walked up to the Quik Mart and left on foot after the transaction. The phone call itself originated from a cell phone tower in an urban part of the county. No other calls had been made to or from that phone.

When the sheriff's office called the number, it immediately rolled over and said the voice mailbox had never been set up. I would be willing to bet the phone now resided at the bottom of one of the lakes or streams around the county.

The thing I couldn't figure out was why someone would go to all that trouble just to tell me where I could find Tommy's body.

"Back again?" The old bootlegger's voice came from behind me.

He was good. I concentrated on listening this time and hadn't heard a twig snap or a leaf crush.

"I'm unarmed." I turned around slowly with my hands in plain sight. "We found the kid in the pickup. He's dead. Three in the head."

"Good riddance." The old man coughed and spit. "Who done it?"

"Don't know. I thought maybe you did."

"Wouldda loved to, but it weren't me."

"Well, then, I don't know. I'm putting Grandpa's house back together. You're welcome to stop by."

"Why thankee, Davie, I just might do that."

He knew my name, but I had no idea what his was. Guess it'll have to stay that way until he offers.

He turned and walked into the forest as silently as a breeze. I waited until he'd disappeared, then slipped into the forest behind him, thinking I would solve who he was once and for all.

He left no trail I could see—not a turned leaf, a broken twig, nothing. So I moved along the path I had seen him travel. A young buck grazed in a small glade. He hadn't heard either one of us. I was in awe of the old man. Somewhere up ahead, I knew he was watching me come up his back trail and laughing at me as I did it.

Then the hair on the back of my neck went up. I've gotten that feeling a hundred times during black ops, and it never failed to save my life—time to go.

I drove over the mountain to the Kubota dealer. They were closing up. I saw Larry walking across the parking lot.

"Larry," I called out.

He froze, then turned around.

"Oh, hi, David." He sounded relieved and suspicious at the same time.

I walked up to him. "Have you ever seen either of these guys?"

I showed him the pictures of Tommy and the guy in the hoody. He gave them a cursory glance, then shook his head. "What'd they do?"

"Well, this one raped Rhiannon McNeil." I held up Tommy's picture. "He'd been shot three times in the head when we found 'im."

I held up the picture of the guy in the hoody. "This one told me where to find 'im. He may also have been the trigger man."

Larry looked at the pictures again. "Rhiannon McNeil. I h'ain't heard that name since high school. Same girl?"

"Yep."

Something about how he was acting got my hackles up. "So you haven't seen either one of 'em?"

"Why you askin' me? I don't hang out with any criminal types. My PO would throw me back in the can if'n I did."

"I thought maybe you might've seen 'em around somewhere."

"Well, I haven't." He walked away without looking back.

Based on his DNA, Tommy Sandouval turned out to be Theodore Santanini. He had a rap sheet longer than my arm. He had been thrown out of the Army for stealing from his company's supply room and assaulting his first sergeant. His fingerprints were the ones on the door to my barn. Eight different states wanted him on various charges, but violent rape seemed to be his favorite. He had managed to stay one step ahead of the law as he jumped from one backwater town to another, always with a different alias. In the last town he'd "visited" before Chambersville, he'd left a woman brain-damaged and paralyzed from the waist down.

Two weeks later, the toxicology report came back. Cocaine and heroin had killed him—way past the lethal level. A history of meth and coke showed up in his hair, but not of opiates. The time of death was approximately three months ago, which put it at about a month after he'd packed up and disappeared. The coroner said he had died before being shot. Head shootings produce lots of blood, and there was very little in the truck. The bullets he'd been hit with, 9mm, were recovered from inside the truck, but all the windows were intact, so someone shot him with the door open, or the windows had been closed afterward. Not a single fingerprint was found inside the truck. Whoever wiped it down knew their job. Even the cigarette lighter was clean. Not a hair or piece of dust remained in the cab. The glove box and console were empty and clean. Even the seats and carpets were scrubbed.

"Why didn't they burn the truck?" the detective at county scratched his head. "Why go to all the trouble of cleaning it? And why shoot 'im after he's already dead? None of this makes any sense."

Tommy wasn't my problem anymore. I could quit spending all my time checking coordinates and visiting bars with a tractor on a trailer. That meant I could spend a lot more time with Rhiannon and working on my house, the two most important things in my life right now.

No one ever claimed Tommy's body. Instead, the county had him cremated and paid for it with the money they made selling his truck. His ashes were stored in the county evidence locker in case someone eventually showed up who wanted them.

Once they had Tommy's real name, Marylou, one of the district attorney's clerks, found Tommy's birth certificate, then his mother. When she learned Tommy's mother had Alzheimer's, she tried to transfer all the remaining money from the sale of Tommy's truck to provide for his mother's care. The transfer was blocked by the insurance company who paid for the repairs on my house. They wanted all of Tommy's estate assets sent to them to offset what they had paid to fix the damage. The DA wanted the money to offset the costs of the investigation. The court would have to decide.

Joan, the billing department clerk in the senior care facility where Tommy's mother was staying, told Marylou about Tommy wiring in money and gave her Tommy's phone number and the bank and account number of where the money came from. That led to the discovery of Tommy's private bank account in his mother's name and social security number. Because the account was in his mother's name, the insurance company and county couldn't touch it. Marylou got that transferred to Tommy's mother's care. No old woman was going to get left out in the cold, not if she could help it. Tommy's mom would be taken care of for at least the next couple of years. After that, who knows? By then, his mother probably wouldn't care either way. She passed Tommy's phone number to the detective handling Tommy's case.

Chapter 17 – Pissing Off the Pope

A gurgling voice on the other end of the line called my name, "Daaavuud!"

The caller ID said "Frank Everest." The clock on the end table displayed 1:31 A.M.

"Frank? What's wrong?"

"Hellllp meee!"

"Are you at home?"

"Yesss." I heard a thunk and a couple of bumps, then nothing.

I tore up the road on my way over to Frank's. He was unconscious by the time I got there, but he still had a pulse and was breathing shallowly. I pressed Chief Parker's number on the speed dial of my cell phone.

"Josh—David. Frank Everest is unconscious. I'm at his house. Meet me at the station so we can transport him over the mountain."

"I'll be there in five minutes."

I called Rhiannon and filled her in as I drove to the station.

"I have an oxygen bottle with a bag valve mask that I got for Grandpa before he died. It should be full. I'll meet you at the station with it."

As I pulled up to the station, Frank stopped breathing. While Rhiannon got the BVM ready, I started mouth-to-mouth, wishing I had a one-way facemask. Josh pulled up with his lights going. We transferred Frank into Josh's patrol car and left Chambersville with the light bar flashing and siren screaming. Rhiannon was pumping oxygen into Frank while I called the ER and told them what we had followed by Frank's pulse rate, respirations, and our ETA. The ER doc got on the phone. I put mine on speaker so Rhiannon and Josh could hear, too.

"Is there any sign of trauma?" he asked.

"No. He was facedown, unconscious on the floor when I found him. The floor was carpeted. There was a small amount of vomit or mucus next to his mouth, but nothing inside. He was breathing then, but he's stopped once already. We were able to restore his respirations. His pulse never stopped. There is a distinct gurgling sound when he breathes, but we have no way to suction him. We're ventilating him with a bag-valve mask and oxygen."

"Have you checked his pupils?"

"They are equal and reactive."

"What is his temperature?"

"I have no way to measure it."

"Feel his forehead."

"It feels hot."

Rhiannon put her hand on her own forehead for thirty seconds, then on Frank's. "He's running about 102, maybe 103," she said.

"How much oxygen are you giving him?"

I checked the regulator. "Ten liters per minute."

"What's the capacity of your oxygen cylinder?"

"Don't know."

Rhiannon spoke up, "It's a D-sized cylinder."

"Is it full?"

"Yes, 2,000 PSI."

"A D cylinder holds about four hundred liters. How far out are you?"

"Fifty minutes, more or less." I looked at Josh for confirmation. He nodded in the rearview mirror.

"Reduce the flow to seven liters per minute, so you don't run out and, if there is a way to do it, elevate his chest to a thirty-degree angle. Do you have any way to monitor his lung sounds or blood oxygen?

"Nope."

"OK. Keep ventilating him with the BVM and monitor his respirations and pulse. If we're lucky, the bag-valve pressure will push some of the fluid in his lungs back into his bloodstream. Not much else you can do. If his pulse stops, immediately start CPR."

Rhiannon and I pulled off our jackets and propped up Frank's torso. He started breathing easier.

I thought I recognized the doctor's voice. "Dr. Chung?"

"Yes. Is this Mr. Peterson?"

"Yes."

"We'll be ready when you get here. Call again when you're five minutes out or if his status changes."

Frank didn't stop breathing again during the trip. The oxygen seemed to be helping. Rhiannon and I took five-minute shifts on the BVM. When we got to the hospital, the ER team was waiting. They transferred Frank to a gurney and ran him into the ER. An hour later, Dr. Chung came out.

"Frank has pneumonia. He would have died in another fifteen minutes. He's stable in our ICU. His oncologist is on the way. He's on the strongest antibiotic we have."

We stuck around to talk to Frank's doctor. After another two hours, he came out. I had just returned from the coffee machine with cups for everyone. He walked up to us in his green scrubs. He was taller than me by six inches, clean-shaven, and looked like he worked out. I figured him to be about fifty-five.

"Frank should've died tonight." He sounded irritated. "If you hadn't brought him over the mountain, he would have. Did you know he had a DNR?"

Rhiannon went white.

"DNR?" I asked, playing dumb.

"Do Not Resuscitate order. Frank's dying. He knows it. I know it. You just prolonged the inevitable and caused him more pain. Now he's going to have to die some other time."

He was talking to us like unruly children at a church social. I wasn't going to have it.

"I don't get it, Doc. Did we interrupt your beauty sleep? Is there somewhere else you'd rather be? Because we just spent two hours driving over the mountain with a friend who asked us to help. It didn't sound to me like he'd given up when he moaned 'David, please help me!' over the phone. But you obviously have. I've never known a doctor who could wash their hands and let a patient die after that patient cried out for help."

The longer I talked, the redder his face got. Before I finished, he had turned on his heel and stalked back into the ER without saying another word. I shouted the last part at him after he disappeared through the door. All three of us stared as it swung shut. The rest of the people in the ER waiting room gave a ragged cheer. The admissions nurse was looking down, trying real hard not to laugh.

"Damn, David," Josh said, amusement all over his face. "You could piss off the Pope."

Frank *did* recover from his pneumonia. He removed the DNR and changed doctors. His new doctor, a young man just out of residency, said he might have a chance to recover with a new experimental treatment he'd gotten permission to use from the FDA. Rhiannon and I crossed our fingers and kept him eating well. Frank bought the city two sets of medical equipment: an oxygen bottle, a BVM to use with it along with an assortment of mask sizes, an Automatic Electronic Defibulator for heart attacks, a stethoscope, and pulse-oximeter to measure blood-oxygen levels. One set would be kept at the police station and the other in Josh's cruiser. The mayor sent him a thank-you letter and a receipt so he could claim the donation on his taxes.

Frank began eating with us regularly. Rhiannon bought him a bong, and I made sure he always had pot to help with his nausea and appetite. He looked like he was gaining weight and had a much healthier glow about him. Maybe it was the food, or perhaps the companionship. Either way, Frank Everest was fighting the good fight, and we weren't giving up on him as his ex-doctor had.

Chapter 18 – An Alternate Reality

The cop class ended with a graduation ceremony. One semester of Cops 101 and I got a Certificate of Completion. I finished first in my class, which sounded impressive until you saw the other class members. Apparently, being an insta-cop didn't seem to require a lot of smarts. Chief Parker attended and shook my hand when the ceremony finished. He presented me with a Chambersville PD baseball cap, made to size instead of adjustable. I was officially a cop.

Sheriff Crook came for the ceremony as well. He took me aside while Chief Parker visited with some other friends. "If you ever get tired of working in a small town, I have a job for you with the sheriff's department. I liked how you ran with the search for Tommy. Our detective branch could use some new blood."

"He's mine, Daniel," Chief Parker declared, walking back to us. "At least let him get some dust on his new hat before you try to recruit him."

"You have a gem here, Josh. Be hard to keep him busy in Chambersville."

I felt like a piece of meat in a dog fight. It wasn't a bad feeling, being appreciated.

On a perfect day two weeks later, Rhiannon and I moved into Grandpa's house. The sky was electric blue with white puffy clouds, about 70 degrees. Rhiannon had requested that we wait until June 21 before we began living there, something about alignment of the planets, summer solstice, or some such. I agreed, of course. Some things aren't worth fighting about. We had worked on the house for almost nine months. If it was important to her, that's all that mattered.

Before the moving party, the house had been ready for a week. All the furniture I put in storage had been cleaned and moved in. Rhiannon "cleansed" the house with a burning bundle of sage with all the windows open, then tied little bundles of sage, holly, and dried wildflowers over each window. It wasn't until she put the bundles in place with a thumbtack through the ribbon that held them together that I remembered my mother doing the same thing when I was a little boy—must be another X-chromosome thing.

Moving day arrived. An army of friends with trucks showed up to move all the remaining items from Rhiannon's house to our new-old one. It's amazing to me how much stuff can be crammed into a little house. After all the trips we made from her home to our new one, carrying truckload after truckload of her stuff, I thought Rhiannon's had to be almost empty. But, instead, what remained had filled six pickups and Rhiannon's Corolla. It's a good thing we had an almost-empty basement. I have no idea where we would have put it all without the black hole at the bottom of the stairs.

Rhiannon had put all her plants into her Corolla. As she unloaded it, the living room slowly became a greenhouse.

By the middle of the afternoon, everything had been placed pretty much where it would be until we developed a plan to bring order out of the chaos. The trucks were empty, and so was my belly. So I asked everyone to come with me out to the barn—time to relax.

I opened the cooler full of burgers and hotdogs. Gus fired up the charcoal barbeques. I turned on the radio and tapped the keg.

We put some bales of hay around for people to sit on, then I drew a beer for Gus, him being the only one still working. Then I drew one for everyone else who wanted a beer. A cooler full of pop, fruit juices, and water sat beside me if someone didn't want to partake of our local brewers' craft.

In the middle of my second beer, I heard a commotion from the front yard. Gina took off toward the noise, barking her head off. It sounded like a motorcycle club had chosen that moment to come up our driveway and investigate. I walked out front, not sure what I would find.

No less than fifty motorcycles, most of them Harleys, pulled up and parked. I had never seen such an accumulation of chrome, leather, and paint. From the back of the pack a rider wove his way through the other bikes and stopped right in front of me. His bike was immaculate! The chrome and polished aluminum glittered in the sun. The rider, a clean-cut young man about twenty-five, handed me the keys. "Thanks for lettin' me ride 'er over the mountain. Gonna be hard to get back on mine. She's one sweet ride."

I stared, speechless. The black paint on the tank was so clear and black it looked to be an inch thick. Embedded in the black, a bald eagle with gold highlights in its feathers stared out at me with a Special Forces patch behind it, surrounded by ghost flames. The painter had painted an image of my weather vane on both sides of the gas tank. It looked so real it could have taken wing, and I would not have been surprised. Its talons were gripping forward through the air, dripping blood, its beak open and screaming, its eyes glowed red. Both fenders were painted the same deep black with ghost flames that only showed up in the bright sun. On the console, a pretty, middle-aged woman's face looked out at me. With a shock, I recognized her—Gina, Rhiannon's grandmother, but not the young woman I had seen in Rhiannon's picture. This Gina was the woman I had met by the river.

Suddenly, Rhiannon was beside me. "Socks wasn't gonna be ready until today. I didn't want to move in until the last part of Tommy's damage had been fixed." She saw me staring at Gina. "I had the artist put Grandma's face on your console because, without her, we never would have met. She aged Grandma to look like you described her. We got to be friends while she did the artwork. Her name is Chloe. You'll have to meet her."

I looked back and forth between her, the bike, and the assembled mass of bikers. It was then I noticed all the riders were packing pistols and the patch on the back of their jackets said "Blue Knights."

An old, grizzled cop with a leather medallion on his jacket that said "Chapter President" walked up to me and gave me a bear hug. "Welcome, brother."

I hugged him back, then Rhiannon was in my arms with a different kind of hug. Hers took a little longer than the first one. She kissed me, and the rest of the world faded out. Kisses like that don't happen every day. It was one of those extended, alternate reality kisses where you lose track of where you end, and she begins. By the time we were done, everyone had moved into the barn, leaving us alone. I was torn between continuing that kiss upstairs or meeting all the friends I never knew I had. Upstairs won, by a large margin.

By the time we came back down, the barbeque was in full swing. The cop who'd ridden my bike over the mountain wanted to know if Rhiannon was an extra cost option that came with the bike. If the Harley shop owner had been at the party, I believe the cop would have ordered one right then. Socks had been pushed into the barn, and everyone was dancing around her to the music from the boom box Gus brought along. Rhiannon was being passed from dance partner to dance partner. I sat back with my cold beer and watched her have fun. Then, when the slow ones came on, she would drag me out onto the floor. She absolutely glowed.

Chapter 19 – Once More unto the Breach

Rhiannon and I settled into life together. I had never believed I would find the happiness other people talked about. My life in the army slowly faded into a distant past that I put into a mental box, then closed the lid. My grandfather's house was on twenty acres in the country, surrounded by thick trees and my eight-foot-high electrified fence. We had all the privacy we needed, so we had sex spontaneously and often. She filled a hole in my soul that I hadn't even known was empty.

We discovered something she loved almost as much as I did—riding motorcycles. We rode Socks everywhere together. I loved having Rhiannon tucked in behind me as we leaned into those curvy roads. We began visiting all the bars and gas stations to collect the pictures of Tommy's truck I put up during my search for him. In each of the bars, we bought a beer and visited with the bartender.

One Sunday morning, after I woke her with a kiss and we made love, Rhiannon rolled over and asked, "Would you teach me how to ride Socks?"

I blinked. Twice. She was doing some amazing things with her fingernails right then, and I was having a little trouble concentrating on anything else. I took a breath and moved her hand away from me, one of the dumber things I've ever done.

"OK, first, you don't know how to drive any motorcycle, let alone a heavy, powerful bike like Socks. Second, you don't have a motorcycle endorsement on your driver's license. You couldn't leave the yard even if you did learn how to ride her."

"So, will you teach me to ride?"

"I'd rather you took the rider's class that is offered at the community college where I took the cop class. They do all their training off the road in a big parking lot at the county fairgrounds. They supply the bikes for you to learn on, and they teach you all the little tricks to stay alive while you share the road with cars and trucks."

"Would you take it with me?"

That actually sounded like fun. "Sure." I had been riding since I was fifteen years old. What could they teach me?

We signed up for the course together. The next class began in one week. The class took place on two weekends, including two Friday nights in the classroom. The first Friday night, they gave a lecture on the theory of staying alive on the highway. I never considered simply changing lanes when a truck or SUV pulled in front of me and blocked my view of the highway ahead. Instead, I bitched and stayed where I was. Changing lanes made a lot more sense. Then they talked about looking two cars ahead instead of only at the car in front of me—another "common sense" idea that I had never thought of before. The second Friday, we took a sample of the written test the state was going to give her. I got two questions wrong.

"You must be an experienced rider," the instructor said, grinning. "They always get those two wrong."

I rolled my eyes and waited for Rhiannon to finish. She got all the questions right.

For the riding portion, we started out getting used to the little 250cc motorcycles they supplied us. My legs stuck out a little, but the bikes were fun to putt around on. I resisted the impulse to stand on the seat or pop a wheelie. We had to stop and start, turn and shift, then weave through a series of cones.

"Use both brakes," the instructor told me.

"The ground's wet—too easy to lose control."

"You should always use both brakes and develop a feel for how much the front can take. It takes practice, but in an emergency stop, it can save your life. Learn how to do it before you have an emergency, then the emergencies aren't quite so scary."

I remembered saying those same words to a Green Beret hopeful during a practice attack.

I started using both brakes. He was right—with a little practice, I could stop much more quickly in all conditions.

Rhiannon took to riding like she always knew and just had to remember. The Monday after the course was finished, we rode together to the DMV license examination storefront. She got her motorcycle endorsement on her first attempt. I pulled into the Honda shop on the way back home.

"What're we doing here?"

"Checkin' out bikes. You're gonna need one."

She sat on every bike in the shop, then selected a used, red, 600cc Shadow. "If I can't have a Harley, I want a bike that looks like one."

It fit her perfectly. She practiced in the dealer's parking lot until she was comfortable with the balance and controls.

"I need to change the seat. The foam in this one's worn-out." The dealer sold us a new seat for his cost as part of the deal. We topped off the gas tanks and headed up the mountain. In the middle of the day, there wasn't much traffic. I let her lead and followed behind, watching proudly. She was a natural, a little hesitant on the hairpin turns, but "cautious," when you're learning, is a good thing.

We pulled through the gate to our house and parked the bikes in the barn. A hundred pounds of shrieking wildcat was suddenly on my back.

"Thank you, thank you, thank you!" she said jubilantly. Her arms and legs were around me like an octopus.

"I guess you like the Shadow."

"Oh, honey, I *love* it! I've never felt freer! It's like I'm flyin'."

"Drive that one for a year, and I'll show you how to ride Socks. You should be ready by then."

"Deal!" She got a sultry look in her eyes. "But right now, I've got something else that needs to be ridden."

She started pulling off her clothes. "If I were any hotter, I'd be on fire. Think you're 'up' for it?"

Who'd have imagined riding her own bike would affect her that way? If I had only known, she would have gotten the Shadow long ago. And we had all summer to ride together!

I rallied the troops. "Once more unto the breach, dear friends!" Shakespeare has always been a favorite of mine.

Chapter 20 – Salt on the Wound

We were about finished with the removal of the "Tommy" flyers. Rhiannon and I had stopped at a little bar not far from where the bootlegger saw Tommy turn up that driveway. The place was about half full. The jukebox sang to us about some guy going crazy over a lost love.

Rhiannon and I found a table in the corner. The barmaid brought us both a beer.

After that first wonderful sip of cold beer, I asked a question that had been bothering me for a while.

"Why did you recommend Tommy to me when I asked if you knew someone who could fix my dad's truck? He was a crook, and you must have known it."

She looked at me without speaking for a moment, took another swig of beer, pursed her lips, and sighed. "He gave me a kickback when I referred someone to him. It was all about the money."

Her answer didn't surprise me. "How much of the $2,000 he charged did you get?"

"Nothing," she said, looking away. "He came over to pay me that night. I said you were a friend and not to cheat you. He accused me of wanting to fuck you. Then he shoved a hundred bucks down the front of my shirt, called me a whore, and backhanded me. I guess he knocked me out for a few minutes. When I came to, he had torn off my clothes and was on top of me. I tried to claw his eyes out. He knocked me out again. When I came to the second time, I kneed him in the crotch. He worked me over good after that. That's when he dislocated my arm."

The barmaid walked back up to us warily, sensing the tension in the air. "Hi, how are your beers? You need anything?"

"No, I think we're OK," I said, trying to dismiss her. I wanted to get back to my conversation with Rhiannon.

"You, you're that cop from Chambersville, aren't you?"

"Yep. My name's David Peterson. Do I know you?"

"No," she said, pausing to look around to see if anyone was watching her talk to me. "I don't know many cops. Most of the time, I try to keep my distance. But Mike, the bartender, wants to talk to you. He told me to ask you to come up to the bar."

I walked up to the bar where Mike waited.

"You know those guys you described last time?" Mike asked in a low voice. "The ones that kept quiet and to themselves, never made trouble, paid their bill, and left?"

I nodded.

"Well, they came in here about a week ago."

"Looks like I might make my twenty bucks after all!" I joked. "Thanks! Did you happen to card any of them?"

"Nah—slow night. I was glad for the business. All of 'em looked over twenty-one to me."

"Which way did they go when they left?"

"Funny you should mention that. I went outside in the alley to have a cigarette when they left. There were about ten of 'em. Four got into an old Chevy sedan, and the rest piled into a ratty old pickup, Chevy or GMC, I think. Then they left, going east. A few minutes later, I saw 'em drive back west real quiet-like. Must've got turned around."

"Did one of 'em have a beard, kinda close-cropped?"

"Yep—had on a hoody an sunglasses, too. Pretty strange in a dark bar. He seemed to be in charge a the group."

"How about the pickup? Did it have a cab-high railing around the bed, old and faded?"

"Yeah, now that you mention it, it did."

"Thanks a lot, Mike."

I shook his hand and walked back to where Rhiannon waited for me.

"Drink up. I have some work to do at home."

"What did the bartender say to you?"

"He said some kids I've been searching for all winter and spring showed up last week."

"Kids? What kids are you searching for?"

I didn't know how to answer her without telling her about the meth lab—the *top-secret* meth lab.

"I can't tell you. It's police business."

I could see the hurt on her face. "Can't or won't?"

"Both. You don't want to know. Your life would be in danger if I told you."

"And yours isn't?"

My life had been in danger for so long I didn't know any other way for it to be. I realized hers was in danger just by being my girlfriend.

"Maybe we need to split up for a little while until this blows over."

She misunderstood. She thought I didn't trust her after her confession about being in league with Tommy.

"Yeah? Well, maybe we do!"

She got up and stalked out of the bar. A moment later, I heard her bike start, then pull away. Part of me cried out in agony at the sound of her bike disappearing into the night.

"Go after her, moron!" the little voice screamed.

I ignored her. Instead, I tried to justify to myself what I had done. Rhiannon wasn't quite the rosy-cheeked high school cheerleader I had a crush on thirty years ago.

"Neither are you, David," the little voice scolded. "Think of the things you've done to survive. How many of them would you tell your mom?"

The ghosts of Colombia rose again in my subconscious.

"She has steel, David. She's raised five kids on her own and put them through college. How do you think a waitress in a roadside diner did that? On tips? Can you really fault her for sending people to Tommy? Hard times make for hard choices. And when she tried to get Tommy *not* to cheat you, she got beaten and raped for it."

And now she had left. I had driven her away from me. I looked down at my hands and wondered if losing them would hurt this much. I went outside and sat on Socks. The air had chilled since we arrived. Alone, I began the long ride home, hoping Rhiannon would be there when I arrived, that I could find some way to apologize to her without compromising Doc's trust in me.

Rock and a hard place. Why do I always end up being right here?

A dark and empty house greeted me when I arrived. Gina ran up as I parked Socks. I sat down on the dusty floor of the barn and pulled her onto my lap. The idea of entering the house Rhiannon had made a home, entering our bedroom where we had made joyous love so many times, was incomprehensible to me. Gina didn't know what was wrong, but she knew I needed caring, and "caring" is what dogs do. Gina began to lick my face. Dogs like salt. I had plenty for her that night.

Chapter 21 – The Question

I studied the photos that I'd taken. Something was wrong, but I couldn't figure out what. The two people were dirty—to be expected, they were working in a garden. The car and pickup matched what the bartender described. But there had to be fifty cars and pickups like them across the county. The rest of the yard looked neat. *So what, lots of people keep neat homesteads.* Then I noticed something. I checked the map and smiled. The ravine ran north and south with the mouth opening on the north end. The walls of the ravine were steep and narrow. No direct sunlight would ever get to the garden. *Why would anyone plant a garden there? And if they did, nothing would grow well.* Then I noticed something else. The tools—they were all new, even the ones in the shed gleamed at me from the doorway. *Why would people who could only afford a beat-up twenty-year-old Chevy Impala have new tools to garden with? And none of the tools in the shed were even dirty.* Then I noticed the windows in the house. The curtains on every window were arranged the same way, with the window shade the same distance from the window sill, about six inches. I looked closely at the two people. I zoomed in, grateful for my 24-megapixel camera. I knew how much work turning over a garden by hand is. Not a drop of sweat on either person. They hadn't been working very long when I took those pictures.

I think another visit might be in order. But I would do it a little differently from the last time. They wouldn't know I was coming or that I had even been there.

I sent an encrypted e-mail to Doc updating him about what I'd found, the coordinates of the homestead, and attached the pictures I took of it. Then I called his cell phone and left a voice mail message telling him to check his e-mail. And to say hi to his wife. He had never been married. His pistol was a .40 caliber Beretta. He'd called it his wife for as long as I knew him. He named her Sarah. She was a protective bitch. Betray Doc, and she would hurt you.

I brought up Google Maps on my computer and studied the area with Google Earth. It showed the same partially turned-over garden, and that data was over a year old. Dumbasses. The first crack in the armor. They should have made it a working homestead.

I got out the boxes of stuff I ordered from the internet. Pretty incredible what you can buy on the internet these days. I had already installed the motion sensors and two-way cameras around my grandpa's property. The cameras were called two-way because they used visible light during the day and infrared at night. All the cameras fed to a central computer that I had tucked into a hidden room in the attic. The laptop kept the picture of anything that moved for as long as it had disc space. And it had a lot of disc space. I must have a thousand pictures of Gina as she prowled around the property at night. I checked and deleted them every day. I couldn't think of a better way to verify the cameras and computer remained operational.

I had camouflaged the remote cameras and motion detectors as birdhouses with the solar panels on the roof and the battery inside the box. Underneath the camera and battery was a real, working birdhouse. A family of barn swallows had already moved in. The cameras sent the pictures via a wireless hookup to the central computer. All the data on the central computer was encrypted. Every five minutes, anything new got sent off-site to another encrypted computer under my desk at the police station. The satellite internet connection that a kid half my age installed on my property worked great.

As I shuffled through the boxes, I searched for the special night vision goggles I ordered. They picked up on several different bands. Infrared, obviously, but they also showed high-frequency-sound motion detector transmitters and laser beam telltales. The goggles were by far the most expensive thing I had bought. I put them into my backpack.

I got out the 1x100,000 map of the area around the homestead and studied it. Behind and south of the house, a 3,500-foot peak had a panoramic view of the entire area. It didn't appear to have a line-of-sight into the ravine. A bunch of radio and TV antennas were clustered on top.

The ridgeline ran down the west side of the ravine—the one that I came up when I visited before. It must be bugged because they knew I was coming. The east side of the ravine had an almost sheer basalt cliff to the ravine floor. I figured they hadn't bugged that one, at least not completely.

I opened another box. Inside were two shoebox-sized, camo-colored, hard-case boxes. Each box contained a digital camera with telephoto lenses. They contained enough internal storage for 100,000 pictures. I could put them up to a mile away from what I wanted to take pictures of and read the headlines of a newspaper. Solar cells on the outside of the containers kept the internal battery charged, even in a low-light situation. The camera and the solid-state storage unit were powered by the battery. The batteries in both boxes were fully charged.

The cameras went into my backpack along with my laptop, a bundle of zip ties, my tree climbing spikes, climber's saddle, and climbing flip line. I set my cell phone on mute, so I wouldn't forget later, and put on my camos, boots, and Boonie hat. Grabbing my backpack and a roll of climbing rope, I walked out to Dad's truck.

As I got into the truck, I considered calling Rhiannon and telling her where I was going but decided not to. She was already in enough danger. Instead, I wrote a letter to Doc, addressed it, and put a stamp on it. On my way through town, I dropped it in the mail drop box in front of the post office. If I didn't come back, Doc would find out why, and I suspected there would be hell to pay.

The approach must be made at night. The big reasons were: one, because I wasn't visible to the naked eye at night, and two, because my night vision goggles didn't work during the day. I wanted to see laser telltales and motion detectors.

If you've never done it, walking along a sheer cliff at night using night-vision goggles is a little surreal. You have a little display in front of your eyes, guiding the way instead of using your unaided eyes. It's like virtual reality goggles but real. The homestead spread out a thousand feet below me—clearly visible in my goggles.

As I walked along the edge of the ravine, I spotted a motion detector where you would have to pass. A large boulder field prevented easy access up the hill. The motion detector showed up on my goggles as a violet cloud. Someone had done their homework: put detectors in all places where someone would pass while they were looking down at the homestead. I turned around and studied the terrain. A motion detector would also have a camera aimed at it.

I saw it above and away from the motion detector, about thirty feet from where I stood, on the other side of the boulder field. The motion detector would turn on the camera and alert the guard, and then the camera would take a picture of whatever had set off the detector and send it to the monitor for the guard to see. I surveyed the area again.

A cluster of hundred-foot-high fir trees stood at the edge of the ravine a couple of hundred yards from where I stood. They would have a clear view of the house. I made my way over there. There were no motion detectors or lasers near the trees.

I got out my flip line, spikes, and climber's saddle. I put on the spikes and saddle, snapped into the flip line, and started up one of the trees. Branches made the flip line unusable about fifty feet up, so I climbed another twenty feet by hand using those branches and looked down—a perfect view.

After snapping back into the flip line for safety, I zip-tied the camera in place. It needed to be hidden from above and below with a clear view of the homestead. I got out my laptop, plugged it into the USB port on the bottom of the box, and then draped my jacket over me to hide the glow from the laptop screen.

Using my laptop, I aimed, zoomed, and focused the camera, so the whole homestead and area in front of it were in the picture. The same half-tilled garden in my other pictures showed clearly on the monitor. The interval between images was set to 15 seconds and the picture density to 2 megapixels. Not as good as a cell phone, but good enough for surveillance. The camera had enough storage to photograph at that density for 17 days and nights.

As I descended the other side of the ravine, I figured most of the bugs were on that side since it was so much easier to access.

Most people, as I had, would go up or down that side of the ravine. I looked for motion detectors as I went down but didn't find any. That made sense—the game trail I came down looked well used. Critters would be setting off the alarms constantly.

I found another tree with a view of the homestead and climbed up it. After I tied down and aimed the second camera, I saw another camera above me by about five feet. Some of the branches were cut off the trunk to give it a clear view up and down the ridgeline. It pointed down the ridgeline, where I had ascended on my first trip. As I watched, it turned and pointed up the hill to where I came down on this trip. It was obviously on a timer because it couldn't see both ways at once. I checked my watch and stayed motionless until it swung around again and aimed downhill. Fifteen minutes, on the nose.

I climbed down from the tree and ran up the hill while the camera watched downhill. Fifteen minutes later, the camera in the tree pointed back up the ridgeline. I was long gone.

I sent an encrypted e-mail to Doc once I got home, telling him I had placed both surveillance cameras and gave him the GPS coordinates of them. Then I told him about the other side of the ridge and the camera I found.

I drove up the driveway to Grandpa's house. Rhiannon had been gone for three days without even trying to contact me. I didn't know where she was or how to contact her. Gus hadn't seen her either. He said he could hang on until the end of the week before he had to hire another waitress to help him at the diner. I parked Dad's truck and began the dismal walk to the dark house, my backpack over my shoulder. Gina ran out to me as she always did. She seemed really excited. I got down on one knee and scratched her ears while she licked my face.

"David?"

I did my automatic drop-roll and came up with my gun pointing at the source. Rhiannon stood there without moving, having expected me to react like that.

"Rhiannon?"

I got up, not knowing what would happen next. She ran to my arms.

"I love you, David. I don't care about what you can't tell me. I don't want to live without you. I've tried to tell myself I could go back to the way I lived before, but I can't. You're a part of me, and I think I'm a part of you. We're a team I don't want to ever break up. Can you forgive me?"

I was so relieved she had come back I couldn't think of anything to say but, "I love you, too. I'm sorry I didn't trust you. Please don't ever leave me again."

How could I tell her how devastated I was when she left, how my life had been on automatic without any joy at all. I didn't know how to begin, not believing I would get a second chance with this beautiful woman.

Instead, I got down on one knee and said the words that I had promised myself I would never speak again: "Will you marry me?"

She pulled me up into her arms and clutched me to her. After a long hesitation, she pulled away and looked at me. Her face didn't have the happy smile I had hoped for. Instead, I saw a mixture of fear and doubt. This wasn't good.

"I have something to tell you first. If you still wanna ask me that question when I'm done, you can."

She stopped again, knowing in her heart this wouldn't end well. "My other job isn't what I said before."

"So you don't clean rooms at a prostitute palace?"

She looked into my eyes again, started to say something, stopped again. Finally, she said, almost deadpan, "No. I don't ... I work there."

"You mean ..."

"Yeah. I'm a prostitute. I fuck people for money."

She might as well have kicked me in the nuts. "Why do you do that?" I asked her.

"To put five kids through top-notch colleges."

"Wasn't there some other way to earn your kids' tuition?"

"Oh, yeah, sure! People are falling all over themselves to hire nurses over here. And even if I could get hired, do you have any idea what college tuition costs these days? Most starting nurses get a little over minimum wage. I earn more at the diner than I would as a nurse."

"How about grants? Tuition assistance? There has to be money for single parents to send kids to school."

"Not if you're white and have a job," she said bitterly. "If I was an illegal, black, Indian, or on welfare, people would have thrown money at me. But there's not any help for an employed white girl, not with the Feds pulling their assistance back from the states, not with people cutting back on donations to the colleges."

She studied my face one more time. I couldn't meet her eyes.

"I'll pay you back for the motorcycle. Give me a couple of days." She reached up to my face, pulled it around so she could look into my eyes once more, and put her hand on my cheek. "Goodbye, David."

Then she turned on her heel and walked away. I heard her motorcycle start, and she was gone again, the taillight disappearing down the driveway.

I stood where she had left me for at least an hour. Three nights a week, Rhiannon was a prostitute. I tried to find a way I could tell her I didn't care. But I did care. I cared a lot. Three nights a week, someone else was having sex with the woman I loved. Maybe more than one guy. Perhaps four or five guys. Maybe two or three at once. I tried to shake the images out of my head: vaginal sex, oral sex, anal sex, cum on her face, men grabbing her breasts.

Lord knows I've used lots of prostitutes as I have traveled around the world. I am sure most of those women had boyfriends or husbands. It was a little different when I was the boyfriend, and someone else was using my woman. My woman! It started to sink in—she wasn't "my woman" anymore, and I wasn't "her man." She had left me and left for good. There wouldn't be any coming back, not after tonight.

Chapter 22 – The Fishing Trip

I was in shock. My brain spun in an unending loop, emotionally paralyzed. This had never happened to me before. Even after blowing up Poco Pito, I still functioned.

"Rhiannon is gone. Where is she? She should be here. But she's gone. And you drove her away. Where is she? She should be here. And she's not coming back."

Over and over and over, it played. No way to end it. No room for anything but the pain and remorse.

When the brain's on tilt, the body goes into autopilot mode. My feet walked into the house. I went along with them, then sat on the first horizontal thing I encountered—the floor. The familiar things in the room had changed somehow, as though I'd never seen them before. I'm sure I had come into the house to gain some level of comfort from the ghosts of comforts past. Unfortunately, those ghosts were somewhere else this lonely night.

"Gone. How can she be gone? Why didn't I reach out for her and tell her I didn't care how she'd done what she had to do? How can I face tomorrow when today hurts this bad?"

I heard an eerie howl, like a cross between a werewolf and a coyote. The hair on the back of my neck stood up. What a strange noise, the analytical part of me observed. It sounds like that poor animal is in horrible pain. What animal could make such a sound? What would make it hurt so badly? I realized the sound had come from me.

I have no idea how long I sat on the floor of Grandpa's house—all night, I suppose. Gina was curled up on the floor next to me when I finally returned to the present. I had left the front door open when I came in. The heat pump was blowing warm air out of the ducts, then out into the chilly night. Apparently, it had been doing that all night. Outside the open door, the sunrise was brightening the horizon to the east.

"I need to get out of here for a while," I told Gina, getting up. She wagged her tail and nuzzled my hand. Absently, I scratched her head between her ears, her favorite spot for me to scratch. "I think a fishing trip is in order, Gina. You up for it, girl?"

She had no idea what I had asked, but her tail wagged, and her ears were at full attention.

Fishing is unlike almost any other activity. Most of the time, you aren't doing anything but sitting still, waiting for a bite. The mechanics of fly fishing become mindless after a while—see a likely spot, get enough line in the air to reach it, and cast the fly. Watching a well-cast fly hit the exact place you intended is a beautiful thing to behold. Your mind can wander wherever it wants while the fly is floating down the river. It is a very healing thing to do.

Taking Gina meant I would be taking Dad's truck. I loaded a cooler full of beer and water, then emptied the ice maker from the fridge on top of it. Next to the cooler, I put the fishing tackle, a sleeping bag, dog food, and my tent. I always keep a plastic storage tub full of camping stuff ready to go. Inside it were all the spices, cooking implements, and camping stuff I always forgot. It even contained some military MREs (Meals Ready to Eat) in case the fishing was less productive than usual. I put that into the back next to the cooler, then wedged in my last bottle of Johnnie Walker and Dad's old Coleman stove.

If I couldn't have Rhiannon to keep me company, Johnnie had done the deed for me all over the world. The most important thing in the whole camping box was toilet paper. I hate forgetting toilet paper. Leaves might work in Ranger school, but I'm too old for that shit now.

I considered stopping at the grocery store in Chambersville as we went through town. I could use some more ice for the beer cooler, then decided not to, too big a chance of meeting Rhiannon. The ice would last as long as it lasted. I've drunk many a warm beer.

As I left the outskirts of Chambersville, I realized I had no destination in mind. Then just as quickly realized, I was autopilot-driving to the old campsite Jack, Larry, and I camped at in high school, the same place where the ghost of Gina had visited me.

"OK. The old campsite it is."

I reached over to Gina and ran my hand down her back, gaining comfort from just her being there. I don't think she even felt me. Her head was out the passenger window with her ears and tongue flapping in the wind. If dogs could smile, hers was ear-to-ear.

The camp was set up by early afternoon. Gina ran around the campsite and nearby area like a hurricane. It looked like she was trying to explore everything all at once. She would sniff a tree and leave her mark, then bark at a bird, then smell a chipmunk hole, then jump at a bug, then run up a deer trail, then hear a fish jump in the river. I opened a beer and sat down to watch her—you can't pay for entertainment like that! After forty-five minutes of exploring, she settled down on the ground next to me, panting contentedly.

"Let's go see if any fish are biting, girl."

I put a couple of beers in my jacket pocket, picked up my tackle box, fishing pole, and a folding chair. Together Gina and I walked down to the river. We stopped at a perfect flat spot, partly in the sun, with the river running deep and swift right beside it. I tied a trolling lure on the line, attached the rod to my chair, and pulled out a beer.

Her reflection in the water fascinated Gina. She gingerly reached out and touched it with her paw as an eagle swooped down right in front of us, skimmed above the water, put its claws in, and came up with a trout. It was back up into the sky long before Gina decided to bark and chase. She jumped into the river with a huge splash.

Before I got my shoes and jacket off, she had been carried fifty feet downstream by the current. I dove in after her. The rapids, a mile downstream, were still a muffled roar. Gina didn't know to swim toward shore. She was trying to swim back toward me, to where she fell in. I swam as fast as my clothes would let me.

I got to her as we passed the first gigantic boulder announcing the beginning of the rapids. White, frothy water and lots of BIG rocks filled the river ahead of us. In her panic, Gina kept trying to climb up on me to get out of the water. Her claws dug into my skin and pushed me under the water as I struggled to keep both of us from drowning and away from the rocks.

We slid around one monstrous boulder and crashed into a second one. Gina was torn from my grip. A whirlpool spun behind the second boulder. I didn't see Gina anywhere. I dove down into the whirlpool. The current fought me fiercely and came from all directions.

I was being pulled downstream when I saw her, still struggling, her collar caught on a submerged branch of a tree. I swam with everything I had back into the whirlpool, then dove down to free her. She wasn't moving when I pulled both of us up into the air. That whirlpool was at least ten feet deep. Then I saw the submerged branch she had been caught on was part of a tree that had fallen into the river—it could be my escape route from this mess! The only way to get to it was to dive down to the branch and use it to pull us both up the tree to the shore.

I blew some air into Gina's nose, then dove down to the branch. Less than a minute later, we were onshore. Gina still wasn't breathing. I held her upside down and drained as much water out of her lungs and throat as I could, then started artificial resuscitation and chest compressions. You have to be careful when resuscitating a small animal, just like you do when resuscitating a child. You can do more damage by blowing in too much air than the water did.

She wasn't responding to my efforts. In my gut, I had that feeling—the feeling that told me I'd lost her. Some soldiers act the same way before they die.

"C'mon, Gina!" I implored between breaths. "Help me! Don't leave me yet."

I worked on her for ten more minutes before I quit. She hadn't regained consciousness. I couldn't find a pulse.

"I'm just not having any luck with females," I told the air, looking at the sky.

I picked her up gently and carried her back to the campsite, her head pressed against my chest, and put her down on my sleeping bag, arranged like she was sleeping. I figured she would like to be buried like that. Then I walked down to the river to collect the fishing stuff I had abandoned when I dove after Gina.

The old bootlegger was sitting next to Gina when I got back.

"I saw yer truck. Thought I might stop for a visit."

He was staring at Gina instead of me.

"My dog died in the river a few minutes ago. Maybe this isn't such a good time."

"Where is it?" he asked.

"Right there." I pointed at Gina. "Are ya blind?" My world had turned to shit. I didn't feel like playing word games with a goddammed recluse moonshiner.

He looked up at me with concern. "This dog ain't daid ... leastways not yct."

He reached over and stroked her head. She opened her eyes and licked his hand.

"Gina?" I called out in disbelief.

She lifted her head, got up onto some unsteady legs, and made her way over to me. I got down on one knee and picked her up. She licked my face as I closed my eyes. I never expected to feel her do that again.

"Had a dog do the same thang," the moonshiner laughed. "Thought he was daid, too. Got his haid caught in a fork of a tree while we was huntin'. Took 'im a couple a hours afore he woke up."

"You want some coffee? I was about to make a pot."

"Why sure, Davie. Coffee'd be right nice."

"There's another folding chair in the truck."

I fired up Dad's stove, got the coffee pot ready, and put it on the burner. The sound of it percolating filled the campsite with a gentle gurgle. Gina had returned to my sleeping bag and curled up again, sound asleep. I pulled some wood out of the back of the truck and set up a campfire for later as the coffee finished, then poured us both a cup and sat down.

Some clouds were moving in from the west, and the temperature was falling—felt like rain. A breeze started up, swaying the tree limbs above us. I was gonna need a jacket soon. The old moonshiner didn't seem to notice.

"Where's that purty woman o' yorn?" he asked.

"She ain't my woman. Leastways not anymore." Jeez, I was even starting to talk like him.

He looked over at me and sipped his coffee in the quiet. "Yer wrong, Davie," he finally said. "That woman an you're cut from the same cloth. You think she ain't yer woman—yer daid wrong. Ain't no other woman in the world more right fer you."

"You know her? How do you know her?"

"Not much goes on in this town without me knowing about it. I knowed her since she were a little girl. I knowed that asshole she married the first time, too. Bought 'shine from me."

"She's a whore and a liar!" I said vehemently.

The old man didn't speak for a while again. "She may be that, Davie, but ya didn't seem to mind when you two was in the sack. Did ya ask her why? She musta had a damned good reason. It weren't fer fun an games, I'm suspectin'."

"She did it to put her kids through college."

I felt lower than whale shit. This whole situation with Rhiannon and how I handled it, or, excuse me, didn't handle it, overwhelmed what little good feelings I had been able to resurrect after Gina had bounced back to life.

"She had five kids, I'm rememberin'," the old man continued. "Five kids and an that asshole husband who left her with nothin', then died." He spit on the ground. "You ever thought about how having five kids trustin' you to provide a good home wouldda changed *your* life, Davie? All that runnin' all over the world and havin' adventures wouldda come to quick stop. You'd a been here with the resta us, scratchin' out a living any way ya couldda. You think she liked them men pawin' at her body before she went back home to be Mom?"

I didn't answer. This day just kept getting worse.

"It mustta been even worse fer her after she met you again."

"How do you figure?" I asked, not really wanting an answer.

"Well she mustta knowed you'd find out, sooner or later. She mustta knowed it would ruin what feelings you had fer her. She musta been scared to death."

I remembered her face before she said the words, fear all over it.

"She told me. I didn't ask."

"An' why did she tell ya, Davie?"

"I asked her to marry me," I said in a voice so quiet I could barely hear it.

"So you asked her to marry ya, and she told ya the one thing she knew would sour the whole deal?"

"Yeah. I guess so."

"Would ya have wanted her not tellin ya? And when you found out later, what would ya have done?"

"I don't know."

"Well, I do. You'd a dumped her—just like her first husband did. Only he did it because he couldn't keep his dick in his pants. You asked her to marry ya and she wouldn't say yes without making sure you knew what you was gettin' into. She laid herself bare. I wish I'd a met 'er when I were a young man. Yer right, Davie. She's too good for ya."

He spit again and stood. "See ya later." He threw what was left of his coffee onto the ground, set the cup next to Dad's stove, and walked down the trail out of sight.

I stared out at the bits of the river I could see through the trees. *Dammit, the old man was right. What the hell was I thinking?*

I packed the camp back into Dad's truck and drove back toward Chambersville with Gina enjoying the ride back as much as when we came out.

Chapter 23 – Thanks for the Offer

The road back to Chambersville had never seemed so long to Rhiannon. She stopped three times to wipe her eyes so she could see well enough to navigate the turns. When she wasn't stopping to wipe her eyes, she was going way too fast.

She slowed down for good when a four-point buck leaped across the path of her motorcycle. She locked up the wheels and almost went down, but she missed the deer. The buck disappeared into the trees beside the road. Rhiannon sat there on her idling motorcycle and waited until her heart rate returned to normal. Then the anger she felt at David filled her up again and overflowed.

"Men are ASSHOLES!" she ranted. "Joe was an asshole! All those horny men are assholes! Now David's an asshole! Why does this keep *happening* to me?"

She started back down the mountain at a reasonable speed.

"Time to get back to business. Time to raise the shutters, do what has to get done, and get on with my life."

Like she needed a man in her life! She had all the men she could use on the other side of the mountain. Another year! One more year, and she could quit being nice to men who only wanted one thing. They didn't care about her. All they cared about was emptying their precious prostate. No one cared about her but her kids. And her last kid finished college in one year.

"This is what happens to me when I let someone in!" she shrieked to the wind as she navigated the last turn and the lights of Chambersville came into sight. The whole idea of returning to David had been a mistake. He didn't care that she still loved him. The only thing he cared about was his goddamned ego.

She parked her bike in the little garage behind her house. The house was for sale, but no one had even asked to see it yet. She walked through the front door into the dark, empty living room. The ghosts of their life together rose from the floor to greet her.

"Fuck this!" she muttered, tossing her jacket and helmet onto the floor in disgust. The bedroom was even worse. The bed sat there, alone in the empty room—the bed she and David had made love on so many times. They had gotten a new bed for the new house. She couldn't even look at this bed without thinking about David and him sharing it with her.

She dug her sleeping bag out of the closet and walked back out to the garage, spreading it out next to the motorcycle, and crawled in, still fully clothed. Part of her rejoiced in the discomfort of sleeping on the concrete floor, almost a penance for failing to win David back, a distraction from the real pain that hid behind it. But it was a small part. The biggest parts of her had been waiting for a quiet time to come forward. And here they came: the part that missed David's arms around her at night, the part that knew he would never be coming back, the part that desperately wanted to kiss him again and again, the part that curled up inside of her and wished it were dead. Yep, here they came. And they weren't happy.

She curled up into a ball, moaned, and started to cry. Once the tears started, there was no stopping them. She cried the tears of the damned. She cried for the husband Joe should have been. She cried for the unfairness of the hand she drew in the poker game of life. She cried at the thought of not sharing the rest of her life with the man she loved. She cried that she loved him at all.

Her last thought before she passed out from emotional exhaustion was, "David, I still love you. I can't not love you. I wish I could."

The next day dawned clear and cold. Rhiannon dragged herself into her house and showered—stiff and sore everywhere. She dressed and went to work at the diner.

Gus smiled at her and poured her a cup of coffee. "You look like shit."

Rhiannon chuckled. "Yeah, but I don't feel that good."

She caught sight of herself in the glass door to the diner, rolled her eyes, and went into the ladies' room to try to put on a little makeup.

The day passed like a blur. It was exactly what she needed—something to hide behind, so the pain couldn't get at her. She was safe here, working, busy, no time to think. Then, suddenly, it was quitting time. Gus closed the door and turned off the neon sign that said "Open."

"Would you like to come over for dinner, Rhiannon? Desireé has made her famous rotisserie chicken. She asked me to ask you."

All day long, he had treated her like a cherished piece of china, beautiful and fragile. She started to say no, then she was in his arms and sobbing again.

"Gus, why are men such assholes?" she asked between sobs.

He held her gently until she stopped.

"I think I need some time alone before I socialize. Tell Desireé, thanks for the offer."

Chapter 24 – One More Time with Feeling

"Rhiannon?"

She jumped like a scalded cat. The pan on the stove slid off the eye, falling onto the floor with a crash and splatter of half-cooked goulash.

"David?" She looked at me, then at the mess on the floor. She picked up the pan and set it in the sink, then turned off the stove. "What are you doing here?"

"I have some questions. Can I ask them?"

She hung her head like her world couldn't get any worse, sat down on one of her kitchen chairs, looked at the mess on the floor, and said, "Sure. Ask away."

"Do your kids know what their education is costing you?"

She glared at me with fire in her eyes and started to get up. "Of course not," she spat.

I understood her reaction. I would feel the same way about my kid finding out about Colombia. I reached out to her and took her hand. She sat back down.

"How do you keep from getting diseases?"

I don't know why I asked that question. I was all out of balance as I tried to get my mind around the situation.

She cocked her head to one side, wondering at my strange question.

"Well, I'm careful. And the people I have as customers make enough money that they're careful, too."

She always insisted we use a condom, which made no sense since I'd had a vasectomy and her tubes were tied. And she always supplied them and put them on me. She had this fantastic technique ... Things were starting to click.

"How much do you make doing this?"

"On a good night, five hundred dollars. I average about three. That's my share after the house collects their percentage. That pays the room, board, books, and tuition for two kids with a little leftover that I put into an emergency account. I live on my diner money."

"Tell me about Tommy."

That made her pause. "Tommy? There's nothing to tell."

"Was he ever a customer of yours?"

"Good God, no!"

"Bullshit!"

She looked into my eyes, then out the window of the kitchen door. She hesitated again, then decided this was a time to tell the whole truth. She started, stopped, then continued in a monotone.

"He was a regular at the 'house' over the mountain. All the girls loved to do him, but not because he was a great lover, he wasn't. We did him because he tipped great and finished quick. When he moved over here, he wanted to continue doing business. I told him he would have to go to the house to do that kind of business. We went out a couple of times, but I left him in his truck and went into my house alone. When I wouldn't take his money for working on your truck, I guess it was the last straw. He went berserk. Rape is never about sex. You understand that, don't you? Rape is about control."

I stopped for a minute, trying to digest what she had said. This was new territory for both of us.

"Have you ever met an old customer? What do you say when you meet him?"

"Most men ignore me. They're usually with friends or family. I'm the last person they would introduce to their daughter, wife, or mother. One guy smiled and said, 'Hi.' He was alone. I smiled back and said, 'Hi, how are you?' Suddenly he had to be somewhere else he had to be."

That made me pause. Finally, I asked the most important question. "If I paid their college expenses, would you stop?"

Her face jerked up in shock to look at mine. "Why would you do that? How would you do that? They aren't your kids. You don't even know them."

"This isn't about them. It's about you and me." I hesitated a minute. "But first, let me say this: I don't have a problem with prostitution. I think it's an honorable profession supplying a needed service that has been outlawed by people who want to force their prejudices on the rest of the world. But the biggest reason I hate that it's not legal is all the money the service generates goes into the hands of criminals, and those criminals manage the women. They get no respect, no health care, no retirement, or even social security credits for the money they earn. And because of who manages them, the women are robbed, abused, beaten, and raped and have no access to the legal system for self-defense."

She stared at me with her mouth open in disbelief, then laughed. "You're preaching to the choir, soldier boy."

"But the biggest problem I have with your being a prostitute is I don't want anyone else making love to you. I'm a monogamous guy, and I want you to be as well."

"You want me to be a monogamous guy?" She giggled. "I didn't know you walked on that side of the street."

"So, will you stop?"

She reached up to my face and put her hand on my cheek, the same loving gesture she used when she left me.

"Yes, my wonderful man. Of course, I'll stop. I had planned to stop as soon as I didn't need the money. Are you sure you can afford their college expenses?"

"I think so. I have my savings and retirement pay from the Army. That should cover it. I've got my income from working for the Chambersville PD to live on. How much longer will they be in school?"

"Jay is a senior. This is his last year. He graduates in two months. Georgia has one more year left."

"Will you promise to never lie to me again?" I picked up her hands and looked into her eyes. "And will you mean it?"

She squeezed my hands, closed her eyes, and took a breath. "I promise never to lie to you again, and I mean it with all my heart."

"So I still have a question you haven't answered. Will you marry me?"

She stood, pulled me into her arms, put her head on my chest, and hugged me. Of all the outcomes that could have happened after I decided to show up at her doorstep, I hadn't even dared to hope for this one. She didn't answer for a few minutes, wondering what the future held for her. Finally, she looked up and said simply, "Yes, I will."

She put her head back on my chest and squeezed me hard enough to take my breath away. We walked together into her living room with our arms around each other and made love on the living room floor.

I lay on my back, one of her favorite places for me to be. Right before we started, I asked, "What about a condom?"

"Not tonight, my lover," she whispered, "and never again. You are mine, and I am yours—two bodies with one heart."

I watched her draw a five-pointed star on my chest and then drew a circle around it. She hugged me fiercely, pressing her breasts into me, and murmured something I couldn't quite make out.

She reached down and guided me into her, held me motionless for a few moments, then began moving. I lay still and enjoyed the incredible feeling of having her make love to me. Her pace increased, her breath coming in short pants until she cried out and came with a force that overwhelmed both of us. About halfway through her orgasm, I joined her with mine. That sent her over the rainbow again. Together we went to a place where I have never been before or since. We were bathed in multi-colored lights as wave after wave of orgasm crashed through us. We became a single being. I felt her orgasms and mine simultaneously, not as hers and mine, but as ours. It might have lasted an hour or ten seconds. There was no way of knowing. The passage of time had no meaning where we were.

When we were done, and the northern lights disappeared, I realized I had passed out kissing her. She was still on top of me— me still inside of her. I think she had passed out as well. All I could do was wonder, "Did that really happen?"

I guess everyone has a high-water mark in their sexual memories, one they look back on with affection and a soft smile in quiet moments. This one became mine. As far as I was concerned, this was the first time we had made love.

Chapter 25 – Pecan Pie

Rhiannon and I had been together for almost a year. Thanksgiving was coming up in a week. I bought all the groceries for the feast and found places to store them.

"Why did you get two turkeys?" she asked, looking at the weights of the birds. "You're too young to start buying things twice."

I looked out the window at the fence separating my place from Mr. Griff's. "It happened a long time ago, about half a mile from where we're standing right here. I was thirteen."

The week before Thanksgiving, Socks and I came down a ravine that bordered a neighbor's cornfield. We worked those edge areas a lot that time of year because the harvesting process always drops some of the corn kernels, and wild turkeys liked to hide in the forest, then run out to eat them. Socks froze in mid-stride. I flicked the safety off my rifle and whispered, "Go, Socks!" She jumped into a bush, followed by a noisy confrontation, then a monstrous wild turkey erupted from behind the bush and took flight. Turkeys fly up to treetop height, stop, then take off horizontally. It's like they're changing gears from vertical to horizontal flight. I waited until it stopped, then got it right through the head. Socks was waiting for me when I climbed out of the ravine, guarding that big tom. It had to weigh thirty pounds. I cleaned it and put it in my game bag. *This* would be a supper to remember. And Thanksgiving was just around the corner.

I amazed Mom with the size of the old boy. She plucked him and singed off the fuzz. We didn't have anywhere to keep him until Thanksgiving, so he went into the oven with a belly full of her sweet potatoes, onions, and chopped-up giblets. Even the dogs feasted on more than they could eat that night.

Three days later, Mr. Griff, our neighbor, came knocking. He was tall and lean with the kind of chiseled, regal face that should have been carved into the rocks on Mt. Rushmore. His white hair was always neatly combed.

"Howdy do, Annalee," he said, smiling at Mom. "Hey, you guys hain't seen nothing of my old tom turkey, have you? I've been fattening him up for Thanksgiving and ain't seen hide 'er hair of him for a couple a days."

I looked at Mom, then at Mr. Griff. She looked back at me, waiting to see what I would do.

"Mr. Griff, I think I shot yer turkey," I said, looking down. "I didn't know he was yers. Me and Socks found 'im in the ravine next to yer cornfield. I thought he were a wild tom."

He looked at me with no expression on his face for a minute, deciding what to do.

"Do you think you could find me another one?" he asked.

Now a turkey is about the hardest critter there is to hunt. They can hear a flea fart at a hundred yards. And when they get to flying, they might as well have an "S" on their chest because your bullet will have a hard time catching up.

"I cain't make no promises, but I'll give 'er a try."

"That's good enough fer me, David."

He shook my hand and began the walk back to his homestead.

Socks and I started the hunt right after lunch. A second turkey sandwich that Mom made for me for lunch in my game bag. We went up and down every ravine I could think of. We skirted cornfields far and wide. We saw grouse, pheasant, doves, squirrels, coons, possum, even a couple of blacktail deer, and a bull elk with a six-point rack. But, not only did we not find a turkey, we didn't even find sign of a turkey, turkeys having a pretty distinctive footprint. There wasn't a turkey print anywhere we went.

Four days Socks and I scoured the countryside and turned up nothing. We hunted from the moment I got home from school until we couldn't see anymore. I believe every turkey in the county had taken off for parts unknown just because I was searching for them so hard. Word gets around the critter grapevine when a hunt's going on, just like with deer on the first day of huntin' season.

Today was the day before Thanksgiving. Socks and I watched the sun go down from the top of the ridge overlooking Mr. Griff's spread. With a hanging head, I began the walk down to Mr. Griff's house empty-handed.

He opened the door when I knocked.

"I hain't been able to find you another turkey, Mr. Griff," I said, on the verge of tears. "Socks and me, we beat them hills from top to bottom, and there ain't a turkey in 'em."

He laughed at that. "Well, that's good!"

I looked at him like I couldn't believe the words that just came out of his mouth.

"My old tom come back last night. He's hanging in my smoke house gettin' a right nice tan. I'll be sure to bring him over tomorra if your momma would like to trade some a his meat fer one o' her pecan pies."

"I'm sure she would, Mr. Griff," the weight of that debt coming off my shoulders like a cool breeze on a hot afternoon.

Mom made an extra pie. It was waiting for Mr. Griff when he showed up with that turkey breast. Both of them thought they got the better part of the deal.

"So every year, I delivered or sent a turkey to Mr. Griff. He'd bring it to Mom on Thanksgiving morning and tell her that some damned fool gave it to 'im again. She would cook and serve it to all of us. She always had a pecan pie for Mr. Griff to take home with 'im."

I picked up the extra turkey I bought, went out the front door with it, and walked down the driveway to Mr. Griff's place. He opened up his door when I knocked. I was shocked at how frail he had become. He had to be over ninety now. His knobby hands shook a little as he held the door.

"Who're you, young man?"

It had been a lot of years since anyone called me "young man." I guess when you're as old as him, almost every man is a young man.

"It's David, Mr. Griff. I brought you a turkey for Thanksgiving."

"What the hell would I do with it? I cain't cook no damned turkey."

I looked at the turkey, then at Mr. Griff.

"You're right. This is for someone else. What I came over for is to ask you if you'd like to have Thanksgiving dinner with us. Thanksgiving's in two days."

"I cain't. I'm having Thanksgivin' with the Petersons like always. But thanks fer askin'."

"OK. I'll tell Annalee to expect you."

"Why thankee, young man. What'd you say yer name is?"

"David, Mr. Griff."

"What a coincidence. The Petersons have a David, too. He's in the Army."

"Small world."

"Thanks again, young man."

I donated the extra turkey to the Abused Women's Shelter—going to make that an annual event.

Rhiannon checked to make sure we had all the ingredients for a couple of pecan pies. She wanted to continue the tradition, and I was sure glad. It wouldn't have been Thanksgiving without the smell of pecan pies cooking in the oven or a large slice of it showing up in front of me after the meal. I made a mental note to pick up some vanilla ice cream to go with it.

Chapter 26 – Southwest

"What do you mean I can't get a license to open a clinic? Do you have any idea of the level of training I've received in the Special Forces? I've been fixing people up for almost thirty years. There've been countless soldiers in the field that would have died if I hadn't been there to work on them. I've delivered twenty-three babies and done a C-section. I've set bones and nursed men while bullets were flying past my head. I've dispensed narcotics and saved lives doing it."

She waited patiently for me to finish my rant.

"Sergeant Major Peterson, I do understand the level of training a Green Beret medic gets. At least I think I do. But a battlefield is different from the backwoods of this state. We require people operating a clinic to have state certifications. That means the clinic has to be run by a registered nurse, a licensed practical nurse, or a nurse practitioner. In addition, the clinic itself must run under the auspices of a doctor who has a diploma from an accredited medical school, a license to practice medicine issued by this state, and a federal narcotics license."

She hesitated and smiled. "I wish I could help. There aren't any medical services within fifty miles of where you want to open your clinic, and God knows those people could use you. But the law is the law. Without a nurse to run it and a doctor to say he'd manage it, my hands are tied."

I was angry. I learned a long time ago I didn't make my best decisions when I was angry. So instead of saying what I thought about the state and its rules for rural clinics, I stood and collected my paperwork. I would have to be a cop for a while longer.

"Is there any way you could convert some of your training into college hours toward a nursing degree?"

"The local branch of the state university told me the Army way and their way were so different nothing would carry over. I'd have to again start from scratch with algebra, English, chemistry, and the history of goddamned nursing."

That made her smile and shake her head a little. "Would you consider running an ambulance service that would be affiliated with the nearest hospital? Then, a paramedic or EMT certification would be a snap for you."

"I'd still need a doc to sign on, and there isn't one." I hesitated for a moment, considering my options. "Could you imagine what it would be like to see someone injured, know I could save their life, and not be allowed to do it because I wasn't a nurse or a doc? Or even worse, what if I ignored all the rules and saved their life anyway, only to be arrested because I did and wasn't authorized to do the procedure?"

She smiled at me sadly. "No. I cannot imagine that. This makes no sense, but I don't make the rules. Why don't you ask the doctors around you in your county if they would consider taking your clinic under their wing? Maybe you'll get lucky."

"I wouldn't have any idea how to contact them. Is there a list somewhere?"

She smiled in relief. "Now *that* I can help you with."

She typed at her computer console for a few minutes. Finally, the printer on her desk began humming, and three sheets of paper came out.

"Here is a list of all the doctors in your county, their addresses, and phone numbers. But you didn't get it from me." She winked and handed me the papers. "It's probably an invasion of their precious privacy, a felony at the least."

I left the state office building shaking my head. Things weren't working out like I envisioned when I left the Army a year ago. But, the long ride back to Grandpa's house gave me some time to think and cool off.

Rhiannon is an RN, and she said she wanted to work at the clinic when it got set up. She would have to take some refresher courses to get current again, and she could do that in one semester. She had already signed up for the coming fall term. The doc-requirement continued to stump me. Where the hell could I find a doctor who would step up to the time it would take them to run the clinic? Every doctor I knew was busier than a one-armed paper hanger.

When I got home, I started calling the doctors on the list.

"Hello, is Dr. Richard Miller there?"

"No," a shaky voice that sounded female and very elderly answered. "He died last year."

"I'm so sorry. Is this Mrs. Miller?"

"Yes. What can I do for you?"

I explained what I wanted to do.

"Well, Dick would have loved to do that. He retired twenty years ago. He almost drove me crazy trying to figure out what to do with himself."

She rambled on for another fifteen minutes, talking about her husband and all the things they did together.

I was able to interrupt when she took a breath and a drink of something. "Would you happen to know of another doctor who might want to let us run the clinic under his or her control?"

She was quiet for a moment. "Well, Stephen Tanger might. But, no, wait, he moved to Phoenix." She paused again. "I'll have to check around. Give me your phone number."

I gave it to her.

"You sound like a nice young man, David. I hope you find someone to help you out."

"Thank you, Mrs. Miller. I look forward to hearing from you."

"Goodbye and God bless."

One off the list—that one only took half an hour.

That call turned out to be the high point of the list. Most of the numbers rolled over to voicemail or answering services. I left messages and marked them that way on the list. Of the forty-one doctors on the list, I reached five. Those five weren't interested. The one call I thoroughly enjoyed making was to the oncologist I "met" in the E.R. when I took Frank over the mountain. He didn't recognize me, then brushed me off, saying he was too busy saving lives from cancer to fool with saving lives in an ambulance. After he said that, he hung up on me.

I had called every number on the list. Nothing left to do but wait to see if anyone called back. There were a couple of other options. I could open a new branch of an existing clinic or start a stabilize-and-transport ambulance service. Maybe the hospital would let me run it as part of them.

While I waited, I got the extension ladder and leaned it on the side of the house, then climbed up to check why the weather vane seemed to be stuck on the southwest. I hadn't had a chance to examine it up close before the roofers fastened it up there. I climbed the ladder and studied the vane carefully. It was truly a work of art—the detail was phenomenal. I spun it on its pivot. It swung through an entire circle. There were no bumps, rubs, or friction I could feel. The bearings were stout and well lubricated. I spun it in the other direction. Again, nothing to make it stick. A puff of wind came from the northeast. The eagle swung to that direction. I stood on the ladder and watched for a while. With every minute change in the breeze, the eagle moved into it.

I climbed down the ladder, collapsed it, then looked up—the eagle had returned to its southwest orientation.

"Bob!" I sighed, giving up.

Bob is the name I gave to my pet ghost. Whenever something happened for no rational reason, I attributed it to "Bob." Who knows? Maybe his name really is Bob. He'd been a part of my life so long I actually viewed him affectionately. Sometimes he played jokes. Sometimes he would try to get my attention before I made a monumental mistake. Sometimes he simply said hi.

I looked southwest. What was so important down there? The only thing I could think of was the homestead where the moonshiner last saw Tommy's truck.

Chapter 27 – En Garde

The wind blew strongly across the ridgeline. My night vision goggles showed the cluster of fir trees that overlooked the ravine. I could see their branches waving as the wind blew through the trees. Another hundred yards and I would be there. I moved from one place of concealment to the next, working my way to the firs. I saw a new set of laser telltales crisscrossing over the ground. I avoided them, wondering why they were added. Routine changing of defenses? A trap for whoever placed the camera?

I stopped at the base of the tree where I had concealed the camera and waited, watching and listening. I would be essentially defenseless when I began my ascent. I could hear or see nothing out of the ordinary. But I sure felt something. Every hair on the back of my neck stood at full attention. I put on my climber's saddle and spikes, then snapped into my flip line—time to go up. An owl hooted high above me. That was *not* what I wanted to hear at that particular moment. I looked around again—still nothing weird I could put my finger on.

"OK, owl. What's up your butt tonight?"

I hesitated and listened yet again—nothing but the wind. Owls had appeared many times in my life and always brought a warning—to be ignored at my peril. My tension was already on high alert. The owl ratcheted it up even higher. About twenty-five feet up, the voice in my head said, "Duck left!" I reacted without thought. The first bullet hit the tree right where my head had been a moment ago. I continued around the tree to the left, so the tree stood between the shooter and me, then pulled out my .45. The second bullet threw bark in my face as it grazed the tree. I saw the shooter from the muzzle flash—crouching between two boulders. I drew a bead on him and waited. The shooter began shooting a steady stream of rounds into the tree directly on the other side of me.

"He's trying to shoot through the tree. What a great idea!" While he did that, I leaned around the tree and emptied my clip. I figured if I didn't get him directly, then a ricochet would. The shooting stopped. I reloaded and went up the tree without waiting. I cut loose the camera, threw it in my backpack, and descended the tree in less than a minute.

The last ten feet were kind of exciting. My flip line parted, and I dropped those ten feet to the ground with my climbing spikes raking down the bark of the tree. I landed an inch to the right of a boulder that would have snapped my leg like a twig.

I heard dogs coming up the ridgeline from the house. The flashlights behind the dogs would be bristling with firearms. I didn't wait around to meet them. Instead of running directly back to the truck, I chose route B. I always started an operation with at least two, sometimes three, escape routes planned. Route B went through a stream for a quarter-mile, then over some hard ground.

I got to Dad's truck, put my stuff behind the seat, and started to drive home, a little below the speed limit. About two miles down the road, I saw some flares and cars stopped in the road at a curve. One car lay on its roof. I stopped.

"Anyone hurt?" I asked the guy who flagged me down.

"No," he said, smiling. "Only some kids going too fast. We'll have it open for you in a minute. Out for a drive?"

"Got to get some groceries. My wife's nursing, and we ran out of milk. She drinks it by the gallon."

While he looked around my truck and in the bed, I studied him. He had a tightly trimmed beard, gray hoody, and sunglasses. I recognized him from the picture of the young man at the Quik Mart buying the GoPhone. He was a little smaller than I expected from the photo—about 5'8"—and appeared to be about thirty with a slightly brownish tint to his skin. Maybe Hispanic or Mediterranean. I flipped the safety off my .45 that I held next to the door of the truck.

"OK, you can go now." He stepped out of the way, and I drove past. He recorded my license number on a piece of paper. It wouldn't do him much good since that plate came off a wrecked car on the other side of the mountain.

I was reminded of the opening stance of two fencers when they crossed swords at the beginning of a match. I had no illusions that the phony license plate would slow them down much. It wouldn't be long before they visited where I lived.

In the Special Forces, what I would do now is turn all this over to the Intel section and call in the gunships. In fact, I did exactly that in Panama.

When I got home, I went directly to my laptop and got out the camera. I couldn't wait to see what pictures were on the camera. I put on latex gloves, plugged the USB cable into the bottom of the camera, and then noticed the master power switch to the camera—in the "off" position. I turned it on. The batteries were gone. Fresh batteries, and I saw what I expected with the master switch being off—nothing. The solid-state storage device was clean—not a single picture—not even the ones I took before setting it on automatic. That explains the guy waiting for me. They had found my camera and cleaned it. Maybe there were some fingerprints.

Rhiannon came up behind me. "What's that? Looks like a camera."

"It *is* a camera."

"You wanna tell me what's going on? Why you're in here playing with a camera on a Wednesday night."

She was about to get into this as deeply as I was. It wouldn't be fair to let her be in danger and not know why.

"I think I've found the meth lab."

"What meth lab?"

"The one that's the subject of a top-secret DEA investigation."

"Maybe you should start at the beginning."

She took it a lot better than I feared.

"You mean Tommy laundered money for those drug manufacturers?"

"Tommy and a lot of others, if the DEA is right in their assessment of the size of the operation. They think this site's supplying meth to the entire three-state region. There would be millions, even tens of millions of dollars rolling through there every month. Tommy had to have been small potatoes. Even when his checking account was closed, he only had a quarter million in it."

I pulled out the second camera. "Let's see what's on this one."

I had hidden it across the cornfield from the entrance to the property. It wouldn't show the actual homestead, but I would see all the vehicle traffic entering and leaving.

Chapter 28 – Just Two More Days

The call came in while Reynolds, the bearded man who ran the meth factory, was having his daily production team meeting in his office at the homestead. The voice on the speakerphone was "management."

"The plate's registered to a 1997 Toyota Camry that was totaled six months ago, a hundred miles from there."

This didn't surprise Reynolds at all. Then Samantha walked into the room.

"Marley's dead."

Blood covered her shirt and pants. The blood on her forehead stood out in stark contrast to her blonde, almost white hair. Her delicate Scandinavian features and sky-blue eyes had the look of numb shock that Reynolds hadn't seen since he'd left Sarajevo.

No surprise about Marley either. He'd taken a round in the chest and another through his jaw.

"Get rid of his body. You know how."

No one said a word for a few moments while the news sunk in, even the management guy on the speakerphone was silent. Samantha walked back out without any change in expression.

Reynolds watched her go with concern. *Sam was one of the happy members of my team*, he thought. *It might have been losing Marley—she had been close to him. But she had been part of the production team for five years and knew the risks—everyone did. She also knew the benefits. Those fat bank accounts didn't happen by accident. But this was the first fatality since Sam had joined the team. This kind of thing didn't happen to us very often, and that was exactly why everyone did their jobs so carefully. The objective didn't change—stay under the radar. The couriers weren't even allowed to carry weapons. No one interfered with them after the first couple of incidents. Our organization had begun as the new kid on the block, and people thought they could horn into our business. The enforcement teams had subsequently cleaned out whole families.*

Now everyone understood. Leave us alone and get rich with us. Cops, politicians, judges, sellers, couriers, suppliers, enforcers, the production team, management, everyone got a cut. And there was so much money to cut up—money beyond belief.

The man on the other end of the phone broke the silence. "I've seen that pickup. He lives in Chambersville somewhere. I should be able to find him."

"How about the phone number from the flyers? Any address on that?"

"Yeah. It's billed to a private account at MacDill air force base."

"No shit! This keeps getting worse. What would the Special Forces have to do with this? They work for the CIA. The CIA isn't allowed to do domestic surveillance." Reynolds came to a decision. "You work on finding the pickup. I'm going to prepare the lab to move to alternate site A."

"You think that's necessary? We'll be out of production for at least two weeks."

"This is at least the second and probably the third visit from this guy. Either we move or wait for the DEA to show up. Your choice, but I'm out of here. This place is hot enough to fry potatoes."

The rest of the team nodded in agreement—every one of them. No one would miss this site. Two years they had been here. Everyone thought this place was haunted. Stuff kept breaking that should never have broken. Animals kept tripping their flares. Fresh batteries were dead the next day. Laser telltales kept moving out of alignment and setting off alarms.

Then Tommy came back from that boondoggle with Marley and Samantha. Not one of them would say what happened, but they never left again. They acted scared to death. Things started going downhill faster after that. Last night had been the final straw. Thank God Marley saw that camera three days ago. Those pictures would have convicted them all.

"For the record, it's my call." The line went silent for a few moments. "OK. You're right. Move. Begin immediately. I'll clear it with upstairs."

No one mentioned Tommy. He had always been the weak link at this site with his attitude and that stupid truck. Nothing Reynolds said would make the voice at the end of the line budge. The voice said they needed a local contact to see if anyone noticed the facility or the traffic into and out of it. After the rape and beating of that waitress and the flyers searching for Tommy and his truck going up all over the county, even management saw there was no other way. The voice gave his approval for the killing.

Tommy was dead within hours. The speedball overdose did the job the way heroin and cocaine are supposed to. Then Marley couldn't resist doing the headshot thing. Tommy instantly went from an accidental overdose to a murder. *Good riddance to both of them—fucking amateurs and hotheads.*

It's just hard to get good help, Reynolds chuckled bitterly to himself. *So now we're moving to a new facility with all the disruption and risk that causes to the supply and distribution couriers. We have a couple of months' production stockpiled. But the replacement for Marley has me concerned. I'm not looking forward to that. Every new guy is a potential informant—no matter how much money they make or how many pictures you show them of their mother, kids, and girlfriends. And a new guy with a gun is an even bigger risk. But it isn't my problem. The enforcement team is tasked with supplying on-site protection. It's up to them to keep the factory and couriers safe. Maybe we'll get lucky this time, and Enforcement will send someone who understands "low profile."*

Reynolds sighed. "OK, everyone. It's been a while since we did this, but you remember the drill. If you don't, work with someone who does. Shut down the production line as soon as the last batch currently cooking is done. Everyone else—start packing. The sooner we're out of this shithole, the better."

He chose three teams to get the U-Haul trucks, then opened the safe and got out a bundle of phony driver licenses and credit cards. He went through them until he found a set that matched the teams.

"Use these credit cards to rent the truck, but pay with this cash when you return them. If you can rent them with cash, do it. Use the credit cards as a last resort."

He handed each team $500 in used twenty-dollar bills.

"Rent the trucks from at least 150 miles away and return them there when we're done, exactly like we did last time. Buy their insurance to cover the truck in case someone has an accident."

The driver teams walked out together to help with the packing. They would get rides from the couriers that night.

"What do you want to do with all the stuff from Tommy's service station?" Samantha walked back into the room.

"Leave it here. When we blow and burn the place, no one will care."

Reynolds looked around the office, sighed again, and walked to the storeroom to get some boxes. *Three shifts of people working on the production line. Three shifts of people to do the cooking and cleaning and set up the entertainment. All the supplies, records, belongings, and equipment. All of it had to fit into three goddamned trucks. At least the next site was ready. It had been for months. Now he'd have to find and outfit another location for the next time they had to jump.*

"Two more days," Reynolds prayed. "Give us two more days before the DEA shows up."

Chapter 29 – They Started It

The second camera showed the same five nondescript cars going in and out of the driveway in the hours between midnight and 6 A.M. The kind of cars you wouldn't give a second glance—all of them with their lights off. Even the brake lights didn't work as they slowed to turn in the driveway. The camera was too far away to see license plates, the make and model of the vehicles, or even how many passengers were in them.

"What do you make of it?" Rhiannon asked.

"Deliveries and pickups."

"Who can we tell?"

"Well, everything is circumstantial. We don't have pictures of anyone doing anything illegal except driving at night with their lights out. We're not going to get a search warrant on that."

"So, what do we do?"

"Well, everything I've heard about these guys is tht they want to stay hidden. With them seeing me four months ago and trading shots with me tonight …"

"Shots? Someone shot at you? Did you shoot at someone? Tonight?"

"Well, they started it."

When I laughed, she looked at me like I was insane. I guess black ops humor is an acquired taste.

"Are you hurt?" She began checking me all over.

I told her the whole story.

"So you don't know if you hit the person who shot at you or not."

"I can only assume I did, or at least scared the hell out of whoever it was—enough to make them quit shooting at me. I wasn't going to stop on my way out of Dodge to see which one it was."

I might as well have been a stranger by the way she stared at me in disbelief.

"What do you think I did in the Army for thirty years?" I asked her. "Play tiddlywinks with the bad guys?"

"This isn't the Army."

"No, it's a drug war. Kids are dying every day, stealin' to get the money to pay these assholes, killin' people while they drive around high, beatin' up their girlfriends because the beer's gone from the fridge, and they're too high to remember drinkin' it. Do you think this only happens in L.A.? It's right here in River City. Yes, sir, we've got trouble. And that begins with T, and that rhymes with M, and that stands for meth."

Rhiannon didn't like my reference to her favorite movie, *The Music Man*. She didn't want to think about drugs and hopped-up kids in Chambersville.

"M doesn't rhyme with T."

"Shoot me."

"Someone already tried that."

"He wasn't the first."

I took her hand in mine. "Back to the problem at hand. Now that we've traded shots, I believe they will bolt. They're successful because they cause no, nada, nein problems near the factory. The DEA hasn't been able to crack their nut for just that reason. These aren't ghetto kids making low-grade speed in motel factories, then smoking half of what they make. These guys are pros. I would be willing to bet none of them use—at all. They don't even let the street people sell within a hundred miles of here. That's how the DEA came to believe they're here. This county is the center of the no-sell circle. And if Tommy hadn't upset the apple cart, we still wouldn't know they were here. They made what appears to be a rare mistake in letting Tommy in. Now they'll move to start over in *another* community that thinks *they* don't have a drug problem either."

"What should we do?" Rhiannon asked, overwhelmed.

"I think it's time to go to the police."

"You are the police."

"I mean the sheriff. I'm going to the sheriff's office tomorrow and give them everything I have."

"Why not the DEA?"

"Because Doc stuck his neck way out giving me that top-secret information. Yeah, we're friends, and both of us have top-secret security clearances, but there are people in jail who've done a lot less. I can't even mention I know about the investigation. And we have no proof that anything to do with drugs is going on in that homestead. All I can do is say somethin' fishy's going on and tell them Tommy was last seen driving up that driveway before I found him murdered. I'll give them the pictures and tell them about me being shot at on national forest land. Maybe that's enough to get someone to nose around before the people leave. Right now, with what we know, it's a county jurisdiction issue."

"How about an anonymous tip to the DEA?"

"Anonymous tip? Is such a thing even possible? We almost got the guy with the GoPhone who told us where to find Tommy. And he is a pro."

I had already considered the tip thing, but I didn't want Rhiannon trying it. She would get caught. There really are untraceable ways to drop a tip. If the sheriff's office didn't work, that was plan B. Besides, I wanted to see what the sheriff's detectives were like and if they would run with good intel.

Rhiannon stared at me, then out the window. I pulled the remaining stuff out of my backpack. When I got to the flip line, I stared at it in disbelief. The line had been cut by bullets. The powder marks the bullets left were still on the rope. *The guy wasn't trying to shoot me through the tree—he was trying to shoot through my flip line. Damn near made it, too. I went up the tree to retrieve the camera without knowing the flip line was hanging on by threads. If it had parted when I was fifty feet in the air instead of ten feet, I wouldn't be here now.*

"That guy was pretty good," I muttered with grudging respect. "Hitting a black half-inch rope against a black tree trunk at night from a hundred and fifty feet again and again with a quarter-inch bullet. I wonder if the rest of them are that good?"

Chapter 30 – Let Me Do My Job

"Why're you sending a security team?" Reynolds asked the Voice. "We'll be gone in two days. They'll just get in the way."

"I don't want any surprises during the move. They're there to make sure everything goes smoothly. With Marley gone, you don't have any security."

"No security? All of us have guns. The last thing I need is a bunch of guys with automatic weapons and hair triggers. They're used to protecting distribution sites with all that cash sitting around. We don't do cash. We do chemicals. The sheriff's covered. The DEA is clueless. No one's gonna bother us."

"Then there won't be a problem."

"Unless these guys *are* the problem."

"They're pros. Let 'em do their job."

The security team walked into Reynolds's office. They were all dressed in military-looking uniforms and body armor. Reynolds felt like saying "Atten-hut!"

"You must be Reynolds. I'm Nesmith. Where do you want us to set up our command center?" Nesmith was all blond crew cut, clean shaven, and square jaw. He looked like a muscular and fortyish GI Joe.

"You can use my office." Reynolds got up. "The last things packed will be the computers and surveillance monitors."

Reynolds didn't have anything close to a high level of confidence as he watched the twelve-person team unpacking and loading their weapons. Each person carried more firepower than had been on the whole site for two years. The soldiers walked outside and began to examine the ravine that camouflaged the factory.

"Joel and Larry, you go up on the west ridge and see what the condition of the cameras and lasers are. I want you to trigger each one. Call me before you do. Work from the top down to the road. Billy and Steve, you do the east ridge. Vera and Shawn, you walk down the driveway and check it out. The rest of you identify probable hiding places for trouble. I want a map of the ravine and where everything is located in my hands in one hour. Keep out of sight, everyone. Sound off for radio check."

Each of the members turned on their headsets and did a communication check, verifying the radios were functional. They walked outside to begin their tasks. Nesmith sat down in Reynolds's chair and began examining the monitors and motion detector pickups.

"Who's the biggest threat?" Nesmith asked Reynolds.

"We've only had one threat. An ex-Green Beret named David Peterson. He got tangled up with our local contact over a woman. We ended up terminating the contact, but Peterson has been back twice since then. He planted a camera above the ravine. Marley found it, erased it, then waited up for Peterson to show up for the recovery. Marley got killed during the firefight."

"Any way to put 'im on hold?"

"Not that I know of. He's the reason we're moving."

"Too bad we weren't called in earlier. We could've taken him out. End of problem. Who's the woman?"

"Local named Rhiannon McNeil. Works at the diner in Chambersville."

Reynolds didn't like the gleam in Nesmith's eye. "I'd leave her alone. There'd be no surer way to get Peterson out here than to snatch her."

"Really? Now why didn't I think of that?"

"Look, we just want to pack and leave. No muss. No fuss. No Green Berets hiding in the woods trying to rescue their girlfriends."

"I understand. Let us do our job."

"That's funny." Reynolds said to him.

"What's funny?"

"Marley said almost those exact same words: 'I understand. Let me do my job.'"

Reynolds knew what *he* thought the security team's job was. He was almost certain *his* perception of their job was more than a little different from *theirs*.

"I hope I'm wrong," Reynolds muttered as he went back to his job of organizing the move. "Please, you guys, amaze me."

Chapter 31 – Kicking Ant Hills

Detective Ives looked again at the pictures from the cornfield camera and the pictures I had taken on my first trip to the homestead. He'd listened to my whole story without comment.

"So someone saw Tommy's truck go up a driveway four months before he was found dead. That's it? It's pretty slim. No judge would give us a search warrant for that. Getting shot at when you were climbing a tree at night sounds like a hunter mistaking you for a critter. Good thing no one got hurt."

I decided not to remind him that we had no evidence someone *didn't* get hurt. "How about all the cameras, lasers, and motion detectors?"

"Nothing illegal there. I expect it's someone feeling like he was vulnerable. You can buy the same stuff on the internet all day long."

"Couldn't you at least visit them and see what they know about Tommy?"

"Yeah, I could do that." He checked his calendar. "How about next Tuesday or Wednesday? I could free up some time then."

Tuesday was four days away. In two days, they would be long gone. "Could someone stop one of those cars for a 'broken' taillight?"

"You want me to have an officer wait for them on a Friday night when we have drunks running all over the county? Have to make it look like a Friday night DUI roadblock. And why would we have a roadblock way out in the country? Roadblocks are something we do between party places and home places. I had one thrown out of court a couple of months ago because the perp claimed entrapment, and the court bought it."

I was beginning to realize why Sheriff Crook wanted some new blood in his detective division.

"Did anyone report an accident on Black Mountain Road last night?"

Detective Ives turned to his computer and typed a query. "Nope. What happened?"

"After I retrieved my second camera from the cornfield, I was stopped by some guy helping some kids with an overturned car. The guy who stopped me looked like the guy in the Quik Mart CCTV photo, the guy who was buying the GoPhone that made the call announcing where to find Tommy."

He rechecked his display. "Nobody reported anything out there. But that's not too unusual by itself. The kids were probably drunk and going too fast. I'll bet they were thrilled someone would help them without calling the cops." He picked up the guy's picture in the gray hoody at the Quik Mart. "This guy could be any of a thousand people within five miles of that Quik Mart."

I got up. "Well, when you go out there, let me know what you find."

"I'll do that, David. Thanks for your help. I'm sure there's a good explanation for all this. We don't have much crime in this county."

"I keep hearin' that." I stood to leave. "By the way, why didn't anyone think to run Theodore Santanini's DNA from Rhiannon's rape through the national criminal database?"

"Don't know. That was being handled from over the mountain. Officer Sanchez, as I remember. Good idea, though— should've been done. But it wouldn't have made any difference. By the time the results would have come back, he was already dead. The lab has at least a one-year turnaround on a noncritical analysis."

"Then why didn't his fingerprints from the door on my workshop get run?"

"Don't know that either. Grant was in charge of that case. Sometimes it takes a while to get them back from the FBI."

Detective Ives smiled at me.

I decided to try something that worked with a reluctant CIA analyst in Brazil. "You think I'm new-copping you, don't you? You think I'm makin' a mountain out of a molehill?"

"The thought had crossed my mind," he said, smiling indulgently.

"Look, Bert. Your name *is* Bert isn't it?"

He nodded.

"I've been chasing bad guys for thirty years. People who make a meth pusher look like a Sunday school teacher. These guys are making drugs. You either don't want to believe it, or you're in on it with 'em. I guess time'll tell which one it is. See ya, Bert."

Detective Ives went white. I couldn't tell if it was from shock or rage. I didn't want to stick around to find out. I smiled and walked back out to my truck. Kicking ant hills was one of my favorite things to do.

Chapter 32 – No One Knows

I drove back toward Chambersville, thinking about Bert and his responses. I stopped in the diner for a cup of coffee.

"What did he say?" Rhiannon was all ears.

"He said he'd drop by on Tuesday or Wednesday."

"They'll be gone by then. Is he stupid?"

"I got the feeling that waiting until they were gone might be the idea. That, or he thinks I'm Barney Fife, and I've uncovered an unlicensed bingo game."

Rhiannon was appalled. "You mean you think the detective might be in on it?"

"I have no proof at all. Maybe he didn't think my intel was very important. Maybe he thinks I'm a new cop and new cops are renowned for seeing major crime behind every blade of grass. Maybe I need to develop some credibility with Detective Ives."

I told her all about my meeting.

"I can't believe you accused him of being in on it."

"I figure one of a couple of things will happen: Option 1—he will get righteously pissed off, and Josh will read me the riot act when I get back to the office or, Option 2—he'll ignore me and not do anything, or Option 3—he'll call the lab, and they'll send out people to kill me."

"Kill you?" Rhiannon said way too loudly.

Everyone in the diner turned to look.

"Either way, we'll know where Bert stands," I said quietly, "and which side he's on."

I went over to the police station. When I walked in the door, Josh had a red face and was talking with someone on the phone.

"He just came in the door. Let me get his side. I'll call you back."

I walked over to his desk—looks like option 1. Option 1 was certainly better than Options 2 or 3.

"Well, it's official. You have all the tact of a water buffalo."

"Was that Bert?"

"No, that was Sheriff Crook. Tell me your side."

I told him all about what I found and about the conversation I had with Bert.

"Couldn't you have at least tried to be polite? Bert's been in the sheriff's department for going on twenty years."

"Are they going to go over to the homestead?"

"I don't know what they're going to do."

"Well, asking politely didn't work. Maybe pissing 'em off will."

"Those guys are on our side!"

"Maybe, maybe not. We'll see which one it is. Hard to believe all this was happening in our county, and no one knew about it." I looked directly at Josh. "Did you know about it?"

Josh gave me a long hard look. "David ..."

"Look, Tommy's been laundering money for them for two years. There's no way his little pissant business made enough for him to save a quarter of a million dollars while he bought toys like that stupid truck. He's also been using meth for at least that long— across the street from here. Didn't you notice? You're a cop. Cops are supposed to notice stuff like that."

"No, I didn't notice. I tried to stay away from Tommy."

"Why?"

Josh stared at me, then out the window. He started to say something, then changed his mind. "I can't tell you."

"OK. Well, I guess I'll see you around."

I walked to the door. Josh was dirty. Damn.

I opened the door and started out. "It's because I still love Rhiannon," Josh said, his voice cracking as he said it.

"*What*?" I closed the door again. "What did you say? I didn't know you had feelings for her. I thought you were happily married."

"OK. I'm sorry. No one else knows. We were lovers for a while when her marriage was breaking up. Her husband had been running around on her for years. I was having trouble with my marriage as well. She broke it off when her divorce went through."

I didn't know what to say. Josh was crushed. His eyes filled with tears he refused to allow himself to shed.

"Does your wife know?"

"No one knows."

I suspected he was wrong about that. Chambersville is a pretty small town.

"Marge and I began counseling after Rhiannon and I quit seeing each other. We were able to turn our marriage around. We had our fortieth anniversary this year. But it broke my heart watching Rhiannon go out with that scum ball, Tommy. Don't get me wrong. I love my wife, too. Just not the same way. Please don't tell anyone. Let this dead dog lie."

I drove back up to the house. Gina ran out to greet me. She was almost full-grown now—her front leg completely healed. She would fill out a lot more, but she was a joy to watch as she ran up to the truck.

I turned on the sprinklers for the lawn. It was green, growing, and healthy—be coming in even better if Gina would stop digging holes in it.

I walked into the kitchen and made some free-form loaves of whole wheat bread dough. Once they were rising, I rolled some beef cubes from the fridge in flour and browned them in bacon fat along with some chopped onions. I let them cook until the onions had caramelized, then I covered them with chicken stock and let them simmer. Then I peeled and cut up some potatoes, carrots, and celery. The beef cubes were starting to smell pretty yummy. I went out to the front porch with a cold beer and waited for the bread loaves to finish rising. Gina carried a tennis ball up to me and dropped it at my feet.

"Is there something you want, girl?" I asked innocently.

She waited almost a whole minute before she nudged it into my feet, then looked up at me again expectantly.

Where do dogs find old tennis balls? I hadn't played tennis in twenty years. I don't think I even owned a tennis racket. I picked it up and turned it over—nothing special—an old, discolored tennis ball. At some point in its past, it might have been yellow. I threw it out into the yard. Gina launched off the porch like a rocket. It must have taken her all of fifteen seconds before she returned, nudging that ball against my feet again. We played that game until I heard the timer in the kitchen announcing the end of the bread rise time.

I painted the loaves with egg white to give them a thick crust, then put them in the oven. I could almost taste the beef stew being served in those bread bowls. Next, I put the vegetables into the pot, put the lid on, and set the timer for the bread.

The aroma of baking bread and beef stew filled the house.

Chapter 33 – Looking Forward to It

Rhiannon left the diner full of anticipation. David had called to tell her what he had fixed for dinner. After his attempt at meatloaf, she began giving him lessons in how to cook. In the Special Forces, most of his cooking was done with a microwave or over a campfire. Once he'd figured out the oven didn't have to be simply on or off, his food improved markedly. While his entrées were getting steadily better, his bread-making had approached excellent. There was something about men and bread. Maybe men's greater upper body strength let them knead the dough more thoroughly. Whatever it was, David could have been a baker in his past life. His bread was pure magic—white, rye, whole wheat, multigrain—each one better than the last. Her stomach growled in anticipation of a rich beef stew served in warm, shiny-brown bread bowls.

She came around a curve and slammed on her brakes. A car was sideways in the road, and people flagged her down. She saw a person lying face up in front of the car in the middle of the road with his arms and legs all scrambled. Without a thought, she jumped out of her car and ran to the accident.

"I'm an RN," she called out to the people standing around, then knelt beside the prostrate man—middle-aged, muscular, crew cut, clean-shaven, good color, no obvious trauma or blood.

As she checked his pulse from the carotid artery in his neck, his eyes came open in a smile. "Hi, Amber." He grabbed both her hands. A man behind her put a cloth bag over her head and held another cloth to her nose. She struggled against the vice grip of the man on the ground until the chloroform on the fabric overcame her, and she lost consciousness.

Slowly she regained consciousness. Her head hurt. She'd had headaches before, but this one was a record-setter. Through the pounding in her temples, she began to hear other sounds—a low conversation from the next room. She couldn't quite understand what they were saying.

"I *told* you not to snatch her, asshole!" one voice said loudly enough for her to make out the words. She heard laughter in response and some more low talking she couldn't make out.

She tried to raise her hand to scratch her nose, but couldn't. It had been tied to the chair she sat on. Her legs were tied to it as well. She tried to speak, but was gagged and blindfolded. "Wha th' fu!" she raged into the gag, trying to kick her legs and pull her arms loose.

"Awake, are we?" a voice asked, coming into the room.

She tried to talk again. The person removed the gag.

"Make any noise, and I'll put it on again. Understand?"

"Yes, I understand. Water!" she pleaded hoarsely. "Could I have some water?"

"Sure." He left the room and returned a minute later. She felt a cup being held to her lips. She drank greedily. Her mouth felt like it was full of chalk.

"Where am I?"

"You don't expect me to answer that, do you?"

"Why am I here?"

"You're bait."

"He'll come for me. You have no idea what you've done."

"I think I can handle one Delta Force puke," the man said with disdain. "Until then, maybe we can have some fun and games like the old days, Amber."

"I remember you," Rhiannon said suddenly. His using her stage name from her prostitution days brought back the memory of him. "I recognize your voice. You're that guy ... Nesmith."

"Yep, that's me," he whispered in her ear, then licked it. "And if you remember me, you remember what I like."

She paled. Nesmith liked to beat up girls. The last time he'd been to the "motel," he'd beaten the woman he'd selected until she was unconscious. Then, when the bouncers tried to eject him, he beat them bloody as well.

"Better than sex!" she recalled him saying as he walked out the door.

The motel "manager" had run into the room with a gun and seen the unconscious bouncers. He'd then run out the door into the street and shot at Nesmith's car as he drove away. The girl and the three bouncers had ended up going to the hospital on stretchers.

Nesmith grabbed her breasts hard. She spit in his face. He twisted her breasts then reached between her legs under her waitress uniform and pulled off her underwear, leaving welts on her legs where the fabric parted. "We'll continue this in a few minutes, bitch."

"FUCK YOU!" Rhiannon screamed at him.

He leaned over and whispered in her ear again, his voice dripping with malice. "Lookin' forward to it, Amber."

He laughed, enjoying himself, then slapped her hard, knocking her head to the side, then wiping her spit off his face with her underwear.

She heard him walk away from her. *Nine-one-one*, she thought. *Why the fuck didn't I call nine-one-one before I got out of the car? Stupid, stupid, stupid.*

"What the fuck is that?" she heard a voice demand from the other room.

"Her underwear, Reynolds."

"I don't like this at all," the other voice said.

"She's toast, and you know it. We can't leave her alive."

"We shouldn't have her at all."

"Well, we do. It's a little too late for whining."

"I want to talk to management."

"Suit yourself. I'll be outside arranging a greeting for our pet Green Beret. As soon as I'm done, we can make the call to him together."

She heard Nesmith leave, shutting the door behind him. The second man came into the room. He took off her blindfold. She recognized him from the picture at the Quik Mart.

"Do you need anything?"

"I need to pee."

"I can't let you up."

"How about another drink of water?"

"Here you go."

After she finished, he said, "I think we have a bedpan. I could slide it under you."

"That'd be nice."

He walked out and returned in a few minutes. "Lift up as far as you can."

She did. He slid the bedpan under her, pulling her skirt out of the way. When she finished, he removed the bedpan, pulled her skirt back down, and left the room. She heard him dial a number and speak into the phone but couldn't make out the words. He was obviously leaving a message on a voice recorder.

Chapter 34 – The Lumberjack

My phone rang from a blocked number. "If ya wanna see yer whore again, come to the house. You know which one."

"I want to talk to her."

The line went dead. The voice had been electronically distorted but was different from the voice I had heard when I got the call telling me about Tommy's truck.

I called the diner.

"She left about an hour ago, David." Gus's voice sounded concerned. "She should've been home long ago."

"Thanks, Gus."

I turned off the oven and the stew, then walked into my bedroom and pulled up a floorboard. Underneath it were two rifles: a Browning .50 caliber sniper's rifle with a scope and a silenced H&K 416 rifle with a scope. The 416 had been developed especially for the special ops teams that were tired of the fouling and jamming of the rifles the rest of the military used. I had "found" the .50 in a Taliban hideout. It could reach out and touch someone from over a mile away. The 416 was a favorite of mine. For close-in fighting, reliability, and accuracy, it couldn't be beaten. I pulled out the 416 along with five clips of ammo and five more for my .45, then got dressed in my DCUs. The clips went in my backpack along with my night vision goggles. In the barn, I added the rest of the case of dynamite John sold me and all the fuse and blasting caps.

I called Josh. "Josh, they have Rhiannon. I'm going out."

"*Who* has Rhiannon?" He sounded panicked.

"The drug factory at 17490 Black Mountain Road. I got a call from them a minute ago telling me to go out there, or they would kill her."

"What do you want me to do?"

"Call the county. See if they'll help."

As I drove out the driveway and turned toward the homestead, I called Doc. "Brother, the balloon is up. They have Rhiannon. Call the DEA and tell them you have confirmed intel on the meth lab. It's at 17490 Black Mountain Road outside of Chambersville. This is a hostage situation. Do *not* send in the stormtroopers. Coordinate with the county sheriff. I'm on-site. They can call my cell phone."

I put in my Bluetooth earbuds so calls could come in without having to dig out a cell phone or have its ringing give my position away. After parking the truck on the other side of the cornfield not far from where I had planted the camera, I walked between the rows of shoulder-high plants toward the driveway to the homestead. I paused across the street, still in the corn. No one was in sight—up and down the road—nothing.

The entrance to the driveway had to be under surveillance, so I crawled through the culvert under the road, the stream washing around me, then waded upstream until I reached about two hundred yards from the homestead. For the next hundred yards, I began putting dynamite loads on trees and connecting them with the fuse as I positioned the charges to knock the trees across the driveway when they blew. With one charge, you place it on the side that you want the tree to fall toward. The explosion knocks the base away, making the top fall in the direction you want—pivoting around the center of mass of the tree. Most of the time, that works. Two charges would have been better, one high and one low—much more reliable to aim—, but I had no way to place the upper charges. I stopped when the homestead came into view. If I could see them, they could see me.

Three U-Haul trucks were parked side-by-side in front of the house with the ramps down the back. A steady parade of people bringing boxes and pieces of equipment streamed out of the house and into the trucks.

I lit the fuse. The ravine had been in the shadow of the mountain for a couple of hours. Sunset was half an hour away.

The fuse was slow-burning, meant for blowing stumps safely. As the almost invisible smoke trail from the burning line went down to the first tree, I took up a position next to a boulder on the hillside with an unblocked view of the whole homestead.

The first load exploded. The tree shook, then fell across the driveway, completely blocking it. People ran out of the house with guns, pointing them all over the place. One guy ran to the shed and emerged with a chain saw. I waited until he began to cut the tree with the saw making a lot of noise, then put a bullet into the saw's engine.

The second load blew—a second tree across the driveway. The man with the chain saw was down, clutching his leg and screaming for help beside the first tree. Through my binoculars, I saw the chain had broken when I shot the saw and wrapped around his leg, which was bleeding profusely.

People ran up to the man next to the tree, looking up the ravine. They began a careful examination of both sides. I was well camouflaged. They carried the injured man back into the house. One of them knelt next to the chain saw and checked it out.

The third tree blew and fell the wrong way.

"It's been shot," the man next to the chain saw called out to the others. "The shot came from that way." He pointed up the hill I was on.

Each of them began firing shots into likely spots on the hillside. I slid down behind the boulder.

The fourth tree blew and landed across the driveway.

A man by the U-Hauls shouted, "Rich, get down the stream and cut that fuse. José and Steve start working up the hillside. See if you can spot 'im."

The guy by the chain saw began running down the road, weaving from place-of-cover to place-of-cover. I shot him in the ass. He went down screaming. While an ass shot is very painful, it is rarely fatal.

"Anyone see 'im?" the man by the U-Haul called loudly. "He's using a silenced rifle. Look for the gas puff."

The fifth tree blew—across the driveway.

Using the noise as it fell and hit the ground, I put a round through one of the front tires of each of the trucks. The guy in charge jumped out of the way as they settled, and I got a good look at him. To my dismay, he appeared to be ex-military. But, then, thinking about it, I was surprised that I was even surprised. Not much else for those highly trained soldiers to do when they came home except become mercenaries, cops, security guards, or criminals.

A guy was working up the hillside toward me. I pulled out my last three sticks of dynamite. The fuse I used burned at about an inch a second, so I cut off all but ten inches, taped the three sticks together, then lit the end, tossing it about halfway between the guy coming up the hill and me. I needed everyone to be looking up the hill when it went off. Eight seconds after I lit the fuse, I screamed, loud and desperate. Everyone looked toward me, thinking I had been hit. I ducked behind the boulder, plugged my ears, and opened my mouth. The dynamite went off with a huge flash, boom, and concussion. While they had lost every bit of their night vision and most of their hearing, I rolled to my secondary position behind a stump from a windfall tree about thirty feet away. It didn't provide much concealment, but it should be enough for a few minutes. I heard a siren in the distance.

"He's behind that boulder!" the man working up the hillside shouted after a few seconds.

"Everyone open up on the boulder," the leader commanded.

Nine people went on full auto, tearing up the ground around the boulder. One of the ricochets hit the man on the hill below. He didn't appear to be badly injured. The leader triggered a remote control device, and the charges he'd planted behind several obvious places of concealment blew, the boulder being one of them. The trunk where I now hid did not explode.

The sixth tree blew and fell across the driveway. That was the last one—but without a chain saw to cut through them or a truck to pull them out of the way, this little ravine might as well have been a prison.

"He isn't here," the first guy to reach the boulder announced to everyone else.

Sunset had finished. The acrid smoke from the explosions and rifle fire filled the ravine and veiled the little light remaining.

"Everyone return to base," the leader commanded.

None of them had night vision goggles. Through mine, I watched them walk back to the house. In Pakistan, I would have killed them all without a second thought. It would have been like shooting fish in a barrel. But we were in the US—unless they're trying to kill you, you can't kill them. Cops have rules, and criminals don't.

I felt the cell phone buzzing in my pocket, and my earbud sounded off.

Chapter 35 – The DEA

"David?"

"Yes, Josh," I answered in a whisper, seeing the caller ID on my phone.

"What's the situation?"

"There are five trees down across the driveway. Everyone is in the house at the end of the driveway. They have three injured men, two hurt bad. Don't know how many people are in the house—at least twenty."

"I heard automatic weapons and an explosion when I drove up."

"Yep. They killed a boulder."

"Excuse me?"

"They have a fire team with eleven people, correction, nine people now. They attacked a boulder they thought I was hiding behind."

"Are you injured?"

"Nope."

"The county's on the way."

"Good. I'll send you the pictures I have of the house and the terrain. I took 'em before the light faded."

"OK."

My phone started buzzing again with another incoming call. "Gotta go. Got another call."

"She's dead, asshole."

"Now, why would you do that? She's the only hostage you have. Kill her, an we come in an' clean out the garbage."

"You and who else?"

"The Army of cops and Feds that's about to descend on your sorry ass."

"Ain't no one out there but you."

"You might look up and smile for the camera."

A helicopter circled the ravine with its spotlight on the house, then hovered over the ridgeline not far from where I placed the camera in the fir tree. I watched ropes get thrown out, and people descend them. I could only assume they were the DEA SWAT team.

I watched them descend, face first, guns at the ready. I always liked deploying like that from a chopper. Hit the ground running and shooting. The shock effect was awesome.

The chopper moved over to the other side of the ravine and dropped more SWAT people down the lines, then hovered with spotlights illuminating the house.

My phone said the conversation was still active. "I'm sure they'll want to talk. Is this a good number?"

The call ended with a click. I have to admit I got some enjoyment out of that click. Lots more sirens were coming down the road. The people in the house were starting to understand the enormity of the shit-storm blowing up the ravine.

My phone rang again.

"David Peterson?"

"Yep."

"This is Agent Fitzgerald of the DEA."

"Hi. Glad you could join the party."

"What have you got?"

I gave him all the details.

"So one fire team of nine people, an undetermined number of workers, one hostage, and three injured."

"Roger that."

"Where are you located?"

I gave him my GPS coordinates.

"Gotcha. Can you extract? I think we can take it from here."

"Roger. Let me know when it's clear."

I heard him talking over the radio.

"You are clear. Come out via the driveway."

"Comin' out."

I shrugged on my backpack, picked up my weapon, and walked down the hill to the driveway, going slowly and making a lot of noise with my arms up and out. Coming into a secure perimeter is dicey. There's always someone who doesn't get the word. I saw the flashes of a vast forest of red and blue lights beyond the last fallen tree.

"Halt right there," a voice commanded. "Lay down your weapon and backpack. Put your hands in the air."

I did.

An armored SWAT soldier with night vision goggles stepped out onto the road, propped his rifle against the hillside, and frisked me, pulling out my .45. I knew no less than ten rifles were pointed at my chest.

"He's clean."

"Can I pick up my stuff and have my .45 back?"

"Can he have his weapons back?"

I couldn't hear the response through his headset.

The soldier handed me back my .45 and picked up his rifle. "Walk that way when you're ready."

I tucked in the .45, put on my backpack, picked up my rifle, and walked to the command center with the SWAT soldier behind me. Josh was in the command center along with Sheriff Crook and a bunch of people in suits—DEA, I supposed. Sheriff Crook looked like he didn't know if he should hug me or shoot me. Bert was nowhere in sight.

"Sergeant Major Peterson," one of the suits walked up. "I'm Agent Fitzgerald. Glad to meet you."

I shook his hand. He could have been any middle-aged businessman walking down the street: fortyish, short hair, clean-shaven, dark blue suit, white shirt with a dark red tie. Except for the bulge under his left arm, I wouldn't have given him a second glance. I could see the butt of a Glock 17 peeking out from under his suit coat.

"I have to admire your style," he said with approval. "We've been searching for these assholes for two years. The trees across the driveway were brilliant. By the way, Doc sends his regards."

"How do you know Doc?"

"Only as a voice at the end of the wire, but when USASOC calls, people tend to listen. This is my first chance to work with the SF."

"We spend most of the time overseas."

"Exactly."

"Aren't you guys worried about a bomb set into the hillside above us?"

Agent Fitzgerald looked up in surprise.

"Agent Henry. Disperse these people and clear a path out of here on this road. Put them in the cornfield. Put them in the trees. But in five minutes, I don't want to see more than two people together or more than twenty people within a quarter-mile of this driveway."

"So, what's next?" I asked him. "How does this get resolved?"

"Typical hostage protocol. We contact the guy in charge and try to negotiate."

"Do you have a negotiator here yet?"

"He's on his way."

"Have you established contact with them?"

"No, not yet. I'll let the negotiator do that."

"Have you shut the cell phone towers so they can't communicate?"

"In the process of doing that. AT&T is resisting. They want a court order."

"Can't you guys claim national security, the Patriot Act, or something?"

"We could if they were terrorists. Not for drug dealers."

I rolled my eyes at that one. Give me a little C-4, and I would shut the tower down for them. Lot's easier to do this stuff in a third-world country.

"How about power? Have you shut off their electricity?"

"The PUD is on their way. But that isn't an issue."

"Why's that?"

"Two of your trees cut the power lines when they fell. The lights are still on in the house. They must have a generator."

There was a lot of noise around the driveway between the chain saws clearing the trees and the chopper circling overhead with its spotlights on the homestead. I got a cup of coffee from the mobile canteen set up at the back of all the cop cars. There was a queue of cops getting donuts, ham-and-egg sandwiches, and lattes. These operations were sure different inside the borders of the US than they were outside. When I asked for an MRE, the canteen operator gave me a bored wave at the menu on the wall behind him. I settled for a cheeseburger, tater tots, a fresh garden salad, a soft-serve ice cream sundae, and a latte. He only let me have one fresh orange juice, though. I figured I would suffer through, somehow.

Chapter 36 – The Back Door

"This is the DEA," the agent broadcast on the loudspeaker. "We want to resolve this situation. Please retrieve the radio on your porch so we can talk."

AT&T finally agreed to shut down the cell phone tower. My phone had no signal. The chopper delivered a package, by rope, to the front porch of the homestead.

The front door to the homestead opened, and a young man darted out to get the package, then darted back in almost as fast.

The radio crackled to life. "This is Joe."

"Hi, Joe. This is Agent Sanders. What are your ideas about how we can end this?"

"You can all go away. We'll leave the hostage here, and you'll never see us again."

"Can we talk to the hostage?"

There was a pause. "Hello." Rhiannon's voice shook with fear.

"Who is this?"

"I am Rhiannon McNeil."

"What's your father's name, Rhiannon?"

"Kenneth."

"Are you hurt?"

"That's enough, Agent Sanders." Joe's voice interrupted her. "I can't let you guys leave, Joe."

"Let us leave, or we kill her."

"Kill her, and we come in. Everyone dies, you included. That can't be what you want."

"We have bombs planted all around the county. Let us go, or I start detonating them."

"You don't have any bombs planted, Joe. Put down your weapons and come out with your hands up. You'll do some jail time and get out. Kill your hostage or blow a bomb, and you're looking at death row."

"How about this? I give you the location of one bomb. You check it out. Once you verify it's there and disable it, you let us go. Or I can start blowing them up. The first one will be during rush hour. There will be a lot of casualties."

"What is the location, Joe?"

"It's in an electrical access panel in the Walmart in Snellville. Look on the ceiling over the checkout area."

I tried to imagine being in that Walmart when the bomb squad showed up in a couple of minutes. Cars with red and blue lights screeching to a stop in front of the store. The manager announced the store was closing and please leave immediately. People running out the door with stuff.

An hour later, Agent Sanders called Joe on the radio.

"Joe, are you there?"

"Yes."

"We found the bomb, Joe. It's been disabled. It would have killed and hurt lots of people, Joe. You would be looking at murder one. Let's find a way to resolve this without a bunch of people on both sides getting hurt. What are your demands?"

"I want a Chinook helicopter to land at the top of the ravine. It should be full of fuel."

"That's going to take a while to set up."

"You have one hour."

"Can't be done, Joe."

"OK. I'll choose the first bomb. Are you going to write condolence letters to the relatives of the people who die? I'll make sure they know you could have avoided it."

"Let me see what I can do."

An hour later, the Chinook settled on the top of the east wall of the ravine. An illuminated *H* on the ground showed it where to land. The SWAT team watched a boulder plop over next to the Chinook and people come out of a passage hidden beneath it. Tarps were put up between the hole and the Chinook, shielding the movements of people into and out of the chopper from the eyes of the SWAT snipers who were watching every move.

Half an hour later, the Chinook pilot was told over the aircraft intercom to take off and proceed to the GPS coordinates she was given. High above it, an F-22 fighter followed along, doing large lazy eights. The Chinook pilot passed the destination coordinates to Agent Sanders.

"They're heading to the airport. Let's get EOD to clear the house, then see what we can find."

About halfway to the airport, the Chinook pilot got new destination coordinates over the intercom from the people in the back. The new coordinates were to a tiny island about thirty miles offshore.

EOD found one bomb after another in the house. Motion detector triggers, laser triggers, taut-line triggers, open-a-door triggers. They would be tied up for hours. If anyone had walked into that house, the whole ravine would have turned into one huge fireball. Everyone in the ravine would have died. In the back wall of the house, they found a doorway that opened into a cave complex. The cave was loaded with explosives as well. The farther they got back into the hillside, the larger the cave got. It housed a massive meth factory, a dormitory, a kitchen, and a recreation hall peppered by a massive set of bombs on top of drums of gasoline. Many had timers on them, set for midnight.

I hadn't seen or heard anything about Rhiannon. I was feeling about as helpless as a horse stuck in a fence. It wasn't a feeling I liked at all.

The command center kept getting updates from the EOD bomb squad as they uncovered and defused one bomb after another. Agent Fitzgerald ordered everyone but the EOD personnel to evacuate the ravine. If a bomb did go off, he didn't want anyone else getting hurt.

"I wouldn't have that job on a bet," Agent Sanders said in a low voice.

"Those guys are the real heroes of this operation," I agreed. "Cojones the size of baseballs. Miss one bomb in that cave, and no one would ever know whose mistake it was." We watched the EOD team work on the closed-circuit TV screens in the command center.

The Chinook reached the island and circled, waiting for further instructions. The intercom crackled to life again, giving new coordinates. They were out in the ocean, about a hundred miles offshore.

"You will rendezvous with the Iranian freighter *Abu Ishmael*," the intercom instructed, giving her the new coordinates.

The pilot relayed the new destination to her command at Fort Lewis. They notified the DEA and the Coast Guard. The Coast Guard cutter *John Fitzsimmons*, on patrol about twenty miles offshore, changed course to intercept *Abu Ishmael*.

"Davie," a quiet voice behind me said my name.

I turned. It was the old moonshiner. I still didn't know his name.

"Hi," I responded, a little shocked he had gotten through all the security around the ravine without being challenged. "Come down to see what all the commotion was about?"

"Not exacly. Once upon a time, I used them caves behind that house to make my, umm, extracts. The whole hill is riddled with them."

"Really?"

"If it were me and I wus trying to get away from these here police, I'd skedaddle out the back door while everyone's busy knocking on the front one. I heared they got your purty woman."

"Yes, they do." I tried not to let my voice show how concerned I was.

"Well, y'all come with me. Let's see if'n they's sneakin' out the back door."

I picked up my backpack and rifle, then followed the old man as he faded into the woods. He set a blistering pace up the hill by the road, angling southwest for fifteen minutes. I had no idea where we were going or even how we got there. He suddenly stopped.

I heard voices below us.

"I tell you I jus' heard somethin' up the hill."

"I don't hear nothin'."

"Is Reynolds almost ready? I wanna get outta here. This place gives me the willies."

"Should be. Let me check."

I put on my night vision goggles. Four old sedans were lined up below us. I could see where a tarp had been over them. It was laying beside the sedans next to a huge pile of brush that must have been on top of the tarps, camouflaging the cars. No one would ever have known they were there. I pulled out my cell phone to call Agent Fitzgerald. No signal. The cell towers were still off-line.

I saw them half-drag, half-carry a person who was tied up. Some cloth, like a burlap sack, was over the person's head. I figured that was Rhiannon. I sighted down my rifle at the head of the man dragging her. His head disappeared after he laid Rhiannon down. Ditto the guy next to him and the two by the door. The clip still had twenty rounds in it, but I put a new full clip in the rifle and handed it to the old man along with my other three full magazines.

"Keep them pinned down. I'm going to get Rhiannon. Push that button on the scope right there to turn on the night vision. Batteries are good for about fifteen minutes."

I pulled out my .45 and ran down the hill with my night vision goggles on. Rhiannon was lying beside the car at the end of the row. I got to her and lay down beside her. She was unconscious. Two more people came out of the tunnel. I heard two soft pops from up the hill, and they fell over. I put the .45 into my belt, picked up Rhiannon, put her over my shoulder, then ran up the hill. I know how difficult that sounds: running up a steep hill with another person over your shoulder. All I can say is adrenaline is a fantastic thing. If I had needed to fly to get her out of there, I had no doubt at that moment I could have sprouted wings. I put her down next to the old man.

"Shoot the headlights, the windshields in front of where the driver sits, and all the tires you can see."

While he was doing that, I did a quick vital signs check on Rhiannon—unresponsive, low respirations, low pulse, pinpoint pupils, sputum coming from out of the side of her mouth. She was drugged.

"What the hell?" I heard voices from down below.

The old man emptied the clip into the opening of the tunnel. He ejected that one, put in a fresh one, and put the empty in the pocket of his jacket.

I put Rhiannon over my shoulder again, and we began the hike back to the command center. She was a lot lighter than many of the men I had carried.

Agent Fitzgerald jumped up in amazement as I entered. His coffee went all over the table and his lap.

"Where're the medics set up?" I asked tersely.

"Over there." He pointed to a tent across the road. "Is that Rhiannon?"

"Yes."

"Is she hurt? I thought she was on the chopper." He was busy mopping up the spilled coffee. When I didn't answer, he looked up and realized I wasn't there anymore.

I told the medics what I had found in my initial assessment. They squirted something up her nose—Narcan probably—started pumping oxygen into her, and began checking her vitals. A moment later, the lead paramedic grabbed the radio and called the Life Flight helicopter in the cornfield across the road to get ready to transport, STAT. The chopper began to spin up its engine—the main blade rotating faster and faster. Two EMTs ran Rhiannon across to the chopper and loaded her in. They lifted off at full throttle before the door was even closed.

I went back to the command center. "Agent Fitzgerald, I suspect you need to ask the Chinook pilot to see who or what he has in the back of his aircraft. I'd get him to jettison everything that isn't human and land as soon as he can. I'd bet he has a bomb on board. And by the way, you have a bunch of bad guys on the other side of this hill that're about to leave. There's a few less than there were before. They won't get far on flat tires and no headlights. The old man over there can show you where they are."

I pointed to where the moonshiner had been a moment ago, but he was gone. My rifle was leaning against my backpack with the two empty clips and two full ones on top.

I led the SWAT team through the woods to the tunnel entrance. They took over.

"You in the cave! This is the DEA. Lay down your weapons and come out with your hands up!"

The people in the cave filed out. Most had their hands on top of their heads. They were searched, cuffed, and moved to the other side of the ravine, where two heavily-armed SWAT members kept watch on them.

I turned the dead guys over and searched them, collecting quite a pile of pistols, rifles, and shotguns. Finally, I turned over the last one, and Larry's empty eyes stared up at me. I didn't know if I had killed him or if it was the old man. I closed his eyes with my hand—what a waste.

"Who's Joe?" I asked the group of cuffed people, getting up and walking over to them.

No one answered or even met my eyes. I went back into the cave and saw them all try to move behind the cars. The cave was booby-trapped. Nothing to do but wait for EOD to clear it. The man with the close-cut beard was not among them. Neither was the fire team commander who had been next to the trucks. I shook my head—should have taken him out when I had the chance—damned lawyers.

In five minutes, the little ravine was full of flashing lights, police, and ambulances. Between the old man and me, we had killed or incapacitated ten of the eleven-man fire team. Then there was the one I shot in the ass. I still laugh about him every time I watch Forrest Gump drop his pants for Lyndon Johnson.

Ghost Ride

I walked back to my pickup on the other side of the cornfield and drove over the mountain to see how Rhiannon was doin', praying she had lived through the flight to the hospital.

Chapter 37 – Grandma's Granddaughter

I held her hand as she woke up.

"David?" she said sleepily.

"I'm right here."

"Where am I?"

"In the hospital."

"What happened?"

"They gave you an injection of cocaine and heroin. You almost died."

"I don't remember."

"That's probably good."

She sat up and pulled me to her. "I thought I'd never see you again."

I had thought the same thing. She had been resuscitated each of the three times her heart had stopped.

She was becoming alert. "I met Gina."

"Tell me about it."

"She held me in her lap. I was a little girl. I told her I was sorry she'd never been my grandmother. She laughed and said she'd always been my grandmother. She said I wasn't supposed to die—that it wasn't my time yet—that there were still things I had to do."

"Did she tell you what those things were?"

"No. I asked, though. She said I'd have to figure them out by myself."

She held me, or I held her—I guess it didn't matter. We held each other for a few minutes in silence.

"I saw the light," she said quietly.

"The one at the end of the tunnel?"

"It wasn't like I expected. There wasn't a tunnel."

"What did you see?"

"I expected a glowing archway or eminence or maybe a bunch of people waiting for me. I walked into a bright spot, like a floor with a spotlight shining on it in the middle of a huge room.

The room was utterly silent—never heard such a quiet, if that makes any sense. Can you hear quiet?"

"I don't think dreams have the same rules as reality."

"This wasn't a dream, David. Did I die?"

"Your heart stopped three times. The Crash Cart resuscitation team is ready to make you their poster child. They've never had three codes on one patient in one shift before."

She held me some more as what I said sank in. I rubbed her back and inhaled the scent of her, listening to her breathe. I think I was making sure she was still in my life.

I whispered, "Thank you." I'm not sure whom I was thanking—I've never been religious. Maybe it was to Gina for sending Rhiannon back to me. Maybe I was so grateful that she didn't die I felt like I had to thank someone. The last time I said "thank you" to anyone, it was to Doc. I had made a mistake, and he'd pulled my ass out of the fire.

"When can I go home?"

"Ask the doc when he comes around. I'll bet he lets me take you home today."

"What day is it?"

"You were unconscious for two days. Today is Monday."

"What happened at the house? Did you get those guys?"

"The two leaders escaped. We got everyone else. They're being arraigned tomorrow, the ones that are alive."

"Reynolds was actually a nice guy, in a criminal sort of way. He's the one with the beard. He ran the factory. The other guy, Nesmith—the one in charge of the soldiers—he was an asshole. I knew him from before—from when I worked at the 'motel.' He's the one who gave me the injection. He said it would calm me down."

"Write down as much as you can remember, right now while it's as fresh as it's ever going to be—every detail—every person— who did what, when, who told whom what to do. Here's a pad of paper."

She looked at the pad, then back at me, as if she couldn't believe I asked her to do this.

"It has to be done. You are going to have to talk to more Feds, cops, detectives, and prosecutors than you've ever seen. It will take weeks. Most of these guys will cop a plea to reduce their jail time. Some may go to trial, and you will be the primary witness."

"What happened to the helicopter? Nesmith put a bomb on it."

"When I discovered all the people who were supposed to be on the chopper were trying to escape out the back door, Agent Fitzgerald called the pilot. She wants to meet you, by the way. Her name is Lieutenant Romero. She unlocked the cabin access door and went back into the cargo area. It was full of rocks to simulate the weight of the people who were supposed to be there. She threw the rocks out into the ocean and found the bomb underneath them. It hit the water also but never went off. The way she described the bomb, it was a plastic explosive, probably C-4, with a timer. Enough to blow her and the chopper to hell all over the ocean. The timer had twenty-two minutes left on the display when she threw it out the door. It would have worked, too. We would have thought something went wrong, and all searching for the druggies would have stopped. All communications with the pilot were through the intercom. They taped a little audio playback device to the intercom mike. All the instructions were recorded. This escape had been planned way in advance. The rendezvous freighter didn't exist. It was just a ploy to get the chopper out into deep water."

"We would never have known about them if Tommy hadn't blown their cover."

"That and me not being willing to shrug and walk away after we found him dead. It almost cost me your life."

"You're not blaming yourself for them kidnapping me, are you?"

I looked at her, then picked up her hand and held it in mine. "I guess I am a little. I knew they were criminals, and I knew you'd be in danger if I pursued them. This is exactly why the SF never lets people participate in operations that have people you care about in 'em. You lose objectivity."

"You know what would've happened to me if you hadn't found me, if you hadn't rescued me, don't you?"

"Of course. You'd be in a morgue or at the bottom of a river somewhere."

"Well, I'm not. And you're the reason why."

"That's funny."

"What's funny? That I'm not dead?"

"No. The words you chose right then."

"Which words?"

"'And you're the reason why.' Those are the same words Gina said to me at the campsite right after I got out of the Army."

"I am my grandma's granddaughter."

"Yep."

Rhiannon picked up the pad of paper and began to write. For the next three hours, I sat in the chair next to her bed and watched her do it.

Chapter 38 – Annalee Peterson

After all the depositions and testimony were finished, our lives began to settle down a little. Rhiannon and I were local heroes. Bert Ives at the sheriff's office will probably forgive me for pushing him so hard in a few years. The DEA wanted to recruit me. I told them no thanks. I was a little tired of people trying to kill me and the people I loved. They offered me a job as a contractor, training their SWAT teams six months a year. The salary was ridiculous—over four times what I had made in the Army as an E-9. I said I would think about it.

We found Rhiannon's old Corolla upside down in a creek not far from where she was stopped. It was totaled. She got a check from her insurance company for $3,501.77. You'd think they would have rounded it up or down, but there it was. Who can explain insurance companies? I'm sure it made sense to them. We bought her a three-year-old Tacoma with four-wheel drive, a V-6, and a stick. She loved it.

I went over the mountain to the Kubota dealer and gave them the bad news about Larry.

The owner remembered me from when I bought my tractor. "I figured he was either dead or back in jail again when he didn't show up for a week."

"Do you know if he had any next of kin?"

"No. I don't. I don't think I ever saw anyone visit him but you. At least not during business hours."

"Could I look through his trailer?"

"What trailer?"

"The one he lived in. He told me you let him live in it at the back of your lot. That he doubled as night watchman."

"He didn't live here. I'd never have let him stay in the lot after hours. I have enough stuff disappearing without giving out invitations."

The way he said it brought up the hair on the back of my neck. "OK, well, thanks again for the tractor. It runs great. See ya."

The trailer I saw Larry point at when he said he was night watchman was gone. I would pass that little tidbit on to Agent Fitzgerald. I wondered if the Kubota dealer did a lot of "cash" business.

I was sitting at the diner having a cup of coffee watching Rhiannon interact with the tourists who were having lunch. She would laugh and flit from one to the next, filling coffee cups, answering questions about local history, and making suggestions about places to visit.

She came back to me and sat down after she was done with her circuit.

"I heard you make three different recommendations to tourists. Do those merchants pay you to recommend them?"

"Sure. Sometimes it's a discount on stuff I buy. Sometimes it's real cash like when people buy some property. This diner is tourist central. All the merchants have offered to pay me for referrals."

"Like Tommy did?"

"Yeah, no, well ... Tommy was a mistake. 'ST'—Since Tommy—I only refer people to merchants whom I would use. I always give some of what I get to Gus. I look at it as a win-win-win. The customer gets what he or she needs without having to shop all over town. The merchant gets the business, which Lord knows *they* need. I get some extra cash to help with the kids' college fund."

I had a thought. "Did Herman Goldstein give you a payment for recommending him?"

"Yeah, well, no, not actually. He offered, but I turned him down. I told him to apply it to your bill. You may have noticed his last bill was about a grand less than he had estimated."

"I thought he was being honest about what it had cost."

"He was. Paying me was part of the estimate. When I declined, he removed it from your bill."

"I'll be damned. I knew I liked him."

"He's a nice guy. His wife Shirley is a sweetheart, too."

Rhiannon's kids contacted her after the drug bust made national news. They were planning to visit over the course of the summer. I was excited to meet them. I had never lived around kids and several of them already had children of their own. I was so ready to have the large family I had never been part of and always wanted to be.

I started training Gina to hunt. She was a natural. I can't think of many things I would rather do than wander around these hills with her. But instead of shooting game with my rifle, I figured I would shoot them with my camera this time. I bought a new 80-400mm zoom lens that was perfect and started practicing on my favorite subject—Rhiannon.

Gina and I were working up a hillside one morning when I realized we were at the mouth of the little ravine where I met the old bootlegger. I decided to wander up and say hi. We followed the old roadway. It was overgrown with weeds and underbrush. Looked like it hadn't been used in years. Way back in the ravine, hidden by the trees, we discovered an aging F-350. It was leaning to one side on two flat tires. The windows were broken out and it was full of bullet holes. A very healthy blackberry bush was growing out of the engine compartment, which had the hood up. The engine, transmission, and most of the accessories were gone. The last time a registration tab had been put on the license plate was twelve years ago.

The next day in the station, I asked Josh, "Do you know an old bootlegger who lives up Shady Road by the Emmersons?"

Josh gave me a strange look, then stared out the front window. "Yes and no."

"You wanna maybe give me a little more info?"

"Why do you ask?"

I told him about my encounters with the old man and how he'd helped me when I rescued Rhiannon.

Josh listened to me without saying a word. When I finished he continued to look out the window then shook his head.

"Damnedest story I've ever heard."

"That he helped me? I'm not sure I could have rescued Rhiannon without his help."

"No. Not that part. At least ... well let me tell you about the old man. He's your uncle. His name is Glen Peterson. He was your father's brother."

"Why do you say 'was'?"

"He died about twelve years ago, a couple of years after your mom passed."

"Why don't I know anything about him? Neither Mom nor Dad ever mentioned him."

"Are you sure you want to know this?"

I considered it. There was something Josh was hiding. I had no idea what it was but it must be pretty big, based on his reluctance to tell me. But I had to find out what the big secret was. "Yeah. Let me have it."

"OK," he paused again collecting his thoughts. "Your mom and Glen were always very close. Both your dad and your uncle were suitors for your mother's hand. ... After she chose your dad, Glen enlisted in the Army and went to Vietnam. When he came back, he went up into the hills and began making moonshine. He would visit your mom and dad every so often but, from what your dad told me, the visits were always strained. When your mom miscarried your sister ..."

"I didn't know anything about a miscarriage."

"I guess that's not a surprise either. It was hard on both of your parents. They would have shielded you from it. It was even harder on your dad than your mom, I think. He withdrew from everyone, but especially her. Somehow I think he blamed her. Or maybe he wanted a daughter so much he didn't know how to deal with the pain of losing her. Then your mom got an infection after the miscarriage that scared her tubes shut. She couldn't have any more children. So your mom reached out to Glen for comfort. They had an affair. Your dad found out and threatened to kill Glen. Glen left their house and never went back. After your mom died, there was a rose on your mom's grave on her birthday every year until Glen died."

It was my turn to look out the window. A new guy was setting up business in Tommy's old service station. I watched him and the high school kids he'd hired working on the station—cleaning and painting.

You never really knew people, even your parents. It was easy to forget parents are people too. I knew about the strain in my parents' relationship. But I had ignored it. They were Mom and Dad, not people with problems.

"If Glen is dead, how did he help me capture the drug people?"

"I don't know." Josh was watching the people across the street also. "If anyone else had told me that story, I would have called him a liar and shown him the door. For now, I'm going to file this under 'Strange things that happen in Chambersville.' It's not the first strange thing and, I suppose, it won't be the last."

That night I went up to Mom's grave behind the house and looked down at it. Rhiannon had cleaned and weeded the family cemetery while she did the landscaping. The freshly painted fence was beautiful. New flowers were blooming.

Mom's headstone simply said: Annalee Peterson. No epitaph. No inscription. No dates. That was what she requested in her will. She died about three years after Dad. Dad's tombstone beside hers said: Amos Peterson—Loving husband and father. His stone listed both his birth and death dates.

Beside Mom's grave was another headstone with the name Dorothy Peterson on it. It had a single date. I was two. Mom always said the person buried there was her sister—that she died in childbirth.

On Mom's grave was a single, fresh, red rose. I realized with a start that today was Mom's birthday.

Chapter 39 – André

Samantha decided she would take the plea bargain. The whole drug factory scene disgusted her. The money was great, but what good was money if you didn't live to spend it? She knew the first name of the cop—the Voice at the End of the Line. She figured she could turn that into a reduction of time for her sentence.

"So what you're telling me," she told her court-appointed attorney, "is, if I tell them the name of the Voice, they will reduce my sentence to one year? With credit for time served and the rest suspended?"

"That's right, kind of. They also want you to tell them all you can about the drug factory and who ran it. And you'd enter the witness protection program. They would set you up with a new identity in a new place with a job. And they would clean your record."

"I want that in writing. Once I give it to them, can they go back on it?"

"Not without a massive lawsuit. And I would really like to represent you on that one. You'd be rich for the rest of your life."

"OK. Tell them I'll give it to them."

Her attorney walked out to deliver the message.

This whole factory thing began going downhill when Marley became friends with that tweaker, Tommy. She tried to tell him Tommy didn't want to be friends. All he wanted was free meth. Marley hadn't bought any of it. Then the two of them talked her into that visit to that fucking Green Beret's house. She knew as soon as they set foot on the property, something was seriously wrong. Sometimes you get a feeling—a GET THE HELL OUT OF HERE! feeling that it's time to go before you get out of the car. She got that feeling and all in caps, too. But Tommy and Marley were so caught up in trashing the place, both of them ignored her. Marley started throwing furniture out the windows and smashing stuff with that goddamned sledgehammer. Tommy went out in the barn to trash it, then he came backi in with a bunch of spray cans and started covering the walls with graffiti. The only part she really got into was when they took a shit in the basement, already being so scared she didn't even have to try. Then when they came back upstairs and walked into the kitchen, things really got weird. An apron started dancing across the floor like it was being worn by an invisible person. All the knives started coming out of the drawers and flying around the room. One buried itself in the wall next to Tommy. Another stopped about half an inch from Marley's neck—floating in mid-air, spinning like a drill. A meat cleaver started swinging back and forth like the pendulum in that book by Edgar Allan something she read in high school. Tommy and Marley had yelled, run out of the house, and jumped into the truck. Tommy started the engine and put it in gear. She had to dive into the bed, or they would have left her there. She began to distance herself from Marley after that.

Her attorney came back in. "Here's the guarantee. Two copies. One for you and one for them."

She read it, signed both. "His first name is André. He's a detective for the Nehalitz County sheriff. When we wanted to contact him, Reynolds would leave a draft e-mail on Andre77@hotmail.com. He would always call us. We never called him."

Agent Fitzgerald walked into the room a day later. "Hi, Samantha. Thanks for agreeing to help us. I have a few questions about the factory. Is that OK?"

"Sure."

"Who was 'Joe'?"

"'Joe' was Nesmith."

"Nesmith who?"

"I have no idea. We never used last names. He showed up with his team of jerks about the time we started packing the trucks."

"Is this Nesmith?" He slid a picture in front of her of a corpse the Los Angeles police had fished out of Los Angeles harbor two days ago.

"Yes."

"Good job on the composite drawing you did with the artist, by the way." He smiled at her approvingly. "The LAPD ID'ed him right away from it. How did you meet Reynolds?"

"In a bar in Vancouver."

"Vancouver, B.C.? In Canada?"

"No. Vancouver in Washington State."

\---------------------------

The questioning of Samantha went on for days. Slowly a picture of life in the factory, recruiting techniques, distribution techniques, payment techniques, and their whole method of operation came to light. Samantha knew a lot more than she had thought.

Chapter 40 – Injun Clothes

"Frank's coming over tonight," Rhiannon said as she came in the door.

"Great! He must be feeling better. He hasn't come over in weeks."

"I hope so. He looked terrible last time. Any word from his doc on that experimental treatment?"

"Not that I've heard," I said thoughtfully. "What do you think he wants to eat? Tacos seemed to upset his stomach last time. And I didn't put any hot sauce or chili powder in at all."

"I thought we should fix breakfast for dinner. Cheese grits, scrambled eggs, fresh biscuits, hash browns, bacon, orange juice."

My stomach started growling as she chose a menu.

"You get my vote. Is it done yet? I could eat two plates."

"I'll make sure there's enough," she promised. She loved that I loved her cooking.

Frank showed up about an hour later. I watched him through the window. He stopped to catch his breath after he walked up the three steps to the porch.

"Hi, Frank. Good to see you. Come on in."

"Hi, David. Hi, Rhiannon."

"Glass of water, Frank?" Rhiannon was already bringing one for him.

"Sure." He sat in a chair without removing his coat. His cheeks were sunken. He'd lost even more weight. His eyes were dull and lifeless. The glass of water sat on the end table next to him, untouched. "The house is really coming along."

"Do you like the new picture I bought?" Rhiannon pointed to a print of a famous Monet water lily scene she bought at the flea market a weekend ago. "I heard about a guy who bought a flea market painting, and it turned out to be a real Renoir. When I saw this one, I had to buy it."

"Maybe you'll get lucky," Frank said, smiling weakly.

"I already am." She smiled at him, then smiled at me. "Lucky enough for the rest of my life."

I blushed. I haven't blushed in twenty years, but I blushed then.

"I'm really glad you two are so happy." He took a breath and swallowed. "I have some news for you. I've stopped the treatment. It wasn't working anyway."

"So, what are you going to do now?" Rhiannon asked. "Is there another treatment you can try?"

"Nope, there is no other treatment. I've stopped all medication."

Rhiannon and I were stunned; we had no idea what to say.

"What that means is I'm going to die," Frank continued. "I have something like three months to live. David, you asked me to be best man at your wedding. I still want to do that, but I won't be alive when you plan to have it at the end of the summer. So if you still want me to do it, you'll have to move up the date."

I looked at Rhiannon. She looked at me, then nodded. I nodded back.

"How about six weeks from now, Frank? Is that too late? Would you be able to do it then?" I checked the calendar. "How about June 21?"

"That'll work."

Rhiannon smiled and picked up his hand. "That's the anniversary of our moving into this house. That'll be perfect." She heard a sound from the kitchen. "Oh my gosh, the bacon!" She ran out of the room.

Dinner seemed a little forced. Frank tried to eat but really only pushed his food around the plate a little. When we were done, he said goodbye and walked slowly out to his car. We watched the taillights disappear down the driveway.

"We have to tell everyone who's coming to move up the date," I said, still watching the driveway where Frank's car had been.

"What reason can we give? Frank won't want us announcing he's dying."

"Tell them you're pregnant," I snickered.

"I wish I could." She looked up into my eyes. "I would have loved to have your baby."

I pulled her to me and held her tightly, trying hard not to release the emotion that threatened to overwhelm me.

"We'll have to make sure we are a big part of our grandchildren's lives."

The plans for the wedding were suddenly on the fast track. Who would have thought two old people who'd already been married once would have so much to do to get married again? We had to get a license, get blood tests, find a band, and choose wedding rings and flowers. Gus said he'd cater it. Because the weather in Washington was so unpredictable, we decided to rent a tent. Luckily the tent people also rented tables, chairs, and port-a-potties. Every time we had reached the end of the list, the list got longer.

Rhiannon and I were walking around the property after dusk one night figuring out where to place the parking and tent when a car I didn't recognize pulled up the driveway. High above us, an owl hooted, then took wing into the night, flying right across the face of the full moon that had cleared the horizon a few minutes before. I braced myself, not sure for what, but knowing it was coming. Rhiannon felt me get tense and looked up into my face, then at the car.

"Hello?" a woman called to us, getting out of the car.

"Hi. What can I do for you?" I asked, walking up to her.

She was young, beautiful, almost as tall as me, and had Asian features with smooth, clean skin, and long wavy black hair that glistened in the moonlight. Her knee-length dark blue silk dress was stunning, but her high heels kept sinking into our lawn.

"Are you David Peterson?"

"Yes, I am. Who are you?"

"I'm Amy Peterson. I'm your daughter."

Seeing the look of complete shock frozen onto my face, Rhiannon took over. "Hi, Amy. I'm Rhiannon."

She gave Amy a quick hug.

"Amy, what are you doing here?" I asked, finally remembering how to talk. "You're the last person in the world I expected to show up. Did my message to your mother get through?"

"I don't know anything about a message to Mom, but I was within a thousand miles, so I thought I'd drop by." Amy tried to laugh at her joke, but it came out a little hollow. "I figured it was time to get to meet you. Gus at the diner said I'd find you guys up here. I got a little lost finding the way. He said to say 'Hi.'"

She laughed again, a little nervously this time.

"Well, welcome," I said. "But first things first."

I held open my arms. Amy walked into them, and I hugged my daughter for the first time in my life.

"I thought I'd never get to get to know you," I whispered into her ear, rubbing her back. Then I kissed the side of her neck and hugged her again, making sure she was real.

"Well, here I am," she spun around then looked at me hopefully. "Disappointed?"

"Surprised. Amazed. Ecstatic. But absolutely not disappointed. I've dreamed of this day for twenty-two years. Let's go inside."

The three of us walked into the house. I sat down and patted the chair next to me. Amy sat down a little awkwardly. She looked like she wasn't sure she hadn't made a mistake coming here. I studied her face for the first time. My daughter! My very own daughter, sitting next to me! I think my staring made her even more uncomfortable.

We had a long pause. No one knew what to say next.

Amy took a deep breath. "Actually, I didn't come up here on a social visit." She hesitated again, like she was having trouble finding the right words. "Mom threw me out." Her chin started to wiggle a little, but her face got hard with resolve. "I'm pregnant, and my boyfriend left when he found out. I don't have anywhere else to go."

Both Rhiannon and I looked at her without a clue what to say.

After another awkward silence, Rhiannon asked, "How long have you been pregnant?"

"About six weeks, according to my OB."

"I take it this wasn't a planned pregnancy?" I asked.

"Nope. Too much wine on a Friday night."

"Well, you can stay as long as you want," I said to her. "The only thing our house is missing is baby noises. Is the father out of the picture?"

"I think the answer to that would be a resounding 'Yes.' He went back to Thailand. His mother has already set him up with another woman, someone from a royal family. They are supposed to get married by the end of the year. I was a dalliance, to be discarded when soiled."

"I think you two have some catching up to do." Rhiannon got up. "I'll make some coffee."

Without trying to be obvious about it, I studied my daughter in the light. She was gorgeous. I could see her mother in her, and I could see me as well.

Both of us sat there in silence, not sure what to say.

"Have you thought of names for your baby?" I asked, trying to put her at ease.

"No. I thought I'd wait until I find out her gender."

Then why are you calling your child a "her," I asked myself. My mother had people coming to her all the time for her to predict their baby's gender. No surprise if Amy had the talent also. She just didn't know it yet.

"What are the names of your parents, grandparents, and great-grandparents?" she asked, looking me straight in the eyes. There was no fear or remorse there. She emanated intelligence and resolve. I felt pride begin to grow inside me.

I started listing them and giving my family history. "Annalee was my mother, Amos my father, Glen my uncle, and my father's brother." I continued with my grandparents, then my great-grandparents. When I got to Itswoot and Duha, Amy started and grabbed my hand.

"Duha? Did you say Duha?"

She pronounced it a little differently than I did. I said great-grandmother's name as DOO-ha with the accent on the first syllable. She put the accent on the last syllable, doo-HA.

"Yes, she was the daughter of two slaves. I think it's an African name. She was born in Independence, Missouri, right after the Civil War. She migrated here with two friends and settled nearby. She was a midwife to this whole area. After she and her friends settled here, she met Itswoot, a member of the local Indian tribe. They fell in love and married."

Amy looked out the window into the night without saying a word, still clutching my hand.

"Why do you ask? Does that name mean something to you?"

"It's the name of my mother's mother. Duha is a Thai name also. She was the only one in my mother's family who supported me when I found out I was pregnant."

The little voice in my head started up. "Your granddaughter will be named Duha. She will ..."

Never mind! I told the voice silently. *I wanna find out for myself.*

For the first time in my life, the voice stopped when I told it to. I thought I heard a chuckle, but I could have been mistaken.

Rhiannon handed us both coffee. "Milk or sugar?"

"Black's fine," Amy said, smiling.

"Yes, it is," I said, taking my cup of black coffee from Rhiannon. "Amy, are you too tired to talk for a while? I'm dying to know about the who, what, where, why, and when of you. But you've just driven a thousand miles. My curiosity will wait until tomorrow."

"Actually, I feel great. I slept in Grants Pass last night. I think I'm still on overdrive from the trip up here."

"Then please start at the beginning. What do you like to do? What do you want to do? What do you read? What movies do you watch? What classes are you taking? What do you do for fun? I have twenty-two years of catchin' up to do."

She smiled at me then, reached out, and squeezed my hand. "I'm a prelaw major. Mother made me do Law, but my first love is marine biology."

She talked about her past, her hopes, and her dreams. I listened, spellbound.

Finally, I noticed Amy had yawned twice in the last sentence. I glanced at the clock on the mantle over the fireplace. It showed past midnight!

"Amy, it's been a big day for everyone. You're staying here, right? Do you have anything in the car? A suitcase?"

"Yeah. Maybe I should get it."

"I don't mind," I said, getting up. "I think I can find a suitcase."

The rear seat of her car was piled with personal belongings, wall-to-wall, floor-to-ceiling. The passenger seat in front overflowed with plants. I got her suitcase from on top of the pile in the back and walked back inside.

"Let me show you to your room. It used to be mine when I grew up here. I'll clean it out tomorrow, and you can move all your stuff in. Will those plants in your passenger seat be all right tonight?"

"I'm sure they will." She yawned again. "How cold will it get tonight?"

"Maybe forty-five."

"Yeah, they'll be fine."

"Do you need anything else out of your car for tonight?"

"Nope."

I carried her suitcase upstairs and showed her to my old room.

"The bathroom is right there—I pointed down the hallway. Why don't you go first? Here's a fresh towel and washcloth."

She hesitated in the doorway to my old room and yawned again. "Dad, I'm glad I finally got to meet you." She hesitated again. "I hope it's OK to call you 'Dad'?"

"Dad is wonderful!"

I had waited twenty-two years to hear my daughter call me "Dad." I hugged her again, and she hugged me back, hard.

Rhiannon made her famous biscuits and gravy for breakfast. We ate quietly, not wanting to wake Amy. She came downstairs as we were finishing up.

"You should have woken me," she said as she rubbed her face. "It's so quiet here! I didn't wake until the sun hit my pillow."

I fixed a plate for her. Rhiannon got her a cup of coffee.

"Was the bed OK? I can get a new mattress if you'd like. That one's at least forty years old."

"The bed's fine. I could have slept on rocks last night."

She took a bite. "Yum! This is fabulous."

Rhiannon smiled at the compliment. "Thanks, honey! How do you like your eggs?"

"Over medium."

After she finished eating, she looked out the window, then looked at me.

"Dad, why didn't you come for me? Why weren't you part of my childhood? I spent my whole life wondering who you were and why I wasn't in your life."

I had been dreading that question since Amy showed up.

"I couldn't," I said sadly. "Your mom took out a restraining order against me. I wasn't allowed within a mile of either one of you."

"Why did she do that?" Amy asked, astonished and obviously doubting what I had said. "She never said anything about it to me."

"I never understood your mother. She wanted to come to the US. As soon as we got here, she split up with me and got that restraining order. I haven't seen her since the divorce."

Both of us were quiet for a while.

"Actually, it's not fair to put all the blame on your mother," I continued. "I tried once to get the court's permission to get visitation rights to see you. You were six at the time. Your mother fought me hard in court. And I gave up. I shouldn't have. Instead, I wrapped myself in a cocoon of self-justification and went heart and soul into being a soldier. It was the easy way out, and I've regretted it ever since." I reached over, picked up her hand, and looked into her eyes. "I'm sorry. I was wrong. Can you forgive me?"

She continued to hold my hand and stared out the window again for a moment. "The way I look at it, we've both just met each other. Let's see what happens."

"OK. I like the sound of that."

We finished our coffee in silence.

I was curious about why she would pack everything into her car and drive from LA to my house, never having met me, not having any idea what her reception would be.

"Why did you decide to come here? I mean, instead of calling? It's a long drive when you didn't know if you were going to stay or even what you'd find."

"Hard times call for hard choices," she said, pursing her lips and looking out the window again. "My first responsibility was to my baby. Mom demanded I get an abortion. I refused. She went ballistic and ordered me out of the house. She stopped paying the rent on my apartment and tuition at school. She said my 'mistake' had embarrassed her to her family, that I was no longer her daughter."

A tear rolled down her cheek as she continued in a monotone. "It was either live on the street, go on welfare, or find someone who would let me move in with them. I wasn't going to live on the street or go on welfare in LA with a new baby. I could only think of two places to go: your house or Seattle to live with an ex-roommate. Seattle was Plan B. She was waiting for me to show up yesterday. After we went to bed, I called her to say I was staying here."

I wondered to myself, *What really happened between Amy and her mom? Who really got her pregnant? Maybe I'll find out someday. Not a bad story, though—royalty in Thailand, my ass! The tear was a nice touch. I think I'll make a couple of phone calls tomorrow.*

I took her hand in mine again and smiled. "Well, as unexpected as you were, I'm thrilled you chose me as Plan A. You can stay as long as you like. As soon as I come back from my run, I'll clean out the bedroom. Let me know if you'd like some help carrying in your stuff or getting organized."

"Do you want some company?" she asked. "On your run?"

"Do you think you should run, being pregnant and all? Couldn't it hurt the baby?"

"My doc says to keep doing what I had been doing. I ran in the LA Marathon last year."

"OK, then. I would love some company."

I braced myself for a loaf run instead of my normal six-minute miles. I needn't have worried. She led as we started. I was still trying to catch up at the end of the first mile. I passed her and led for mile two. She passed me on a long uphill and led for two more miles, her ponytail bouncing in front of me effortlessly. I passed her at mile four. We ran the last two miles at marathon speeds, neck and neck. I would like to say I let her win or cop an excuse about being fifty, but the truth is: she beat me. Gonna have to work on that. I'm gettin' soft when a cute Asian girl half my age and pregnant can run my ass into the ground.

Plans for the wedding were slowly coming together until the day I found Rhiannon and Amy sitting in the living room with Rhiannon in tears. She had the box with her mother's wedding dress open. Sometime in the last fifty years, the mice had destroyed it. She had been planning to wear that dress at our wedding.

"Would you consider something a little out of the ordinary?" I asked, my eyes twinkling.

"What do you mean 'out of the ordinary'?" Rhiannon asked, knowing that look. Amy stared at me with no idea what to expect from my warped sense of humor.

"How *far* out of the ordinary are we talking about?" Rhiannon continued. "Swimming suits? Tie-die? In the buff?" She got a twinkle in *her* eyes. "You wear the dress, and I wear the tux?"

"No, nothing like that." I giggled a little, enjoying the image of her walking down the aisle, naked in a white veil. "My great-grandmother, Duha married Itswoot not far from where we're sitting." Both women stared at me without understanding. I decided some family history needed to be shared.

"Duha was a midwife. Long before Itswoot proposed to Duha, Duha and Lawis, the tribal midwife, became close friends. Lawis and Lawis's mother had made the dress Lawis was married in. It took the two of them over a year to do all the beading. Lawis never had a daughter of her own to pass it on to. When Itswoot asked Duha to marry him, Lawis gave Duha her handmade wedding dress as a wedding present. I've only seen it twice. Mom showed it to me when I was a kid. I found it vacuum-sealed in a watertight trunk in the attic. It was in perfect condition, the leather as supple and beautiful as it must have been a hundred years ago."

I could see in her eyes that Rhiannon wasn't convinced.

"Let me see it before I decide," she said.

"OK." I went upstairs and retrieved the dress.

Both Rhiannon and Amy gasped when they saw it.

"Mom told me Lawis even cured the leather herself—that her husband shot the deer with his bow before he became her husband."

It was white deerskin with beading up both sides in the front, then continued over the shoulders and down the back. Six-inch fringe went up both sleeves and around the bottom of the skirt. It had a beaded belt to match. Rhiannon put it on. It fit her trim figure like it had been made for her.

"I absolutely love it, David." She spun around, looking at herself in the mirror. "Could we have an Indian theme for the wedding?"

"Sure. What would I wear?"

"Well, what would an Indian groom have worn?"

"Hard to say. Before white settlers made first contact, the local Indians wore leather clothes in the winter and nothing much beyond a breechclout, kind of a loincloth, in the summer—both men and women. Along came the first white settlers, and suddenly everyone was wearing pants, shirts, and dresses. The Indians pretty much fell all over themselves to dress like the settlers—like they were in a contest to out-white each other. They gave up living in their traditional multifamily cedar lodges and started living in single-family houses. The whole tribal community slowly disintegrated until some far-seeing tribal members said 'screw this' and started organizing the tribe into a cohesive unit again."

"Do you know how to tan deerskin?"

"Yes."

"Well, we'll make you a wedding outfit to match mine."

"We have three weeks. That's not nearly long enough. Mom said Lawis and her mother spent a year making that dress. I have another idea. How about we go to the local tribal headquarters and ask them? I would be willing to bet they could help us out, especially if we lend that dress to them to display in their museum after the ceremony."

The next day we visited the tribal headquarters, which doubled as a tribal heritage museum. The tribal leader (they don't call them "chiefs" anymore) also doubled as curator. He walked up to us and introduced himself. He was a little smaller than me but looked more muscular.

"I am Roy Whitedeer. What can I do for you?" He had salt-and-pepper braids down both sides of his round, almost Asian face that was deeply creased. Around him was an aura of peace and humor.

I explained what we wanted and showed him my great-grandmother's dress. He was astonished at its beauty, artistry, and perfect condition. Lawis, as it turned out, was his great-great-aunt.

"The tribe will be thrilled to add this to our display of tribal clothing."

He allowed us to borrow a beaded leather tunic and pants that fit me perfectly. He also allowed me to use a matching leather headband.

Amy walked up to me, excited. "That basket looks like the one we have in the living room!" She pointed across the room at one on display in a sealed case.

"A master basket weaver named Mary Kiona made that basket," Roy explained. "If you have one of her baskets, be very careful with it. It is very valuable. She was one of the last weavers in our tribe who could make watertight baskets."

"Maybe you would like to have it on loan to display next to the other one?" I suggested. I could see Amy's child wanting to play with the pretty basket.

"That would be wonderful! We have only one sample of her work. She died forty-three years ago when she was one hundred and twenty-one years old. All the rest of her baskets were sold or lost before she died."

"I'll bring the basket when I return the tunic and pants. We'll have a baby in the house soon, and I'd hate to have that basket ruined as a plaything. Tell me about the feathers men wore during ceremonies. Should I wear one or not? Could you loan me one to wear in this headband?"

"I cannot give you an eagle feather to wear in it because that can only be worn after it is awarded by the tribal council."

"I have my grandfather's feather. He was Black Eagle."

"That does not matter. You still cannot wear it. Only tribal members can wear such a thing."

"I understand," I said, disappointed. "I will honor your traditions. There is a right way and a wrong way to do everything."

He looked me in the eye without blinking for several breaths.

"You are David Peterson, the Green Beret. The tribe knows of you and your grandfather. Black Eagle was like a father to me. He taught me to shoot a bow when I was a boy. Let me contact the rest of the council and see if anything can be done. I will let you know."

Rhiannon and I dove into finishing the rest of the arrangements for the wedding. I resigned myself to wearing my headband without a feather. All of Rhiannon's children were coming, along with all of their children. We got Frank to the tux rental place and had him measured.

Frank shook his head when they took his measurements. "All my life, I would have killed to have this waist size. Now it just means I'm dying. Sometimes life isn't fair."

Rhiannon asked Amy to be the Maid of Honor. She allowed Amy to pick any dress she wanted. So, Amy scheduled a weekend in Seattle by herself to visit some friends and go shopping.

Doc planned to fly in the Friday before the wedding. Four other A-team members were also coming. They would drive up from the airport together.

Rhiannon seemed quiet at dinner that night. "David?" she finally asked me.

"What's up?"

"I want to invite some of the girls I used to work with at the 'motel.' Would you mind?"

"Of course not. Any friend of yours..."

"Great!" She leaned over and kissed me. And I kissed her back.

On the third kiss, Amy looked out the window, sighed, and said, "OK, you two. Get a room!"

The Wednesday night before the wedding, a knock sounded at the door. Five brown-skinned men, including Roy Whitedeer, stood outside.

"David Peterson, you must come with us."

I looked back at Rhiannon. She smiled and motioned for me to go with them. I did. They put a bag over my head, tied my hands and feet, then put me into the back of a truck. The last time this happened to me did not end well. I was more than a little nervous at being tied up but tried to relax. Knowing the knots were so loose I could easily pull my hands out helped a little.

The truck drove for a while, then stopped. They carried me into a building and sat me on the floor. My hands and feet were untied, then they removed the bag. We were in a low cedar building that reeked of sweat, smoke, and fish.

All the men removed their clothes and put on breechclouts. I was handed one also. I did as they did. A low fire was burning in the middle of the hut. Roy removed some of the rocks surrounding the fire with wooden tongs and dropped them into a bucket of water.

Steam filled the air. Another man started intoning a chant. Another put some sage on the fire—the room filled with fragrant smoke.

Sweat covered us. The men picked up small drums about the size of a phonograph album and started rhythmic drumming. The man next to me gave me one and motioned for me to join in.

That went on for hours—drumming and sweating. One of the men started chanting. I listened to the words but had no idea what they meant. One by one, the other men joined in. The man next to me nudged me in the ribs. I tried to say the same words. No one seemed bothered by my bumbling along. Roy seemed to waver in the air in front of me.

The smoke was thick. There seemed to be some other smells besides the sage. I felt light—like I was floating.

A ghostly image appeared in front of me—my uncle, Glen. None of the other men in the sweat lodge paid him any attention at all—almost as if they didn't see him.

"Hi, Davie," the image spoke.

"Uncle Glen. Why didn't you tell me you were my uncle?"

"I ain't your uncle, Davie."

I frowned, trying to make sense of what he'd said. The analytical side of my mind did not cooperate. "Yes, you are," I managed. "Josh told me you are. You're Dad's brother."

"Josh wus wrong, Davie. Amos was my brother, but he's not your pa. I'm your pa."

"So you're telling me ..."

"Me and your ma, we always loved each other. I ain't proud of it, but there it is."

In a moment of clarity, I realized that explained a lot of things.

"So that's why Dad was so torn up when Dorothy died. She would have been his only blood child."

"Yep."

"And then Mom couldn't have any more children."

"Yep."

I thought about what he'd told me, revisiting all the memories of Mom and Dad and the interactions between them. He waited for me to work through it.

"Why didn't Mom marry you?" I asked.

"We had a stupid fight. She were mad at me and told him yes, out of spite. Once she said them words, there weren't no going back. Not in them days."

I thought about that also.

"Why're you still here?"

"I figured, being your pa, you'd need me sooner or later. We kicked the ass o' them drug runners, didn't we?" He cackled a little.

"Yeah, I guess we did."

"I believe I can go now, Davie. Never really got to be 'pa' to you. That little time we had together was all I'll ever have." He sighed, then smiled. "Gonna miss that sweet rifle of yers, too. Hope they got something jus as good on the other side."

"Goodbye, Pa," the first and last time in my life I ever got to say that to my biological father.

"Goodbye, Son."

"David Peterson." I blinked and saw Roy looking at me. Pa was nowhere in sight. "You have been brought here because you are a warrior who has brought great honor to your tribe. Your grandfather is Black Eagle. He has spoken to us from the afterlife. He is proud to have you in his clan, proud to claim you as his grandson. Tonight we make official what has always been. You are a member of our tribe. Your Indian name is Black Grizzly. Black because your grandfather is Black Eagle. Grizzly because your enemies quake before you as you cut them down without fear. Such an animal does not exist in nature. It only exists in your heart. Now it exists in our tribe as well. Welcome, brother."

Each of the men stood and clasped me to their chest. When we were done, Roy presented me with a single eagle feather. He tied it with a leather thong around my head then we filed out of the sweat lodge. The sun was coming up. We had been in there for the entire night. I felt like I was walking two feet above the ground. I started to remove my breechclout.

Roy stopped me with a serious expression on his face. "You are Indian now. You must wear that for the rest of the day and at all Indian functions."

When they dropped me off at the house, Rhiannon ran out to greet me. She wrinkled her nose at the smoky smell I brought along, then waved at the men in the truck.

"Thank you," she told them.

They smiled and waved back as they left. She pulled me into the house and then started taking off her clothes. I cocked my head and watched what she was doing. My mind still spun from the night of smoke and sweat.

"I have my own tribal induction ceremony all planned," she explained, her face flushed with excitement. "Is my brave too worn-out?"

"I'm just old." I made a muscleman pose. "I'm not dead."

I looked around for Amy.

"She went to Seattle for a couple of days. Remember?"

I found out one thing about Indian clothes I liked a lot. The breechclout made making love a lot more convenient than pants and underwear. A little tuck and pull, and we were ready for business. And white people think they have all the answers.

Chapter 41 – Handcuffs

"Grant, could you step into my office for a second?" Sheriff Crook's voice came over the intercom on the phone.

"Oh, shit," Bert said to him. "What'd you do now?"

"Don't know. Guess I'll find out. Maybe he has a new case he wants to assign to me."

Bert looked at the piles of cases on both of their desks and sighed.

When Grant came into Sheriff Crook's office, two other men in suits were there.

"Hi, Grant. Have a seat. These two fellows are from the DEA. They have some questions for you."

"Detective Burnett, do you know your rights under the Fifth Amendment?"

Grant looked back and forth between the two men. "What's this about? Do I need a lawyer?"

"You have the right to remain silent. Anything you say can and will be used as evidence against you. ..."

Grant sat down heavily while the DEA agent finished his Miranda statement.

"Detective Burnett, you are under arrest for conspiracy to manufacture, distribute and sell a controlled substance ..."

Sheriff Crook sat watching Grant with his lips pursed while the charges were read to him, another good cop falling for the lure of easy money. He unsnapped his gun and held it on Grant under his desk. "Let me have your gun and badge, Grant. I don't think you'll need them for a while. The one on your ankle, too. You are suspended with pay until the outcome of the investigation."

Grant reached under his jacket for his gun.

"Real easy, Grant. Two fingers."

Grant stared at the sheriff in disbelief. "After all these years? You believe them?"

"I don't know who to believe, Grant. Let the investigation run its course. I truly hope you are cleared, and this is complete bullshit. If you are cleared, your job is here for you. Until then, you are still being paid. Everyone is innocent until proven guilty. Treat this as a vacation."

"The last time I started a vacation in handcuffs, I was in Vegas, and she was a lot prettier than these guys."

No one laughed.

The entire sheriff's office watched in silence while the agents led Grant out in handcuffs to the unmarked gray sedan waiting outside. Two other DEA detectives unplugged and bundled up Grant's computer. After Bert moved all Grant's casework onto his own desk, they packed everything that remained into boxes. Outside, a tow truck loaded Grant's car for transportation to the DEA impound lot.

Two other DEA agents had already executed a search warrant at Grant's rental house and were in the process of cleaning out Grant's home office and safe. The Nehalitz County Sheriff's Office tied Grant to André Ivanovich, one of their detectives, on the basis of phone calls between the two. The two of them had apparently worked together to hide the meth lab.

Chapter 42 – Can I Get That in Writing?

Grant watched Agent Fitzgerald from across the stainless steel table. A piece of paper and a pen were the only things on the table. Neither of the men said anything. The table was in an investigation room, bolted to the floor, as were the chairs the men sat on. On the wall behind Agent Fitzgerald was a mirrored window.

Grant had been in the room being questioned all day. He'd been in this same kind of room hundreds of times over the course of his career—only he'd been the one sitting with his back to the mirror. Behind that mirror, a camera recorded them sitting here and every word they said. The Assistant US Attorney for the district was probably in there also, hoping for a crack in the armor to appear.

Grant closed his eyes and thought back to when this began. Someone broke into his house. His cop's house! Who the hell breaks into a cop's house? His new TV had been stolen along with his spare pistol. That was all they took, which said a lot about the value of the rest of his shit. Even a tweaker wouldn't steal it.

His wife, or ex-wife, to be exact, had taken everything else of value. What he had left was a pile of shit you couldn't even give away at a garage sale—the kind of furniture you see on the side of the road with a homeless person sleeping on it. He hadn't owned anything that wasn't chipped, scarred, or broken. And his ex-wife got most of his salary to pay for their kids' child support and her goddamned alimony.

It had been right after the divorce. His oldest son came for a weekend visit. Grant found some cocaine in the boy's book bag. When Grant raised hell with his ex, somehow the whole thing turned out to be Grant's fault: he was never home, his cop life was more important than his family life, he didn't show any emotion, he never *hugged* his kid, for God's sake. Suddenly, Grant had to pay for his son's rehab on top of everything else. People on welfare took home more money than Grant had left in his paycheck. What remained after gas and food barely paid the rent on this roach palace in the ghetto.

Then one day, he'd met Reynolds. They met in a bar not far from the shithole that Grant lived in, a bar where the owner still gave Grant free beer so he'd have a cop hanging out there in case one of the tweakers who frequented the place got out of hand. Grant appreciated it and ended up spending a lot of time in that dive. It beat the hell out of sitting in his worn-out living room and staring at the mounting bracket on the wall where his TV had been.

Reynolds began hiring Grant to provide security at various social functions Reynolds put on. He bought Grant new clothes to wear because his old clothes were so ratty. He paid Grant well.

"Just look silent and tough like a Secret Service agent and keep the parties from getting out of hand," Reynolds had told him.

Grant learned how to ignore when people at the parties nudged over the legal line. He wasn't on duty or in uniform. This was way past the end of his shift. Who cares what people did in the bathrooms? As long as someone wasn't raping a child, beating up a girlfriend, or waving a gun around, Grant turned a blind eye.

Reynolds always paid Grant in cash, and he often included a little extra. Then, he showed Grant how to hide the money: always pay in cash, never be too flashy, never buy a new car, let other people pay as often as you do when you go out together.

Under the radar—Grant understood "under the radar" ever since his ex-wife found out about his other moonlighting jobs and got the alimony and child support increased. "Under the radar" was just fine.

Grant's life slowly improved, just like the safe deposit box at the local bank slowly filling with cash. The twenties became hundreds. The hundreds added up. His shithole furniture hit the curb, replaced with good quality used stuff Reynolds let him have for almost nothing. The tweakers began giving his house a wide berth, not even rummaging through his garbage anymore. It was like someone or something had told them, "leave this one alone." His closet filled up with nice clothes, replacing his worn-out shit. The hookers at the parties would throw him a freebie more and more often. Grant got so he liked his "nightlife" better than his day job at the sheriff's office. He was actually excited about getting off work. He hadn't felt that way since long before his ex-wife left him.

While he sat a bar having a beer with Reynolds, one day, Grant mentioned the DEA suspected a meth lab was operating out near where he worked. Grant thought they were full of shit. Nothing like that could be operating under their noses without the sheriff's office knowing about it. There would be meth everywhere out there, and there wasn't. They both exchanged stories about the inept DEA and how much a waste of taxpayer's money the agency was.

Reynolds revealed to Grant that he was a writer—that he wrote investigative articles for newspapers around the country. Reynolds said he would pay Grant a thousand dollars a tip for anything that led to an exposé. He was particularly interested in drug investigations because the drug manufacturers and importers seemed to operate with such impunity. If there was an actual operation, Reynolds would pay Grant two thousand dollars to know about it before it happened so he could be there when it went down. Reynolds handed Grant ten one hundred dollar bills under the table to clinch the deal.

Grant pocketed the money. Fuck the DEA. Those bastards couldn't find their dick in a snowstorm. And the ever-growing pile of cases on his desk at the Sherriff's office didn't seem quite so irritating when balanced with the ever-growing pile of cash in his safe deposit box.

The money rolled in faster after that. Some of the tips only generated a couple of hundred dollars—some, a lot more. Sometimes a detective in the Nehalitz County Sherriff's Office would call him and shoot the shit about joint operations with the DEA. He would pass that along to Reynolds also.

Until the lab bust in Chambersville—until Agent Fitzgerald had led him out of the sheriff's office in handcuffs—until the bartender had ID'ed Reynolds's picture and told the agents about the two of them talking together many times—until André decided to cop a plea and turned over all the phone recordings he'd made of their conversations—until the DEA pulled his private cell phone records and saw all the calls to a number that didn't exist anymore right after all the calls from André. At least he'd cleaned out the safe deposit box and buried the money where no one would find it.

So they had André telling another cop about some DEA operations. They didn't have a smoking gun. They didn't have Grant speaking to Reynolds about classified operations. All they had was a record of phone calls that could have been him talking about the weather or the next moonlighting gig.

Me? Grant thought to himself. *I was doing my job, hanging out with criminals, and trying to get inside their organization. Fucking incompetent DEA! If they had only waited a couple of weeks, Reynolds would have been back in business somewhere else, and he would have contacted me. They could have put a wiretap on my phone and got me cold. Dumbasses.*

"When will my lawyer be here? I'm not saying shit until I talk with him."

"He said he's on his way," Agent Fitzgerald said. "You know André recorded his conversations with Reynolds also. They were testing you. He would give you intel, then Reynolds would verify you'd given it to him."

Grant went white.

"Yep, you smell that? It's called a smoking gun. So I'll give you a one-time offer: tell us everything, and you'll get ten years, out in two, with credit for time served and good behavior."

Grant thought about what they had. *Fucking André. What was he thinking! Recording his own conversations?*

"I'll take two years, but I want minimum security. Cops don't live long doing hard time."

"I think I can do that if what you give us is valuable."

"Can I get that in writing?"

"Sure. Give me a few minutes."

Chapter 43 – Making Music

Saturday, June 21, dawned clear and cool. The big white and red tent we rented made our property look like a traveling carnival had arrived. People started showing up about 10 o'clock. John Nelson, Jack's son who worked in the hardware store, agreed to manage the car parking. He'd brought two of his friends along to help him. Gus was busy with a couple of kids he'd hired from the high school getting the food and barbeques going. The Blue Knights made quite a stir when they showed up on their motorcycles.

Rhiannon's children—their husbands, wives, and children—had camped out at the local motel. Our little house on the hill was overflowing with people.

A crew of young Indians erected a tipi next to the altar. In Indian marriages, the bride and groom enter the ceremonial tipi immediately after the marriage ceremony while the rest of the people begin the feast and party, which typically continues for at least a day—sometimes several. The bride and groom might return to the party or not—it was up to them.

A drum circle that performed regularly at the Indian Heritage Lodge was going to provide music during the ceremony. Roy Whitedeer would perform the marriage, being an ordained minister. He was greeting people and explaining the history and traditions behind the ceremony.

While everyone settled in, some very talented horsemen from the tribe displayed their riding ability. The air filled with oohs and ahs as they jumped from horse to horse at a gallop and stood on the backs of their bareback horses as the horses circled the yard. An archery range had been constructed behind the barn, and people were trying their skill while the archery master from the tribe gave them pointers.

The local newspaper had sent a reporter and a photographer to cover the event. The photographer shared ideas with the tribal photographer, here to make a photo history for the tribe. The reporter was interviewing people for the body of the article.

High above us, a Blackhawk helicopter circled.

The National Guard must be having some exercises, I thought, glancing up. Then I heard a gasp from the crowd.

"Look up there," John shouted from the parking area, pointing up.

Beside the Blackhawk, five small dots fell. They joined into a star that plummeted straight toward us. At two thousand feet above my yard, the star broke apart, and five square parachutes opened simultaneously with USASOC on the side of each of them. Five Green Berets landed on my lawn in single file as gently as if they were taking a stroll on a Saturday afternoon, one behind the other.

Doc was grinning from ear to ear when I walked up to him.

"You always knew how to make an entrance, Doc," I said, giving him a big hug.

"Nothing but the best for my brother."

"How'd you get the Blackhawk?"

"A return favor from a crazy man I knew in Afghanistan. He was needin' some air time to stay current. The maintenance platoon had just released that bird back to the flight line. It needed a test flight. We killed two birds, so to speak."

"How would the Army run without favors?"

"It wouldn't!"

Most of the single women, and a lot of the married ones, clustered around the five men as they collected their 'chutes. Amy was right in the thick of them, everyone talking at once and getting pictures taken with the five Green Berets who fell out of the sky. Pretty soon, Doc had his arm around one of Rhiannon's friends from the "motel."

The drum circle began shortly after Doc's arrival, signaling the beginning of the ceremony. Everyone quickly took their seat.

Roy stood at the altar dressed in a leather tribal tunic, pants, and breechclout. His hair was braided under a single leather thong around his forehead, with three eagle feathers tucked in behind. He beseeched the Great Spirit loudly to bless the participants of this marriage with long life, happiness, and prosperity. He sang a song in native Indian words no one but him could understand, then called us to the altar.

I went first in my ceremonial leather clothes and breechclout, my newly earned eagle feather proudly displayed in my beaded headband. Frank decided he didn't feel strong enough to stand for the whole ceremony. So I pushed him ahead of me in his wheelchair. His rented tuxedo was already too loose.

Amy came next in a low-cut, grayish pink, knee-length silk dress that swirled beautifully around her. The color of Frank's boutonniere matched Amy's dress.

Rhiannon came last, following two of her granddaughters, spreading rose petals from her new rose bushes on the ground in front of her. Her golden hair was divided into two braids that hung down each side of her face. A beaded headband around her forehead matched the beading on her dress.

I still had trouble believing this beautiful woman wanted to be my wife. I kept wanting to ask her, "Are you sure?"

Everyone stood, even Frank, as she walked to me.

Roy talked about the history of marriage in tribal lore, about the commitment of a man to a woman and a woman to a man in Indian history. He told Rhiannon to love and support me and work hard to make a good home. He told me to love and protect Rhiannon and be a good provider for her. Roy looked at me sternly. "Do you have any words you would like to say to the Great Spirit about this woman you have chosen?"

I turned to her, face to face, and picked up her hands in mine. "I've waited for you my whole life. You fill a part of me that I didn't know was empty. I will love you, support you, and protect you for the rest of my life." Then I looked up and shouted happily, "I am a lucky man!"

Roy turned to Rhiannon. "Do you have any words you would like to say to the Great Spirit about this man you have chosen?"

She looked at me, still holding my hands. "I understand about waiting. I have waited for you also. We will walk together into the end of our lives as one." She looked up into the sky and smiled. "So mote it be."

Frank handed Roy our wedding bands. Roy handed Rhiannon's to me—I slid it onto her finger. Roy gave mine to Rhiannon. She looked up into my eyes as she slid it onto my finger. I pulled her to me, and we kissed.

Roy bound our hands together and held them up to the Great Spirit to see and bless. Then he opened the door to the tipi and motioned for us to enter. Rhiannon and I crouched over and passed through the portal. Roy closed the flaps, tied them with rawhide thongs. The drum circle started a rhythmic beat. Four lines of costumed Indians from the heritage center entered the altar area from four different directions to form a dance circle. They performed the Marriage Dance.

When they were done, Gus announced the food was ready. Doc tapped the keg, the band tuned up, and the party began.

Rhiannon looked at me inside the tent. "This is pretty strange."

We could hear everyone moving around outside, laughing and talking, their shadows on the tent walls as they walked by.

"We can go back out and join the party."

"Maybe later. Right now, I have some other plans for you. We *did* just get married, after all. It would be a shame to waste these costumes."

"Me heap big Chief. You Injun maid. You mine now." I crossed my arms and waited to see if she would run with it.

She gave me a sly smile, liking this game, then held out her dress from her chest and gave a gasp. "Chief! Someone stole all under clothes. Injun maid naked under dress."

"Ugh. Must find thief and thank."

"So, Chiefie," she stepped up to me and ran her fingernails up my thigh, then underneath my breechclout. "Looks like you've got your own tipi growing down there. I've got a drum for that tom-tom. Feel like making some music?"

Chapter 44 – Mrs. Miller Comes Through

Two weeks later, my cell phone rang. Amy answered it.

"Could I speak to David Peterson, please?"

"Dad! Phone call."

I walked out of the bathroom with a towel around my waist. Amy handed me my cell phone, trying hard to look away. She wasn't used to semi-naked men walking around the house. Sometimes I wondered how she *did* get pregnant.

"Hi, this is David."

"David, you may not remember me, but my name is Dr. Chung. We met in the ER a couple of times."

"Hi, Dr. Chung. Of course, I remember you. What can I do for you?"

"Well, the Board of Directors of the hospital had a meeting last night. Do you know a Mrs. Miller?"

I thought a moment. "Not offhand. Who is she?"

"She was married to a doctor who once practiced here at the hospital."

"Oh, sure," I said, remembering the old woman's voice at the end of the line. "I talked to her when I tried to find an MD who would sponsor a clinic over here in Chambersville. She said her husband had died."

"Did you know she was on the hospital Board of Directors?"

"No, I sure didn't."

"Well, her husband gave a bunch of money to the hospital while he was a doctor. The hospital board added Mrs. Miller to the board as a way of saying thanks. She never came to a single board meeting until last night. Not only did she show up, which surprised everyone, she also came with the idea of creating a stabilize-and-transport clinic to be placed in Chambersville. The board loved the idea since Chambersville is at least a four-hour round trip from the hospital, and we keep getting calls from over there. With the ski resorts getting more popular, the board approved it on the first vote. The clinic would house an emergency response ambulance and have a helipad for critical Life Flight transportation. She said she wanted you to run it with your wife. Your wife's an RN, isn't she?"

"Yes, she is."

Dr. Chung left out the part about the board being worried about an ex-Green Beret medic exceeding his authorized procedures. "Is this something you'd be interested in?"

"Yes, it sure is," I said, not believing this conversation was taking place.

"Could the two of you come over here tomorrow and talk about it? Dr. Blessing, the hospital manager, wants to get it started. There are lots of planning, licenses, and approvals that need to be acquired."

"What time?"

"How about 10 A.M.?"

"We'll be there."

"Do you have an EMT or Paramedic license?"

"Nope. Thirty years of Green Beret medic training but no certifications."

"Would you consider taking the classes to get those certifications?"

I thought about that. "Sure. That should be fun, actually. I planned to do that when I first got out of the Army but abandoned the idea when I couldn't find an MD who would let us run a clinic under his auspices."

"OK. See you tomorrow."

"There's only one fly in the ointment," I said.

"What's that?" I could hear the wariness in his voice.

"My wife and I have to spend six months a year working for the DEA, training their SWAT teams." Rhiannon decided she didn't want me to leave for six months at a time. I made her part of my deal with the DEA, that she would accompany me to provide first-line medical support during the training, at full journeyman nurse's pay, of course.

"I don't see that as a problem." Dr. Chung sounded relieved. "Which six months would you be gone?"

They're worried about me overstepping my legally-defined "medic" boundaries—got it. "I will be gone October through March."

"Could you and your wife fill in during the spring and summer months? Those months when you are back in Chambersville?"

"Absolutely!"

"Perfect. Those are our busy months from that side of the hill. We can supply a team to run the service year-round, then use you guys when you're home."

I hung up the phone, feeling a little dazed. Rhiannon was looking at me with her raised eyebrow thing.

"Are you doing anything tomorrow? About 10 A.M.?" I asked her.

"Workin' at the diner training Amy. Why?"

Amy had decided to take a break from college to have her baby. Then she would change majors and schools to Marine Biology at Washington State when she restarted next year.

"Maybe you should call Gus and tell him he needs to think about hiring Amy full time."

"Who was on the phone?"

"Dr. Chung from the hospital."

I related the conversation to her. The further I got into the phone call, the more excited she got.

"Oh, honey! That's *wonderful*!" she shrieked, jumping into my arms. She had finished her classes to bring her RN up to date last spring. "But what about the DEA? You told them we'd work for them for six months a year, didn't you? We're supposed to start in October."

"Yeah, I told 'im about that. He didn't seem to think it was a problem. He said he'd use us in the summer and have a regular team run the service year-round."

And I was worried about what I would do after I retired!

Chapter 45 – Death and Birth

Frank was looking very sick. He didn't come to eat with us much anymore. Rhiannon took him food from the diner after work every day. He gave her a sealed envelope when she visited the last time.

"What's this, Frank?"

"My will. It's all notarized. I have no family. I'm leaving everything to you and David."

She hugged him. He hugged her back, then whispered in her ear, "Thanks, Rhiannon. Thanks to both of you for helping me through this. You've made this past year the best of my life."

"Is there anything you want? Anything we can do for you?"

"It's all in my will. I want my body used in any way it can be. Organs, eyes, research. What's left, I'd like cremated and the ashes spread at the campout site by the river."

"Is there any special kind of ceremony you'd like? Any special words or song played?"

"You're gonna laugh."

"I promise I won't."

"Remember the movie *O' Brother Where Art Thou?*"

She nodded.

"I'd like the song Alison Krauss sang, *Let's Go Down to the River to Pray.*"

"Is there anyone you'd like to officiate? A minister or priest? Anyone else you'd like to have present?"

"Nope. Only you guys—never been religious—seems like a copout to ask for safe passage now."

She hugged him again, struggling to hold back the tears that flooded her eyes.

"Frank thinks he's dying." She served the pot roast I had smelled cooking all day.

"He is."

"I know, but I hate to see it. He's such a nice guy." She handed me the envelope. "He's left everything to us. He says he has no other family."

"Damn. Have you talked to his doctor?"

"Yeah. He says the same thing."

"How much longer did he say Frank can expect?"

"Maybe tomorrow, maybe two weeks, maybe a month. He doesn't know."

"Damn." I couldn't think of anything else to say.

"Yep." She told me what Frank wanted for a burial.

"I love that song."

Both of us were quiet for a while. Then I said the words I was thinking. "I hate that Larry, Jack, and I never invited Frank to one of our campouts."

She blinked then handed me the phone. "It's not too late."

I hesitated a moment, collecting my thoughts, then came to a decision. "You're right." I took the phone from her and dialed Frank's number. "Frank, David."

"Hi, David. What's up?" He sounded exhausted.

"Rhiannon and I are going camping by the river this weekend. So we wondered if maybe you'd like to join us."

There was a long pause. "I'd like that. What should I bring?"

"Nothing but you." I gave Rhiannon a thumbs-up. "We'll take care of everything else."

"What time should I be ready?"

"How about 9 A.M. Saturday mornin'?"

"That'll work. See you then ... and thanks, you two."

"Good night, Frank."

"'Night."

Saturday morning, we picked up Frank. He put his overnight bag into the truck's bed and slid in next to Rhiannon. He was pale and sweating slightly, his breath coming in shallow gasps.

"Good morning, Frank."

"If you say so."

The sky was so blue it hurt to look at it. The weather forecast said it was supposed to be a perfect weekend, temperature in the low eighties. We got to the campsite and set up. My lean-to was still there from when I had camped three years ago. Many people had used and improved it since I built it. It was bigger now. Some corrugated metal had replaced my poncho. Both the tents fit underneath it. I had brought my warmest sleeping bag for Frank with an insulating pad underneath.

Rhiannon and I unloaded the firewood I brought along with us, figuring the area around the lean-to would be picked clean. Rhiannon pulled out lunch. She was a magician with chicken salad sandwiches. Frank ate about two bites, then leaned over and puked. "I'm sorry, David," he said, wiping his mouth.

"Do what you have to do, Frank. I'll take care of it."

The pot wasn't working anymore. In fact, nothing was working anymore. Frank had put the DNR back into effect. He was in the final stretch. I kicked some dirt over the puke and rubbed it into the ground.

"Feel like taking a walk, Frank?"

"No." He smiled weakly. "Just sittin' here in the sun is about all I wanna do."

The happy noise of children playing in the water reached our campsite from the river. A soft breeze blew up the hillside to us, full of the smell of wildflowers and healthy forest. Frank closed his eyes and napped in the recliner we brought for him, a smile on his face even in his sleep.

We let him sleep all afternoon. Then, a little after 5 P.M., Rhiannon and I fixed dinner, making as little noise as we could. Burgers and potato salad. When they were done, I picked up Frank's hand and realized he had died sometime that afternoon while he'd sat in the sun. His arm was stiff with rigor mortis.

"Frank's dead," I said.

"I thought he might be."

"When it's my time, I hope I go as peacefully."

"Me, too."

"You want me to go peacefully?"

Rhiannon gave me a quizzical expression, then giggled. "Yes, idiot. And me too."

We got out Frank's sleeping bag and tucked it around him. "This is pretty dumb," I said. "He's already dead."

"It's more a statement than a need," Rhiannon responded, stepping back to look at Frank with the sleeping bag around him. "I hope he's warm and comfortable in whatever's next."

"Should we call someone?"

"Who?"

"The coroner? His doctor? I don't know."

"I'll call his doctor tomorrow. There's no point in getting everyone out here tonight and ruining their Saturday evening. It won't change anything. Tomorrow's as good as now."

We held hands and watched the sun go down.

"Hello, the camp."

I sat bolt upright. I knew that voice. Gina! Rhiannon sat up, too, with wide-open eyes.

"Get up, Rhiannon. I think there's someone out there you want to meet."

We struggled into our clothes.

"Give us a second," I called. "We'll be right out."

Gina was waiting for us when we opened the tent.

"Hi. Cool tonight. Can I warm up by your fire?"

"Sure." I began to throw more wood on the coals. "You're Gina."

"Yes, I am. Do I know you?"

"We met a couple of years ago. I'd just gotten out of the Army."

"Maybe you know my husband, William. He was a Marine."

"I never met him, but I've heard of him, that he was a wonderful man, but I do have someone else I think *you* would like to meet."

Rhiannon stepped out of the tent.

"Gina, this is your granddaughter, Rhiannon. She's Delilah's daughter."

"Granddaughter? I didn't know Delilah was married."

"She's been married a long time," I said.

"Hello, Grandmother," Rhiannon said, not believing what she was seeing.

"Hello, dear. I can see Delilah in you. How is she?"

"She's dead, Grandmother. She passed ten years ago."

"Dead? How did she die?"

"She was old and wanted to be with Dad."

"I can understand that. I've been waiting for William so long."

"William's waiting for you."

"No, he's not! He can't be. I would know!"

"Grandma, when he was dying, he held my hand and smiled at me. He said it wouldn't be long until he held you again."

Gina put her hand to her mouth in dismay. "All these years, I've been waiting for him, and he's already gone through!"

"You had other things to worry about." Rhiannon reached out to her. "Do you know how many people you've helped while you waited?"

"Did I help anyone? I don't remember."

"You helped David and me find each other. I've heard about so many others as well."

"Enough of that!" Gina said sharply. "How do I pass over? William needs me. I've waited long enough."

"Can you stay for a few minutes more?" Rhiannon asked, thinking this was her last chance. "I have so many questions I wanted to ask you."

Gina looked around anxiously, then sighed, walked over to Rhiannon, and hugged her.

"What do you want to know, dear? Is this man the one? What mistakes will your children make? When will you die? All those answers will come as they are needed."

"No, Grandmother. Nothing like that. I want to know what it was like being a midwife when you were alive. And when did you decide you loved William? What was Great Grandma like?"

"I actually had *four* mothers," Gina said, smiling softly and sighing again. "I haven't thought about those wonderful women since I died—my birth mother, my grandmother, my spirit mother, and my guide mother. Charlotte was my birth mother, Duha was my spirit mother, Georgia was my grandmother, and Lawis was my guide mother. All four of them were midwives and healers. David, don't you want to ask about Duha?"

"My great-grandmother? I don't know much about her, except she was the child of two slaves, was born in Missouri, and came out here at the end of the 19th century. She married an Indian and had my grandfather Jacob."

"Yes, she married Itswoot and had Jacob, your grandfather. It's from her, you got that beautiful hair and your guide owl."

"So your mother and grandmother and Duha did know each other!" Rhiannon said. "I knew it!"

"Of course we did. Duha and Georgia came here together from Wyoming with Henry, my grandfather. No one wanted a black woman and a white woman to be friends back then. So the three of them fought that battle their whole lives. Those three didn't care. That's why they settled out here. There weren't enough white people to matter. And when the people that *were* here found out how good a midwife Duha was, they were willing to overlook that she was black."

Gina gave Rhiannon another hug. "I have to go, dear."

"Just one more question, Grandmother, please. When did you decide you loved Grandfather?"

That got another smile. "It was when he sent me a poem."

"Which one was it, Grandmother? I've read all his letters to you."

That made her laugh. "Both of us saved them. And they survived all these years?"

"Yep. I found them in mother's things with a ribbon around them after she died. I think she loved reading them as much as I did. Which poem was it that made the difference to you?"

"The one he read me when he came home from the war was amazing. But the one that I fell in love with him, he sent me from Okinawa. I still remember opening that letter. It was a beautiful day at the end of June in 1945. None of the other men I wrote to wrote letters like William. Most of them were stiff and formal. William's were full of gentleness, caring, and introspection. I could see the war through his eyes. Each time I opened the mailbox, I hoped a letter from William was there. But that letter from Okinawa was special in a lot of ways. It was only one page. Most of his letters were fat with descriptions of the war and his longing for home. And they always contained at least one poem. He was good at writing them. He'd written this particular letter from Okinawa after the battle was over. I think he was trying to escape from the horrors he'd seen there. The poem was named 'Petals.' It went like this:

> I always thought that
> > it's not OK to need anyone.
> That when you want to reach out,
> > you're being weak.
> But I want you to hold me, and
> > tell me you love me, and
> Somehow, that doesn't feel weak to me.
> > It feels whole.

Rhiannon said the last two lines together with her.

Gina hugged Rhiannon one more time. "Do either of you know how to pass over?"

Rhiannon looked at me and shrugged. "I saw a light when I died. Then you sent me back."

"It wasn't your time yet, dear." Gina smiled and touched Rhiannon's cheek. Then she looked around. "I don't see any lights."

"Well, Frank died this afternoon." I motioned to Frank's body. "Can you follow him?"

"Hi, Gina," a voice said from the darkness. Gina looked around in confusion. Frank walked up to her. Not the dying Frank we had brought to the campsite. This Frank was young, plump, and healthy. "Come with me, Gina. I know the way. Before I crossed over, William asked me to come back for you. He's waiting on the other side. I figured you'd be here."

He held out his hand. Gina took it eagerly, and they walked away into the night. Right before he was out of sight, Frank turned and mouthed "Thank you" to us, then they were gone.

Rhiannon turned to me and put her head on my chest, crying softly. "My whole life, I wanted to meet her. Now she's gone forever."

"Not forever, sweetheart," I whispered in her ear. "Just until you pass over."

Two weeks later, we spread Frank's ashes around the campsite. Alison Krauss serenaded us while we did it.

That night as we snuggled in front of the fire, Rhiannon looked up at me. "What do you think it's like on the other side?"

I looked at her and wondered what my life would have been if I had never met this beautiful, intelligent woman—if I had spent the rest of my life running from one war to another instead of settling back into my grandfather's house. I kissed her cheek and sighed. "I'd like to think it's a lot like right here, right now."

She was quiet for a while and then squeezed me. "I love you."

Three words I thought I would never hear in this life. I squeezed her back. "I know. I love you, too."

Author's Notes

If you liked this book, please do a review of it on
GoodReads.com
or Amazon.com, if you bought it from them.
It's reviews that sell books and help me fund my next
novel.
Thanks - Fred

I would like to thank the people who were instrumental in my finishing this novel. Melvina R. Hudgin, my wife and best friend, read each chapter as it was finished. Her input, enthusiasm, and feedback were invaluable. M. Kay Howell was my second reader and source of continuous advice. Gina Farago was my beloved editor and resident grammar cop.

Fredrick Hudgin

I have been writing poetry and short stories since I took a Creative Writing class at Purdue University in 1967. Unfortunately, that was the only class I passed and spent the next three years in the army, including a tour in Viet Nam. After leaving the army, I earned a BS in Computer Science from Rutgers and struck off on a career as a computer programmer.

I find that my years of writing poetry have affected how I write prose. My wife is always saying to put more narrative into the story. My poetry side keeps trying to pare it down to the emotional bare bones. What I create is always a compromise between the two.

Short stories and poems of mine have been published in Biker Magazine, two compilations by Poetry.Com, The Salal Review, The Scribbler, That Holiday Feeling, a collection of Christmas short stories, and Not Your Mother's Book on Working for a Living.

My home is in Ariel, Washington, with my wife, two horses, two dogs and three cats.

My website is **fredrickhudgin.com**. All of my books and short stories are described with links to where you can buy them in hardcopy or e-book form. I've also included some of my favorite poems. You can see what is currently under development, sign up for book announcements, or volunteer to be a reader of my books that are under development.

Books by
Fredrick Hudgin
All are available at Amazon.com

Sulfur Springs – Historical Fiction — Set in Lewis county, Washington

A novel about two women who settle in the Northwest.

Duha (pronounced DooHa) is the daughter of a slave midwife. Her mother and she are determined to escape the racism in Independence, Missouri, by migrating to Washington State in 1895. But her mother dies in Sheridan, Wyoming, leaving Duha with no money, no job, and no future beyond working in the brothels. She meets Georgia Prentice, a nurse in the hospital where her mother dies. Georgia takes her in and, together, they begin a life together that spans sixty years and three generations.

They settle in the quiet, idyllic settlement of Sulphur Springs, Washington, nestled between three volcanoes—Mt Rainier, Mt Adams, and Mt St Helens. The beautiful fir covered hills and crystal clear rivers belie the evil growing there that threatens to swallow Duha's and Georgia's families. Three generations must join together as a psychotic rapist/murderer threatens to destroy everything that they have worked and suffered to create.

School of the Gods – Fantasy

A novel about the balance between good and evil.

The idea for ***The School of the Gods*** began with a series of "What if…"s. What if we really did have multiple lives? What if God made mistakes and learned from them? What if our spiritual goal was to become a god and it was his job to foster us while we grew? What if we ultimately became the god of our own universe, responsible for fostering our own crop of spirits to godhead? If all that were true, there would have to be a school. I mean, that's what schools do … give us the training to start a new career.

The School of the Gods is not a book about God, religious dogma, or organized religion. Instead, it's a story about Jeremiah—ex-Marine, bar fly, and womanizer. Jeremiah's life of excess leads to an untimely end. There is nothing unusual about his death other than he is the 137,438,953,472nd person to die since the beginning of humanity. That coincidence allows Jeremiah to bypass Judgement and get a free pass into Heaven. It also begins the story.

Jeremiah's entry into the hereafter leads to him becoming the confident of the god of our universe. As Jeremiah begins his path toward godhead, he discovers the answer to many questions about God that have confounded humanity from the beginning of time: why transsexuals exist, the real reason for the ten commandments, why the Great Flood of Noah actually happened, and where the other species that couldn't fit on the boat were kept. Along the way, God, Jeremiah, and three other god-hopefuls throw the forces of evil out of God's Home, create a beer drinker's guide to the universes, and become all-powerful gods of their own universes.

Four Winds – A collection of Poetry

A collection of poetry in two parts: Poems about love, tears, hope, and fears. Poems that are *not* about love, tears, hope, and fears. Some rhyme—some don't. Some are silly—some are serious. They encompass the beginning of my written career through my current efforts. They lay the groundwork for the prose that I have created. If you can't write about things you experience, you probably need to do something else. And like anything else, you get better with practice. I was tempted to put them into chronological order but after so many years of polishing and correcting, who knows what the actual date should be. Or I could have put them in order of my most favorite to my less favorite. But your order would be different because everyone resonates to poems differently. So I decided to make them alphabetical.

Green Grass – Fantasy/Adventure

This is my first young reader book. My grandkids kept asking me for one of my books and they were all full of adult words, thoughts, and actions—clearly not appropriate for young readers. So I wrote this one.

I'm sure you've heard the cliché about the grass always being greener. Sometimes it's true—sometimes it's not. It's usually a little more complicated than that.

There are no adult words beyond what I hear tweens use every day. And no sex beyond holding hands, giving hugs, and kissing. While the book contains some violence and death, it is not graphic and I feel it is presented in a way that most young readers would understand without getting disturbed.

However, being a young reader book doesn't mean that the plots and subplots are not interesting. Susannah and her friends are dropped into the middle of a civil war. There are good people and bad people on both sides of the portal. Deciding who is whom becomes a pretty important question to figure out. After the Earthlings get cloned, things really get complicated. Imagine saying "Hi!" to yourself!

So pull up a chair and enter a world of Magic with dragons, mages, and swords. It is called Gleepth. You can only get there once a year, and only for a few minutes. But no one told Susannah that when she stepped into the portal and into a life beyond anything she had ever dreamed. And there was no way back beyond waiting a year for the next window.

A Rainy Night and Other Short Stories – Fiction/Non-fiction

The little girl who greets Frank on **A Rainy Night** told him about her father and uncle who had not come home from Afghanistan. But there was more to the story than she said … a lot more. Frank had already lost his wife and family. The girl's loss reached out to him until the men appeared.

In **Ashes on the Ocean**, her husband of forty-three years has died. Suddenly she was free of his strict ways. She rebuilds her life, filling the void he left with bright happy things. But she still had one remaining obligation—to get his ashes to the ocean. The temptation was to repay his years of intolerance in kind, but a promise is a promise.

Being Dad is about healing. How do you bury the memories along with your son when he comes home from the war with an honor guard instead of a bear hug?

This collection of short stories are my favorite of the stories I have I written. Some are twisted. Some are fun. Some are sad and some are happy — kind of like life. I hope you enjoy them.

The End of Children Trilogy – Science Fiction

The End of Children has SEX. It has ALIENS WHO WANT TO CRUSH US and ALIENS WHO WANT TO HELP. It has

VIRUSES. It has PRESIDENTIAL CORRUPTION. It has GALACTIC WARS. It has KIDNAPPED BABIES. It has INTELLIGENT PORPOISES and they don't hitchhike!

Some kids find out how to open a wormhole, the government weaponizes it, the wormhole detectors on the moon announce the discovery to the rest of the galaxy, and after the aliens make humanity sterile for being too warlike and put us in an airtight quarantine, we have World War III. It takes three hours to decimate almost the governments and military of the world – thank god for Canada! The male leaders of the world have failed us and the galaxy won't talk to us about a second chance.

But it all ends happily. A brave young woman finally convinces the galaxy we have something to contribute by performing *Romeo and Juliette* by herself in a space capsule with two weeks food and no way to return to Earth. Our galaxy gets attacked by another galaxy. We save the emperor of our galaxy, show his generals how to fight after ten thousand years of peace, and kick the other galaxy's ass. The emperor offers us another world. We turn over Earth to the porpoises, emigrate to the new world (named Atlantis), and get admitted to the Ur with the woman as our representative.

OK. I left out a little. It's a big story, told in three volumes, each with over 100,000 words.

This is the story of how it all unfolds.

Book 1 – The Beginning of the End

Book 2 – The Three-Hour War

Book 3 – The Emissary

Made in the USA
Middletown, DE
15 January 2022